TH

ALTER DE LA MARE

ZINC READ

Published by
This edition copyright © 2023 by Zinc Read
Design and setting By Zinc Read
Email- zincread@gmail.com
ISBN-978-93-5974-882-5

CONTENTS

CHAPTER ONE

The churchyard in which Arthur Lawford found himself wandering that mild and golden September afternoon was old, green, and refreshingly still. The silence in which it lay seemed as keen and mellow as the light—the pale, almost heatless, sunlight that filled the air. Here and there robins sang across the stones, elvishly shrill in the quiet of harvest. The only other living creature there seemed to Lawford to be his own rather fair, not insubstantial, rather languid self, who at the noise of the birds had raised his head and glanced as if between content and incredulity across his still and solitary surroundings. An increasing inclination for such lonely ramblings, together with the feeling that his continued ill-health had grown a little irksome to his wife, and that now that he was really better she would be relieved at his absence, had induced him to wander on from home without much considering where the quiet lanes were leading him. And in spite of a peculiar melancholy that had welled up into his mind during these last few days, he had certainly smiled with a faint sense of the irony of things on lifting his eyes in an unusually depressed moodiness to find himself looking down on the shadows and peace of Widderstone.

With that anxious irresolution which illness so often brings in its train he had hesitated for a few minutes before actually entering the graveyard. But once safely within he had begun to feel extremely loth to think of turning back again, and this not the less at remembering with a real foreboding that it was now drawing towards evening, that another day was nearly done. He trailed his umbrella behind him over the grass-grown paths; staying here and there to read some time-worn inscription; stooping a little broodingly over the dark green graves. Not for the first time during the long laborious convalescence that had followed apparently so slight an indisposition, a fleeting sense almost as if of an unintelligible remorse had overtaken him, a vague thought that behind all these past years, hidden as it were from his daily life, lay something not yet quite reckoned with. How often as a boy had he been rapped into a galvanic activity out of the deep reveries he used to fall into—those fits of a kind of fishlike day-dream. How often, and even far beyond boyhood, had he found himself bent on some distant thought or fleeting vision that the sudden clash of self-possession had made to seem quite illusory, and yet had left so strangely haunting. And now the old habit had stirred out of its long sleep, and, through the gate that Influenza in departing had left ajar, had returned upon him.

'But I suppose we are all pretty much the same, if we only knew it,' he had consoled himself. 'We keep our crazy side to ourselves; that's all. We just go on for years and years doing and saying whatever happens to come up—and really keen about it too'—he had glanced up with a kind of challenge in his face at the squat little belfry—'and then, without the slightest reason or warning, down you go, and it all begins to wear thin, and you get wondering what on earth it all means.' Memory slipped back for an instant to the life that in so unusual a fashion seemed to have floated a little aloof. Fortunately he had not discussed these inward symptoms with his wife. How surprised Sheila would be to see him loafing in this old, crooked churchyard. How she would lift her dark eyebrows, with that handsome, indifferent tolerance. He smiled, but a little confusedly; yet the thought gave even a spice of adventure to the evening's ramble.

He loitered on, scarcely thinking at all now, stooping here and there. These faint listless ideas made no more stir than the sunlight gilding the fading leaves, the crisp turf underfoot. With a slight effort he stooped even once again;—

'Stranger, a moment pause, and stay;
In this dim chamber hidden away
Lies one who once found life as dear
As now he finds his slumbers here:
Pray, then, the Judgement but increase
His deep, everlasting peace!'

'But then, do you *know* you lie at peace?' Lawford audibly questioned, gazing at the doggerel. And yet, as his eyes wandered over the blunt green stone and the rambling crimson-berried brier that had almost encircled it with its thorns, the echo of that whisper rather jarred. He was, he supposed, rather a dull creature—at least people seemed to think so—and he seldom felt at ease even with his own small facetiousness. Besides, just that kind of question was getting very common. Now that cleverness was the fashion most people were clever—even perfect fools; and cleverness after all was often only a bore: all head and no body. He turned languidly to the small cross-shaped stone on the other side:

'Here lies the body of Ann Hard, who died in child-bed.
Also of James, her infant son.'

He muttered the words over with a kind of mournful bitterness. 'That's just it—just it; that's just how it goes!'... He yawned softly; the pathway had come to an end. Beyond him lay ranker grass, one and another obscurer mounds, an old scarred oak seat, shadowed by a few everlastingly green cypresses and coral-fruited yew-trees. And above and beyond all hung a pale blue arch of sky with a few voyaging clouds like silvered wool, and the calm wide curves of stubble field and pasture land. He stood with vacant eyes, not in the least aware how queer a figure he made with his gloves and his umbrella and his hat among the stained and tottering gravestones. Then, just to linger out his hour, and half sunken in reverie, he walked slowly over to the few solitary graves beneath the cypresses.

One only was commemorated with a tombstone, a rather unusual oval-headed stone, carved at each corner into what might be the heads of angels, or of pagan dryads, blindly facing each other with worn-out, sightless faces. A low curved granite canopy arched over the grave, with a crevice so wide between its stones that Lawford actually bent down and slid in his gloved fingers between them. He straightened himself with a sigh, and followed with extreme difficulty the well-nigh, illegible inscription:

'Here lie ye Bones of one,
Nicholas Sabathier, a Stranger to this Parish,
who fell by his own Hand on ye
Eve of *Ste.* Michael and All Angels.
MDCCXXXIX

Of the date he was a little uncertain. The 'Hand' had lost its 'n' and 'd'; and all the 'Angels' rain had erased. He was not quite sure even of the 'Stranger.' There was a great rich 'S,' and the twisted tail of a 'g'; and, whether or not, Lawford smilingly thought, he is no Stranger now. But how rare and how memorable a name! French evidently; probably Huguenot. And the Huguenots, he remembered vaguely, were a rather remarkable 'crowd.' He had, he thought, even played at 'Huguenots' once. What was the man's name? Coligny; yes, of course, Coligny. 'And I suppose,' Lawford continued, muttering to himself, 'I suppose this poor beggar was put here out of the way. They might, you know,' he added confidentially, raising the ferrule of his umbrella, 'they might have stuck a stake through you, and buried you at the crossroads.' And again, a feeling of ennui, a faint disgust at his poor little witticism, clouded over his mind. It was a pity thoughts always ran the easiest way, like water in old ditches.

'"Here lie ye bones of one, Nicholas Sabathier,"' he began murmuring again—'merely bones, mind you; brains and heart are quite another story. And it's pretty certain the fellow had some kind of brains. Besides, poor devil! he killed himself. That seems to hint at brains... Oh, for goodness' sake!' he cried out; so loud that the sound of his voice alarmed even a robin that had perched on a twig almost within touch, with glittering eye intent above its dim red breast on this other and even rarer stranger.

'I wonder if it is XXXIX.; it might be LXXIX.' Lawford cast a cautious glance over his round grey shoulder, then laboriously knelt down beside the stone, and peeped into the gaping cranny. There he encountered merely the tiny, pale-green, faintly conspicuous eyes of a large spider, confronting his own. It was for the moment an alarming, and yet a faintly fascinating experience. The little almost colourless fires remained so changeless. But still, even when at last they had actually vanished into the recesses of that quiet habitation, Lawford did not rise from his knees. An utterly unreasonable feeling of dismay, a sudden weakness and weariness had come over him.

'What is the good of it all?' he asked himself inconsequently—this monotonous, restless, stupid life to which he was soon to be returning, and for good. He began to realize how ludicrous a spectacle he must be, kneeling here amid the weeds and grass beneath the solemn cypresses. 'Well, you can't have everything,' seemed loosely to express his disquiet.

He stared vacantly at the green and fretted gravestone, dimly aware that his heart was beating with an unusual effort. He felt ill and weak. He leant his hand on the stone and lifted himself on to the low wooden seat nearby. He drew off his glove and thrust his bare hand under his waistcoat, with his mouth a little ajar, and his eyes fixed on the dark square turret, its bell sharply defined against the evening sky.

'Dead!' a bitter inward voice seemed to break into speech; 'Dead!' The viewless air seemed to be flocking with hidden listeners. The very clearness and the crystal silence were their ambush. He alone seemed to be the target of cold and hostile scrutiny. There was not a breath to breathe in this crisp, pale sunshine. It was all too rare, too thin. The shadows lay like wings everlastingly folded. The robin that had been his only living witness lifted its throat, and broke, as if from the uttermost outskirts of reality, into its shrill, passionless song. Lawford moved heavy eyes from one object to another—bird—sun-gilded stone—those two small earth-worn faces—his hands—a stirring in the grass as of some creature labouring to climb up. It was useless to sit here any longer. He must go back now. Fancies were all very well for a change, but must be only occasional guests in a world devoted to reality. He leaned his hand on the dark grey wood, and closed his eyes. The lids presently unsealed a little, momentarily revealing astonished, aggrieved pupils, and softly, slowly they again descended....

The flaming rose that had swiftly surged from the west into the zenith, dyeing all the churchyard grass a wild and vivid green, and the stooping stones above it a pure faint purple, waned softly back like a falling fountain into its basin. In a few minutes, only a faint orange burned in the west, dimly illuminating with its band of light the huddled figure on his low wood seat, his right hand still pressed against a faintly beating heart. Dusk gathered; the first white stars appeared; out of the shadowy fields a nightjar purred. But there was only the silence of the falling dew among the graves. Down here, under the ink-black cypresses, the blades of the grass were stooping with cold drops; and darkness lay like the hem of an enormous cloak, whose jewels above the breast of its wearer might be in the unfathomable clearness the glittering constellations....

In his small cage of darkness Lawford shuddered and raised a furtive head. He stood up and peered eagerly and strangely from side to side. He stayed quite still, listening as raptly as some wandering night-beast to the indiscriminate stir and echoings of the darkness. He cocked his head above his shoulder and listened again, then turned upon the soundless grass towards the hill. He felt not the faintest astonishment or strangeness in his solitude here; only a little chilled, and physically uneasy; and yet in this vast darkness a faint spiritual exaltation seemed to hover.

He hastened up the narrow path, walking with knees a little bent, like an old labourer who has lived a life of stooping, and came out into the dry and dusty lane. One moment his instinct hesitated as to which turn to take—only a moment; he was soon walking swiftly, almost trotting, downhill with this vivid exaltation in the huge dark night in his heart, and Sheila merely a little angry Titianesque cloud on a scarcely perceptible horizon. He had no notion of the time; the golden hands of his watch were indiscernible in the gloom. But presently, as he passed by, he pressed his face close to the cold glass of a little shop-window, and pierced that out by an old Swiss cuckoo-clock. He would if he hurried just be home before dinner.

He broke into a slow, steady trot, gaining speed as he ran on, vaguely elated to find how well his breath was serving him. An odd smile darkened his face at remembrance of the thoughts he had been thinking. There could be little amiss with the heart of a man who could shamble along like this, taking even pleasure, an increasing pleasure in this long, wolf-like stride. He turned round occasionally to look into the face of some fellow-wayfarer whom he had overtaken, for he felt not only this unusual animation, this peculiar zest, but that, like a boy on some secret errand, he had slightly disguised his very presence, was going masked, as it were. Even his clothes seemed to have connived at this queer illusion. No tailor had for these ten years allowed him so much latitude. He cautiously at last opened his garden gate and with soundless agility mounted the six stone steps, his latch-key ready in his gloveless hand, and softly let himself into the house.

Sheila was out, it seemed, for the maid had forgotten to light the lamp. Without pausing to take off his greatcoat, he hung up his hat, ran nimbly upstairs, and knocked with a light knuckle on his bedroom door. It was closed, but no answer came. He opened it, shut it, locked it, and sat down on the bedside for a moment, in the darkness, so that he could scarcely hear any other sound, as he sat erect and still, like some night animal, wary of danger, attentively alert. Then he rose from the bed, threw off his coat, which was clammy with dew, and lit a candle on the dressing-table.

Its narrow flame lengthened, drooped, brightened, gleamed clearly. He glanced around him, unusually contented—at the ruddiness of the low fire, the brass bedstead, the warm red curtains, the soft silveriness here and there. It seemed as if a heavy and dull dream had withdrawn out of his mind. He would go again some day, and sit on the little hard seat beside the crooked tombstone of the friendless old Huguenot. He opened a drawer, took out his razors, and, faintly whistling, returned to the table and lit a second candle. And still with this strange heightened sense of life stirring in his mind, he drew his hand gently over his chin and looked unto the glass.

For an instant he stood head to foot icily still, without the least feeling, or thought, or stir—staring into the looking-glass. Then an inconceivable drumming beat on his ear. A warm surge, like the onset of a wave, broke in him, flooding neck, face, forehead, even his hands with colour. He caught himself up and wheeled deliberately and completely round, his eyes darting to and fro, suddenly to fix themselves in a prolonged stare, while he took a deep breath, caught back his self-possession and paused. Then he turned and once more confronted the changed strange face in the glass.

Without a sound he drew up a chair and sat down, just as he was, frigid and appalled, at the foot of the bed. To sit like this, with a kind of incredibly swift torrent of consciousness, bearing echoes and images like straws and bubbles on its surface, could not be called thinking. Some stealthy hand had thrust open the sluice of memory. And words, voices, faces of mockery streamed through without connection, tendency, or sense. His hands hung between his knees, a deep and settled frown darkened the features stooping out of the direct rays of the light, and his eyes wandered like busy and inquisitive, but stupid, animals over the floor.

If, in that flood of unintelligible thoughts, anything clearly recurred at all, it was the memory of Sheila. He saw her face, lit, transfigured, distorted, stricken, appealing, horrified. His lids narrowed; a vague terror and horror mastered him. He hid his eyes in his hands and cried without sound, without tears, without hope, like a desolate child. He ceased crying; and sat without stirring. And it seemed after an age of vacancy and meaninglessness he heard a door shut downstairs, a distant voice, and then the rustle of some one slowly ascending the stairs. Some one turned the handle; in vain; tapped. 'Is that you, Arthur?'

For an instant Lawford paused, then like a child listening for an echo, answered, 'Yes, Sheila.' And a sigh broke from him; his voice, except for a little huskiness, was singularly unchanged.

'May I come in?' Lawford stood softly up and glanced once more into the glass. His lips set tight, and a slight frown settled between the long, narrow, intensely dark eyes.

'Just one moment, Sheila,' he answered slowly, 'just one moment.'

'How long will you be?'

He stood erect and raised his voice, gazing the while impassively into the glass.

'It's no use,' he began, as if repeating a lesson, 'it's no use your asking me, Sheila. Please give me a moment, a...I am not quite myself, dear,' he added quite gravely.

The faintest hint of vexation was in the answer.

'What is the matter? Can't I help? It's so very absurd—'

'What is absurd?' he asked dully.

'Why, standing like this outside my own bedroom door. Are you ill? I will send for Dr. Simon.'

'Please, Sheila, do nothing of the kind. I am not ill. I merely want a little time to think in.' There was again a brief pause, and then a slight rattling at the handle.

'Arthur, I insist on knowing at once what's wrong; this does not sound a bit like yourself. It is not even quite like your own voice.'

'It is myself,' he replied stubbornly, staring fixedly into the glass. You must give me a few moments, Sheila. Something has happened. My face. Come back in an hour.'

'Don't be absurd; it's simply wicked to talk like that. How do I know what you are doing? As if I can leave you for an hour in uncertainty! Your face! If you don't open at once I shall believe there's something seriously wrong: I shall send Ada for assistance.'

'If you do that, Sheila, it will be disastrous. I cannot answer for the con—. Go quietly downstairs. Say I am unwell; don't wait dinner for me; come back in an hour; oh, half an hour!'

The answer broke out angrily. 'You must be mad, beside yourself, to ask such a thing. I shall wait in the next room until you call.'

'Wait where you please,' Lawford replied, 'but tell them downstairs.'

'Then if I tell them to wait until half-past eight, you will come down? You say you are not ill: the dinner will be ruined. It's absurd.'

Lawford made no answer. He listened a while, then he deliberately sat down once more to try to think. Like a squirrel in a cage his mind seemed to be aimlessly, unceasingly astir. 'What is it really? What is it really?—really?' He sat there and it seemed to him his body was transparent as glass. It seemed he had no body at all—only the memory of an hallucinatory reflection in the glass, and this inward voice crying, arguing, questioning, threatening out of the silence—'What is it really—really—*really*?' And at last, cold, wearied out, he rose once more and leaned between the two long candle-flames, and stared on—on—on, into the glass.

He gave that long, dark face that had been foisted on him tricks to do—lift an eyebrow, frown. There was scarcely any perceptible pause between the wish and its performance. He found to his discomfiture that the face answered instantaneously to the slightest emotion, even to his fainter secondary thoughts; as if these unfamiliar features were not entirely within control. He could not, in fact, without the glass before him, tell precisely what that face *was* expressing. He was still, it seemed, keenly sane. That he would discover for certain when Sheila returned. Terror, rage, horror had fallen back. If only he felt ill, or was in pain: he would have rejoiced at it. He was simply caught in some unheard-of snare—caught, how? when? where? by whom?

CHAPTER TWO

But the coolness and deliberation of his scrutiny, had to a certain extent calmed Lawford's mind and given him confidence. Hitherto he had met the little difficulties of life only to vanquish them with ease and applause. Now he was standing face to face with the unknown. He burst out laughing, into a long, low, helpless laughter. Then he arose and began to walk softly, swiftly, to and fro across the room—from wall to wall seven paces, and at the fourth, that awful, unseen, brightly-lit profile passed as swiftly over the tranquil surface of the looking-glass. The power of concentration was gone again. He simply paced on mechanically, listening to a Babel of questions, a conflicting medley of answers. But above all the confusion and turmoil of his brain, as a boatswain's whistle rises above a storm, so sounded that same infinitesimal voice, incessantly repeating another question now, 'What are you going to do? What are you going to do?'

And in the midst of this confusion, out of the infinite, as it were, came another sharp tap at the door, and all within sank to utter stillness again.

'It's nearly half-past eight, Arthur; I can't wait any longer.'

Lawford cast a last fleeting look into the glass, turned, and confronted the closed door. 'Very well, Sheila, you shall *not* wait any longer.' He crossed over to the door, and suddenly a swift crafty idea flashed into his mind.

He tapped on the panel. 'Sheila,' he said softly, 'I want you first, before you come in, to get me something out of my old writing-desk in the smoking-room. Here is the key.' He pushed a tiny key—from off the ring he carried—beneath the door. 'In the third little drawer from the top, on the left side, is a letter; please don't say anything now. It is the letter you wrote me, you will remember, after I had asked you to marry me. You scribbled in the corner under your signature the initials "Y.S.O.A."—do you remember? They meant, You Silly Old Arthur!—do you remember? Will you please get that letter at once?'

'Arthur,' answered the voice from without, empty of all expression, 'what does all this mean, this mystery, this hopeless nonsense about a silly letter? What has happened? Is this a miserable form of persecution? Are you mad?—I refuse to get the letter.'

Lawford stooped, black and angular, against the door. 'I am not mad. Oh, I am in the deadliest earnest, Sheila. You *must* get the letter, if only for your own peace of mind.' He heard his wife hesitate as she turned. He heard a sob. And once more he waited.

'I have brought the letter,' came the low toneless voice again.

'Have you opened it?'

There was a rustle of paper. 'Are the letters there underlined three times—"Y.S.O.A."?'

'The letters are there.'

'And the date of the month is underneath, "April 3rd." No one else in the whole world, living or dead, could know of this but ourselves, Sheila?'

'Will you please open the door?'

'No one?'

'I suppose not—no one.'

'Then come in.' He unlocked the door and opened it. A dark, rather handsome woman, with sleek hair, in a silk dress of a dark rich colour entered. Lawford closed the door. But his face was in shadow. He had still a moment's respite.

'I need not ask you to be patient,' he began quickly; 'if I could possibly have spared you—if there had been anybody in the world to go to... I am in horrible, horrible trouble, Sheila. It is inconceivable. I said I was sane: so I am, but the fact is—I went out for a walk; it was rather stupid, perhaps, so soon: and I think I was taken ill, or something—my heart. A kind of fit, a nervous fit. Possibly I am a little unstrung, and it's all, it's mainly fancy: but I think, I can't help thinking it has a little distorted—changed my face; everything, Sheila; except, of course, myself. Would you mind looking?' He walked slowly and with face averted towards the dressing-table.

'Simply a nervous—to make such a fuss, to scare!...' began his wife, following him.

Without a word he took up the two old china candlesticks, and held them, one in each lank-fingered hand, before his face, and turned.

Lawford could see his wife—every tint and curve and line as distinctly as she could see him. Her cheeks never had much colour; now her whole face visibly darkened, from pallor to a dusky leaden grey, as she gazed. It was not an illusion then; not a miserable hallucination. The unbelievable, the inconceivable, had happened. He replaced the candles with trembling fingers and sat down.

'Well,' he said, 'what is it really; what is it really, Sheila? What on earth are we to do?'

'Is the door locked?' she whispered. He nodded. With eyes fixed stirlessly on his face, Sheila unsteadily seated herself, a little out of the candlelight, in the shadow. Lawford rose and put the key of the door on his wife's little rose-wood prayer-desk at her elbow, and deliberately sat down again.

'You said "a fit"—where?'

'I suppose—is—is it very different—hopeless? You will understand my being... O Sheila, what am I to do?' His wife sat perfectly still, watching him with unflinching attention.

'You gave me to understand—"a nervous fit"; where?'

Lawford took a deep breath, and quietly faced her again. 'In the old churchyard, Widderstone; I was looking at—at the gravestones.'

'A fit; in the old churchyard, Widderstone—you were "looking at the gravestones"?'

Lawford shut his mouth. 'I suppose so—a fit,' he said presently. 'My heart went a little queer, and I sat down and fell into a kind of doze—a stupor, I suppose. I don't remember anything more. And then I woke; like this.'

'How do you know?'

'How do I know what?'

'"Like that"?'

He turned slowly towards the looking-glass. 'Why, here I am!'

She gazed at him steadily; and a hard, incredulous, almost cunning glint came into her wide blue eyes. She took up the key carelessly, glanced at it; glanced at him. 'It has made me—I mean the first shock, you know—it has made me a little faint.' She walked slowly, deliberately to the door, and unlocked it. 'I'll get a little sal volatile.' She softly drew out the key, and without once removing her eyes from his face, opened the door and pushed the key noiselessly in on the other side. 'Please stay there; I won't be a minute.'

Lawford's face smiled—a rather desperate, yet for all that a patient, resolute smile. 'Oh yes, of course,' he said, almost to himself, 'I had not foreseen—at least—you must do precisely what you please, Sheila. You were going to lock me in. You will, however, before taking any final step, please think over what it will entail. I did not think you would, after such proof, in this awful trouble—I did not think you would simply disbelieve me, Sheila. Who else is there to help me? You have the letter in your hand. Isn't that sufficient proof? It was overwhelming proof to me.

And even I doubted too; doubted myself. But never mind; why I should have dreamed you would believe me; or taken this awful thing differently, I don't know. It's rather awful to have to go on alone. But there, think it over. I shall not stir until I hear the voices. And then: honestly, Sheila, I couldn't face quite that. I'd sooner give up altogether. Any proof you can think of—I will... O God, I cannot bear it!' He covered his face with his hands; but in a moment looked up, unmoved once more. 'Why, for that matter,' he added slowly, and, as it were, with infinite pains, a faint thin smile again stealing into his face, 'I think,' he turned wearily to the glass, 'I think, it's almost an improvement!'

Something deep in those dark clear pupils, out of that lean adventurous face, gleamed back at him, the distant flash of a heliograph, as it were, height to height, flashing 'Courage!' He shuddered, and shut his eyes. 'But I would really rather,' he added in a quiet childlike way, 'I would really rather, Sheila, you left me alone now.'

His wife stood irresolute. 'I understand you to explain,' she said, 'that you went out of this house, just your usual self, this afternoon, for a walk; that for some reason you went to Widderstone—"to read the tombstones," that you had a heart attack, or, as you said at first, a fit, that you fell into a stupor, and came home like—like this. Am I likely to believe all that? Am I likely to believe such a story as that? Whoever you are, whoever you may be, is it likely? I am not in the least afraid. I thought at first it was some silly practical joke. I thought that at first.' She paused, but no answer came. 'Well, I suppose in a civilised country there is a remedy even for a joke as wicked as that.'

Lawford listened patiently. 'She is pretending; she is trying me; she is feeling her way,' he kept repeating to himself. 'She knows I *am* I, but hasn't the courage... Let her talk!'

'I shall leave the door open,' Sheila continued. 'I am not, as you no doubt very naturally assumed—I am not going to do anything either senseless or heedless. I am merely going to ask your brother Cecil to come in, if he is at home, and if not, no doubt our old friend Mr. Montgomery would—would help us.' Her scrutiny was still and concentrated, like that of a cat above a mouse's hole.

Lawford sat crouched together in the candlelight. 'By all means, Sheila,' he said slowly choosing his words, 'if you think poor old Cecil, who next January will have been three years in his grave, will be of any use in our difficulty. Who Mr. Montgomery is...' His voice dropped in utter weariness. 'You did it very well, my dear,' he added softly.

Sheila gently closed the door and sat down on the bed. He heard her softly crying, he heard the bed shaken with her sobs. But a slow glance towards the steady candle-flames restrained him. He let her cry on alone. When she had become a little more composed he stood up. 'You have had no dinner,' he managed to blurt out at last, 'you will be faint. It's useless to talk, even to think, any more to-night. Leave me to myself for a while. Don't look at me any more. Perhaps I can sleep: perhaps if I sleep it will come right again. When the servants are gone up, I will come down. Just let me have some—some medical book, or other; and some more candles. Don't think, Sheila; don't even think!'

Sheila paid him no attention for a while. 'You tell me not to think,' she began, in a low, almost listless voice; 'why—I wonder I am in my right mind. And "eat"! How can you have the heartlessness to suggest it? You don't seem in the least to *realize* what you say. You seem to have lost all—all consciousness. I quite agree, it is useless for me to burden you with my company while you are in your present condition of mind. But you will at least promise me that you won't take any further steps in this awful business.' She could not, try as she would, bring herself again to look at him. She rose softly, paused a moment with sidelong eyes, then turned deliberately towards the door, 'What, what have I done to deserve all this?'

From behind her that voice, so extraordinarily like—and yet in some vague fashion more arresting, more resonant than her husband's, broke incredibly out once more. 'You will please leave the key, Sheila. I am ill, but I am not yet in the padded room. And please understand, I take no further steps in "this awful business" until I hear a strange voice in the house.' Sheila paused, but the quiet voice rang in her ear, desperately yet convincingly. She took the key out of the lock, placed it on the bed, and with a sigh, that was not quite without a hint of relief in its misery, she furtively extinguished the gas-light on the landing and rustled downstairs.

She speedily returned. 'I have brought the book.' she said hastily. 'I could only find the one volume. I have said you have taken a fresh chill. No one will disturb you.'

Lawford took the book without a word. And once more, with eyes stonily averted, his wife left him to his own company and that of the face in the glass.

When completely deserted, Lawford with fumbling fingers opened Quain's 'Dictionary of Medicine.' He had never had much curiosity, and had always hated what he disbelieved, but none the less he had heard occasionally of absurd and questionable experiments. He remembered even to have glanced over reports of cases in the newspapers concerning disappearances, loss of memory, dual personality. Cranks... Oh yes, he thought now, with a sense of cold humiliating relief, there *had* been such cases as his before. They were no doubt curable. They must be comparatively common in America—that land of jangled nerves. Possibly bromide, rest, a battery. But Quain, it seemed, shared his prejudices, at least in this edition, or had hidden away all such apocryphal matter beneath technical terms, where no sensible man could find it, 'Besides,' he muttered angrily, 'what's the good of your one volume?' He flung it down and strode to the bed, and rang the bell. Then suddenly recollecting himself, he paused and listened. There came a tap on the door. 'Is that you, Sheila?' he called, doubtfully.

'No, sir, it's me,' came the answer.

'Oh, don't trouble; I only wanted to speak to your mistress. It's all right.'

'Mrs. Lawford has gone out, sir,' replied the voice.

'Gone out?'

'Yes, sir; she told me not to mention it; but I suppose as you asked—'

'Oh, that's all right; never mind; I didn't ring.' He stood with face uplifted, thinking.

'Can I do anything, sir?' came the faint, nervous question after a long pause.

'One moment, Ada,' he called in a loud voice. He took out his pocket-book, sat down, and scribbled a little note. He hardly noticed how changed his handwriting was—the clear round letters crabbed and irregular.

'Are you there, Ada?' he called. 'I am slipping a note beneath the door; just draw back the mat; that's it. Take it at once, please, to Mr. Critchett's, and be sure to wait for an answer. Then come back direct to me, up here. I don't think, Ada, your mistress believes much in Critchett; but I have fully explained what I want. He has made me up many prescriptions. Explain that to his assistant if he is not there. Go at once, and you will be back before she is. I should be so very much obliged, tell him. "Mr Arthur Lawford."'

The minutes slowly drifted by. He sat quite still in the clear untroubled light, waiting in the silence of the empty house. And for the first time he was confronted with the cold incredible horror of his ordeal. Who would believe, who could believe, that behind this strange and awful, yet how simple mask, lay himself? What test; what heaped-up evidence of identity would break it down? It was all a loathsome ignominy. It was utterly absurd. It was—

Suddenly, with a kind of ape-like cunning, he deliberately raised a long lean forefinger and pointed it at the shadowy crystal of the looking-glass. Perhaps he was dead, was really and indeed changed in body, was fated really and indeed to change in soul, into That. 'It's that beastly voice again,' Lawford cried out loud, looking vacantly at his upstretched finger. And then, hand and arm, not too willingly, as it were, obeyed; relaxed and fell to his side. 'You must keep a tight hold, old man,' he muttered to himself. 'Once, once you lose yourself—the least symptom of that—the least symptom, and it's all up!' And the fools, the heartless, preposterous fools had brought him one volume!

When on earth was Ada coming back? She was lagging on purpose. She was in the conspiracy too. Oh, it should be a lesson to Sheila! Oh, if only daylight would come! 'What are you going to do—to do—to DO?' He rose once more and paced his silent cage. To and fro, thinking no more; just using his eyes, compelling them to wander from picture to picture, bedpost to bedpost; now counting aloud his footsteps; now humming; only, only to keep himself from thinking. At last he took out a drawer and actually began arranging its medley of contents; ties, letters, studs, concert and theatre programmes—all higgledy-piggledy. And in the midst of this childish strategem he heard a faint sound, as of heavy water trickling from a height. He turned. A thief was in one of the candles. It was guttering out. He would be left in darkness. He turned hastily without a moment's heed, to call for light, flung the door open and full in the flare of a lamp, illuminating her pale forehead and astonished face beneath her black straw hat, stood face to face with Ada.

With one swift dexterous movement he drew the door to after him, looking straight into her almost colourless steady eyes. 'Ah,' he said instantly, in a high faint voice, 'the powder, thank you; yes, Mr Lawford's powder; thank you, thank you. He must be kept absolutely quiet—absolutely. Mrs Lawford is following. Please tell her that I am here, when she returns. Mr Critchett was in, then? Thank you. Extreme, extreme silence, please.' Again that knotted, melodramatic finger raised itself on high; and within that lean, cadaverous body the soul of its lodger quailed at this spectral boldness. But it was triumphant. The maid at once left him and went downstairs. He heard faint voices in muffled consultation. And in a moment Sheila's silks rustled once more on the staircase. Lawford put down the lamp, and watched her deliberately close the door.

'What does this mean?' she began swiftly, 'I understand that—Ada tells me a stranger is here; giving orders, directions. Who is he? where is he? You bound yourself on your solemn promise not to stir till I returned. You... How can I, how can we get decently through this horrible business if you are so wretchedly indiscreet? You sent Ada to the chemist's. What for? What for? I say.'

Lawford watched his wife with an almost extraneous interest. She was certainly extremely interesting from that point of view, that very novel point of view. 'It's quite useless,' he said, 'to get in the least nervous or hysterical. I don't care for the darkness just now. That was all. Tell the girl I am a strange doctor—Dr Simon's new partner. You are clever at conventionalities, Sheila. Invent! I said our patient must be kept quiet—I really think he must. That is all, so far as Ada is concerned.... What on earth else *are* we to say?' he broke out. 'That, for the present to *everybody*, is our only possible story. It will give us what we must have—time. And next—where is the second volume of Quain? I want that. And next—why have you broken faith with me?' Mrs Lawford sat down. This sudden and baffling outburst had stupefied her.

'I can't, I can't make head or tail of what you say. And as for having broken faith, as you call it, would any wife, would any sane woman face what you have brought on us, a situation like this, without seeking advice and help? Mr Bethany will be perfectly discreet—if he thinks discretion desirable. He is the only available friend we have close enough to ask at once. And things of this kind are, I suppose, if anybody's concern, his. It's certain to leak out. Everybody will hear of it. Don't flatter yourself you are going to hush up a thing like this for long. You can't keep *living* skeletons in a cupboard. You think only of yourself, only of your own misfortune. But who's to know, pray, that you really are my husband—if you are? The sooner I get the vicar on my side the better for us both. Who in the whole of the parish—I ask you—and you must have the sense left to see that—who will believe that a respectable man, a gentleman, a Churchman, would deliberately go out to seek an afternoon's amusement in a poky little country churchyard? Why, apart from everything else, *that* was absolutely mad to start with. Can you really wonder at the result?'

Probably because she still steadfastly refused to look at him, her memory kept losing its hold on the appalling fact facing them. She realised fully only that she was in a great, unwarrantable, and insurmountable difficulty, but until she actually lifted her eyes for a moment she had not fully realised what that difficulty was. She got up with a sudden and horrible nausea. 'One moment,' she said, 'I will see if the servants have gone to bed.'

That long saturnine face, behind which Lawford lay in a dull and desperate ambush, smiled. Something partaking of its clay, some reflex ghost of its rather remarkable features, was even a little amused at Sheila.

She returned in a moment, and stood in profile in the doorway. 'Will you come down?' she remarked distantly.

'One moment, Sheila,' Lawford began miserably. 'Before we take this irrevocable step, a step I implore you to postpone awhile—for what comes, I suppose, may go—what precisely have you told the vicar? I must in fairness know that.'

'In fairness,' she began ironically, and suddenly broke off. Her husband had turned the flame of the lamp low down in the vacant room behind them; the corridor was lit obscurely by the chandelier far down in the hall below. A faint, inexplicable dread fell softly and coldly on her heart. 'Have you no trust in me?' she murmured a little bitterly. 'I have simply told him the truth.'

They softly descended the stairs; she first, the dark figure following close behind her.

CHAPTER THREE

Mr Bethany sat awaiting them in the dining-room, a large, heavily-furnished room with a great benign looking-glass on the mantelpiece, a marble clock, and with rich old damask curtains. Fleecy silver hair was all that was visible of their visitor when they entered. But Mr Bethany rose out of his chair when he heard them, and with a little jerk, turned sharply round. Thus it was that the gold-spectacled vicar and Lawford first confronted each other, the one brightly illuminated, the other framed in the gloom of the doorway. Mr Bethany's first scrutiny was timid and courteous, but beneath it he tried to be keen, and himself hastened round the table almost at a trot, to obtain, as delicately as possible, a closer view. But Lawford, having shut the door behind him, had gone straight to the fire and seated himself, leaning his face in his hands. Mr Bethany smiled faintly, waved his hand almost as if in blessing, but certainly in peace, and tapped Mrs Lawford into the chair upon the other side. But he himself remained standing.

'Mrs Lawford has, I declare, been telling family secrets,' he began, and paused, peering. 'But there, you will forgive an old friend's intrusion—this little confidence about a change, my dear fellow—about a ramble and a change?' He sat down, put up his kind little puckered face and peered again at Lawford, and then very hastily at his wife. But all her attention was centred on the bowed figure opposite to her. Lawford responded to this cautious advance without raising his head.

'You do not wish me to repeat all that my wife tells me she has told you?'

'Dear me, no,' said Mr Bethany cheerfully, 'I wish nothing, nothing, old friend. You must not burden yourself with me. If I may be of any help, here I am.... Oh, no, no....' he paused, with blinking eyes, but wits still shrewd and alert. Why doesn't the man raise his head? he thought. A mere domestic dispute!

'I thought,' he went on ruminatingly, 'I thought on Tuesday, yes, on Tuesday, that you weren't looking quite the thing. Indeed, I remarked on it. But now, I understand from Mrs Lawford that the malady has taken a graver turn—eh, Lawford, an heretical turn? I hear you have been wandering from the true fold.' Mr Bethany leaned forward with what might be described as a very large smile in a very small compass. 'And that, of course, entailed instant retribution.' He broke off solemnly. 'I know Widderstone churchyard well; a most verdant and beautiful spot. The late rector, a Mr Strickland, was a very old friend of mine. And his wife, dear good Alicia, used to set out her babies, in the morning, to sleep and to play there, twenty, dear me, perhaps twenty-five years ago. But I did not know, my dear Lawford, that you—' and suddenly, without an instant's warning, something seemed to shout at him, 'Look, look! He is looking at you!' He stopped, faltered, and a slight warmth came into his face. 'And and you were taken ill there?' His voice had fallen flat and faint.

'I fell asleep—or something of that sort,' came the stubborn reply.

'Yes,' said Mr Bethany, brightly, 'so your wife was saying. "Fell asleep," so have I too—scores of times'; he beamed, with beads of sweat glistening on his forehead. 'And then? I'm not, I'm not persisting?'

'Then I woke; refreshed, I think, as it seemed—I felt much better and came home.'

'Ah, yes,' said his visitor. And after that there was a long, brightly lit, intense pause; at the end of which Lawford raised his face and again looked firmly at his friend.

Mr Bethany was now a shrunken old man; he sat perfectly still, his head craned a little forward, and his veined hands clutching his bent, spare knees.

There wasn't the least sign of devilry, or out-facingness, or insolence in that lean shadowy steady head; and yet he himself was compelled to sidle his glance away, so much the face shook him. He closed his eyes, too, as a cat does after exchanging too direct a scrutiny with human eyes. He put out towards, and withdrew, a groping hand from Mrs Lawford.

'Is it,' came a voice from somewhere, 'is it a great change, sir? I thought perhaps I may have exaggerated—candle-light, you know.'

Mr Bethany remained still and silent, striving to entertain one thought at a time. His lips moved as if he were talking to himself. And again it was Lawford's faltering voice that broke the silence. 'You see,' he said, 'I have never... no fit, or anything of that kind before. I remember on Tuesday... oh yes, quite well. I did feel seedy, very. And we talked, didn't we?—Harvest Festival, Mrs Wine's flowers, the new offertory-bags, and all that. For God's sake, Vicar, it is not as bad as—as they make out?'

Mr Bethany woke with a start. He leaned forward, and stretched out a long black wrinkled sleeve, just managing to reach far enough to tap

Lawford's knee. 'Don't worry, don't worry,' he said soothingly. 'We believe, we believe.'

It was, none the less, a sheer act of faith. He took off his spectacles and took out his handkerchief. 'What we must do, eh, my dear,' he half turned to Mrs Lawford, 'what we must do is to consult, yes, consult together. And later—we must have advice—medical advice; unless, as I very much suspect, it is merely a little quite temporary physical aberration. Science, I am told, is making great strides, experimenting, groping after things which no sane man has ever dreamed of before—without being burned alive for it. What's in a name? Nerves, especially, Lawford.'

Mrs Lawford sat perfectly still, absorbedly listening, turning her face first this way, then that, to each speaker in turn. 'That is what I thought,' she said, and cast one fleeting glance across at the fireplace, 'but—'

The little old gentleman turned sharply with half-blind eyes, and lips tight shut. 'I think,' he said, with a hind of austere humour, 'I think, do you know, I see no "but."' He paused as if to catch the echo and added, 'It's our only course.' He continued to polish round and round his glasses. Mrs Lawford rather magnificently rose.

'Perhaps if I were to leave you together awhile? I shall not be far off. It is,' she explained, as if into a huge vacuum, 'it is a terrible visitation.' She moved gravely round the table and very softly and firmly closed the door after her.

Lawford took a deep breath. 'Of course,' he said, 'you realise my wife does not believe me. She thinks,' he explained naively, as if to himself, 'she thinks I am an imposter. Goodness knows what she does think. I can't think much myself—for long!'

The vicar rubbed busily on. 'I have found, Lawford,' he said smoothly, 'that in all real difficulties the only feasible plan is—is to face the main issue. The others right themselves. Now, to take a plunge into your generosity. You have let me in far enough to make it impossible for me to get out—may I hear then exactly the whole story? All that I know now, so far as I could gather from your wife, poor soul, is of course inconceivable: that you went out one man and came home another. You will understand, my dear man, I am speaking, as it were, by rote. God has mercifully ordered that the human brain works slowly; first the blow, hours afterwards the bruise. Oh, dear me, that man Hume—"on miracles"—positively amazing! So that too, please, you will be quite clear about. *Credo*—not *quia impossible est*, but because you, Lawford, have told me. Now then, if it won't be too wearisome to you, the whole story.' He sat, lean and erect in his big chair, a hand resting loosely on each knee, in one spectacles, in the other a dangling pocket handkerchief. And the dark, sallow, aquiline, formidable figure, with its oddly changing voice, re-told the whole story from the beginning.

'You were aware then of nothing different, I understand, until you actually looked into the glass?'

'Only vaguely. I mean that after waking I felt much better, more alert. And my thoughts—'

'Ah, yes, your thoughts?'

'I hardly know—oh, clear as if I had had a real long rest. It was just like being a boy again. Influenza dispirits one so.'

Mr Bethany gazed without stirring. 'And yet, you know,' he said, 'I can hardly believe, I mean conceive, how—You have been taking no drugs, no quackery, Lawford?'

'I never dose myself,' said Lawford, with sombre pride.

'God bless me, that's Lawford to the echo,' thought his visitor. 'And before—?' he went on gently; 'I really cannot conceive, you see, how a mere fit could... Before you sat down you were quite alone?' He stuck out his head. 'There was nobody with you?'

'With me? Oh no,' came the soft answer.

'What had you been thinking of? In these days of faith-cures, and hypnotism, and telepathy, and subliminalities—why, the simple old world grows very confusing. But rarely, very rarely novel. You were thinking, you say; do you remember, perhaps, just the drift?'

'Well,' began Lawford ruminatingly, 'there was something curious even then, perhaps. I remember, for instance, I knelt down to read an old tombstone. There was a little seat—no back. And an epitaph. The sun was just setting; some French name. And there was a long jagged crack in the stone, like the black line you know one sees after lightning, I mean it's as clear as that even now, in memory. Oh yes, I remember. And then, I suppose, came the sleep—stupid, sluggish: and then; well, here I am.'

'You are absolutely certain, then,' persisted Mr Bethany almost querulously, 'there was no living creature near you? Bless me, Lawford, I see no unkindness in believing what the Bible itself relates. There *are* powers supernatural. Saul, and so on. We are all convinced of that. No one?'

'I remember distinctly,' replied Lawford, in a calm, stubborn voice, 'I looked up all around me, while I was kneeling there, and there wasn't a soul to be seen. Because, you see, it even then occurred to me that it would have looked rather queer—my wandering about like that, I mean. Facing me there were some cypress-trees, and beyond, a low sunken fence, and then, just open country. Up above there were the gravestones toppling down the hill, where I had just strolled down, and sunshine!' He suddenly threw up his hand. 'Oh, marvellous! streaming in gold—flaming, like God's own ante-chamber.'

There was a very pregnant pause. Mr Bethany shrunk back a little into his chair. His lips moved; he folded his spectacles.

'Yes, yes,' he said. And then very quietly he stole one mole-like look into his sidesman's face.

'What is Dr Simon's number?' he said. Lawford was gazing gloomily into the fire. 'Oh, Annandale,' he replied absently. 'I don't know the number.'

'Do you believe in him? Your wife mentioned him. Is he clever?'

'Oh, he's new,' said Lawford; 'old James was our doctor. He—he killed my father.' He laughed out shamefacedly.

'A sound, lovable man,' said Mr Bethany, 'one of the kindest men I ever knew; and a very old friend of mine.'

And suddenly the dark face turned with a shudder from the fire, and spoke in a low trembling voice. 'Only one thing—only one thing—my sanity, my sanity. If once I forget, who will believe me?' He thrust his long lean fingers beneath his coat. 'And mad,' he added; 'I would sooner die.'

Mr Bethany deliberately adjusted his spectacles. 'May I, may I experiment?' he said boldly. There came a tap on the door.

'Bless me,' said the vicar, taking out his watch, 'it is a quarter to twelve. 'Yes, yes, Mrs Lawford,' he trotted round to the door. 'We are beginning to see light—a ray!'

'But I—*I* can see in the dark,' whispered Lawford, as if at a cue, turning with an inscrutable smile to the fire.

The vicar came again, wrapped up in a little tight grey great-coat, and a white silk muffler. He looked up unflinching into Lawford's face, and tears stood in his eyes. 'Patience, patience, my dear fellow,' he repeated gravely, squeezing his hand. 'And rest, complete rest, is imperative. Just till the first thing to-morrow. And till then,' he turned to Mrs Lawford, where she stood looking in at the doorway, 'oh yes, complete quiet; and caution!'

Mrs Lawford let him out. He shook his head once or twice, holding her fingers. 'Oh yes,' he whispered, 'it is your husband, not the smallest doubt. I tried: for *myself*. But something—something has happened.

Don't fret him now. Have patience. Oh yes, it is incredible... the change! But there, the very first thing to-morrow.' She closed the door gently after him, and stepping softly back to the dining-room, peered in. Her husband's back was turned, but he could see her in the looking-glass, stooping a little, with set face watching him, in the silvery stillness.

'Well,' he said, 'is the old—' he doggedly met the fixed eyes facing him there, 'is our old friend gone?'

'Yes,' said Sheila, 'he's gone.' Lawford sighed and turned round. 'It's useless talking now, Sheila. No more questions. I cannot tell you how tired I am. And my head—'

'What is wrong with your head?' inquired his wife discreetly.

The haggard face turned gravely and patiently. 'Only one of my old headaches,' he smiled, 'my old bilious headaches—the hereditary Lawford variety.' But his voice fell low again. 'We must get to bed.'

With a rather pretty and childish movement, Sheila gently drew her hands across her silk skirts. 'Yes, dear,' she said, 'I have made up a bed for you in the large spare room. It is thoroughly aired.' She came softly in, hastened over to a closed work-table that stood under the curtains, and opened it.

Lawford watched her, utterly expressionless, utterly motionless. He opened his mouth and shut it again, still watching his wife as she stooped with ridiculously too busy fingers, searching through her coloured silks.

Again he opened his mouth. 'Yes,' he said, and stalked slowly towards the door. But there he paused. 'God knows,' he said, strangely and meekly, 'I am sorry, sorry for all this. You will forgive me, Sheila?'

She looked up swiftly. 'It's very tiresome, I can't find anywhere,' she murmured, 'I can't find anywhere the—the little red box key.'

Lawford's cheek turned more sallow than ever. 'You are only pretending to look for it,' he said, 'to try me. We both know perfectly well the lock is broken. Ada broke it.'

Sheila let fall the lid; and yet for a while her eyes roved over it as if in violent search for something. Then she turned: 'I am so very glad the vicar was at home,' she said brightly. 'And mind, mind you rest, Arthur. There's nothing so bad but it might be worse.... Oh, I can't, I can't bear it!' She sat down in the chair and huddled her face between her hands, sobbing on and on, without a tear.

Lawford listened and stared solemnly. 'Whatever it may be, Sheila, I will be loyal,' he said.

Her sobs hushed, and again cold horror crept over her. Nobody in the whole world could have said that 'I will be loyal' quite like that—nobody but Arthur. She stood up, patting her hair. 'I don't think my brain would bear much more. It's useless to talk. If you will go up; I will put out the lamp.'

CHAPTER FOUR

One solitary and tall candle burned on the great dressing-table. Faint, solitary pictures broke the blankness of each wall. The carpet was rich, the bed impressive, and the basins on the washstand as uninviting as the bed. Lawford sat down on the edge of it in complete isolation. He sat without stirring, listening to his watch ticking in his pocket. The china clock on the chimney piece pointed cheerfully to the hour of dawn. It was exactly, he computed carefully, five hours and seven minutes fast. Not the slightest sound broke the stillness, until he heard, very, very softly and gradually, the key of his door turn in the oiled wards, and realized that he was a prisoner.

Women were strange creatures. How often he had heard that said, he thought lamely. He felt no anger, no surprise or resentment, at the trick. It was only to be expected. He could sit on till morning; easily till morning. He had never noticed before how empty a well-furnished room could seem. It was his own room too; his best visitors' room. His father-in-law had slept here, with his whiskers on that pillow. His wife's most formidable aunt had been all night here, alone with these pictures. She certainly was... 'But what are *you* doing here?' cried a voice suddenly out of his reverie.

He started up and stretched himself, and taking out the neat little packet that the maid had brought from the chemist's, he drew up a chair, and sat down once more in front of the glass. He sighed vacantly, rose and lifted down from the wall above the fireplace a tinted photograph of himself that Sheila had had enlarged about twelve years ago. It was a brighter, younger, hairier, but unmistakably the same dull indolent Lawford who had ventured into Widderstone churchyard that afternoon. The cheek was a little plumper, the eyes not quite so full-lidded, the hair a little more precisely parted, the upper lip graced with a small blonde moustache. He tilted the portrait into the candlelight, and compared it with this reflection in the glass of what had come out of Widderstone, feature with feature, with perfect composure and extreme care. Then he laid down the massive frame on the table, and gazed quietly at the tiny packet.

It was to be a day of queer experiences. He had never before realized with how many miracles mere everyday life is besieged. Here in this small punctilious packet lay a Sesame—a power of transformation beside which the transformation of that rather flaccid face of the noonday into this tense, sinister face of midnight was but as a moving from house to house—a change just as irrevocable and complete, and yet so very normal. Which should it be, that, or—his face lifted itself once more to the ice-like gloom of the looking-glass—that, or this?

It simply gazed back with a kind of quizzical pity on its lean features under the scrutiny of eyes so deep, so meaningful, so desolate, and yet so indomitably courageous. In the brain behind them a slow and stolid argument was in progress; the one baffling reply on the one side to every appeal on the other being still simply. 'What dreams may come?'

Those eyes surely knew something of dreams, else, why this violent and stubborn endeavour to keep awake.

Lawford did indeed once actually frame the question, 'But who the devil are you?' And it really seemed the eyes perceptibly widened or brightened. The mere vexation of his unparalleled position. Sheila's pathetic incredulity, his old vicar's laborious kindness, the tiresome network of experience into which he would be dragged struggling on the morrow, and on the morrow after that, and after that—the thought of all these things faded for the moment from his mind, lost if not their significance, at least their instancy.

He simply sat face to face with the sheer difficulty of living on at all. He even concluded in a kind of lethargy that if nothing had occurred, no 'change,' he might still be sitting here, Arthur Rennet Lawford, in his best visitor's room, deciding between inscrutable life and just—death. He supposed he was tired out. His thoughts hadn't even the energy to complete themselves. None cared but himself and this—this Silence.

'But what does it all mean?' the insistent voice he was getting to know so well began tediously inquiring again. And every time he raised his eyes, or, rather, as in many cases it seemed, his eyes raised themselves, they saw this haunting face there—a face he no longer bitterly rebelled at, nor dimmed with scrutiny, but a face that was becoming a kind of hold on life, even a kind of refuge, an ally. It was a face that might have come out of a rather flashy book; or such as is revered on the stage. 'A rotten bad face,' he whispered at it in his own familiar slang, after some such abrupt encounter; a fearless, packed, daring, fascinating face, with even—what?—a spice of genius in it. Whose the devil's face was it? What on earth was the matter?... 'Brazen it out,' a jubilant thought cried suddenly; 'follow it up; play the game! give me just one opening. Think—think what I've risked!'

And all these voices thought Lawford, in deadly lassitude, meant only one thing—insanity. A blazing, impotent indignation seized him. He leaned near, peering as it were out of a red dusky mist. He snatched up the china candlestick, and poised it above the sardonic reflection, as if to throw. Then slowly, with infinite pains, he drew back from the glass and replaced the candlestick on the table; stuffed his paper packet into his pocket, took off his boots and threw himself on to the bed. In a little while, in the faint, still light, he opened drowsily wondering eyes. 'Poor old thing!' his voice murmured, 'Poor old Sheila!'

CHAPTER FIVE

It was but little after daybreak when Mrs Lawford, after listening at his door a while, turned the key and looked in on her husband. Blue-grey light from between the venetian blinds just dusked the room. She stood in a bluish dressing-gown, her hand on her bosom, looking down on the lean impassive face. For the briefest instant her heart had leapt with an indescribable surmise; to fall dull as lead once more. Breathing equably and quietly, the strange figure lay stretched upon the bed. 'How can he sleep? How can he sleep?' she whispered with a black and hopeless indignation. What a night she had had! And he!

She turned noiselessly away. The candle had guttered to extinction. The big glass reflected her, voluminous and wan, her dark-ringed eyes, full lips, rich, glossy hair, and rounded chin. 'Yes, yes,' it seemed to murmur mournfully. She turned away, and drawing stealthily near stooped once more quite low, and examined the face on the pillow with lynx-like concentration. And though every nerve revolted at the thought, she was finally convinced, unwillingly, but assuredly, that her husband was here. Indeed, if it were not so, how could she for a single moment have accepted the possibility that he was a stranger? He seemed to haunt, like a ghostly emanation, this strange, detestable face—as memory supplies the features concealed beneath a mask. The face was still and stony, like one dead or imaged in wax, yet beneath it dreams were passing—silly, ordinary Lawford dreams. She was almost alarmed at the terribly rancorous hatred she felt for the face... 'It was just like Arthur to be so taken in!'

Then she too remembered Quain, and remembered also in the slowly paling dusk that the house would soon be stirring. She went out and noiselessly locked the door again. But it was useless to begin looking for Quain now—her husband had a good many dull books, most of them his 'eccentric' father's. What must the servants be thinking? and what was all that talk about a mysterious visitor? She would have to question Ada—diplomatically. She returned to her room and sat down in an arm-chair, and waited. In sheer weariness she fell into a doze, and woke at the sound of dustpan and broom. She rang the bell, and asked for hot water, tea, and a basin of cornflour.

'And please, Ada, be as quiet as possible over your work; your master is in a nice sleep, and must not be disturbed on any account. In the front bedroom.' She looked up suddenly. 'By the way, who let Dr Ferguson in last night?' It was dangerous, but successful.

'Dr Ferguson, ma'am? Oh, you mean... He *was* in.'

Sheila smiled resignedly. 'Was in? What do you mean, "was in"? And where were you, then?'

'I had been sent out to Critchett's, the chemist's.'

'Of course, of course. So cook let Dr Ferguson in, then? Why didn't you say so before, Ada? And did you bring the medicine with you?'

'It was a packet in an envelope, ma'am. But Cook is sure she heard no knock—not while I was out. So Dr Ferguson must have come in quite unbeknown.'

'Well, really,' said Sheila, 'it seems very difficult to get at the truth sometimes. And when illness is in the house I cannot understand why there should be no one available to answer the door. You must have left it ajar, unsecured, when you went out. And pray, what if Dr Ferguson had been some common tramp? That would have been a nice thing.'

'I am quite certain,' said Ada a little flatly, 'that I did shut the door. And cook says she never so much as stirred from the kitchen till I came down the area steps with the packet. And that's all I know about it, ma'am; except that he was here when I came back. I did not know even there was a Dr Ferguson; and my mother has lived here nineteen years.'

'We must be thankful your mother enjoys such good health,' replied Mrs Lawford suavely. 'Please tell cook to be very careful with the cornflour—to be sure it's well mixed and thoroughly done.'

Mrs Lawford's eyes followed with a certain discomfort those narrow print shoulders descending the stairs. And this abominable ruse was—Arthur's! She ran up lightly and listened with her ear to the panel of his door. And just as she was about to turn away again, there came a little light knock at the front door.

Mrs Lawford paused at the loop of the staircase; and not altogether with gratitude or relief she heard the voice of Mr Bethany, inquiring in cautious but quite audible tones after her husband.

She dressed quickly and went down. The little white old man looked very solitary in the long, fireless, drawing-room.

'I could not sleep,' he said; 'I don't think I grasped in the least, I don't indeed, until I was nearly home, the complexity of our problem. I came, in fact, to a lamppost. It was casting a peculiar shadow. And then—you know how such thoughts seize us, my dear—like a sudden inspiration, I realised how tenuous, how appallingly tenuous a hold we every one of us have on our mere personality. But that,' he continued rapidly, 'that's only for ourselves—and after the event. Ours, just now, is to act. And first—?'

'You really do, then—you really are convinced—' began Mrs Lawford.

But Mr Bethany was too quick. 'We must be *most* circumspect. My dear friend, we must be *most* circumspect, for all our sakes. And this, you'll say,' he added, smiling, stretching out his arms, his soft hat in one hand, his umbrella in the other—'this is being circumspect—a seven o'clock in the morning call! But you see, my dear, I have come, as I took the precaution of explaining to the maid, because it's now or never to-day. It does so happen that I have to take a wedding for an old friend's niece at Witchett; so when in need, you see, Providence enables us to tell even the conventional truth. Now really, how is he? has he slept? has he recalled himself at all? is there any change?—and, dear me, how are *you*?'

Mrs Lawford sighed. 'A broken night is really very little to a mother,' she said. 'He is still asleep. He hasn't, I think, stirred all night.'

'Not stirred!' Mr Bethany repeated. 'You baffle me. And you have watched?'

'Oh no,' was the cheerful answer; 'I felt that quiet, solitude; space, was everything; he preferred it so. He—he changed alone, I suppose. Don't you think it almost stands to reason that he will be alone...when he comes back? Was I right? But there, it's useless, it's worse than useless, to talk like this. My husband is gone. Some terrible thing has happened. Whatever the mystery may be, he will never come back alive. My only fear is that I am dragging you into a matter that should from the beginning have been entrusted to—Oh, it's monstrous!' It appeared for a moment as if she were blinking to keep back her tears, yet her scrutiny seemed merely to harden.

Only the merest flicker of the folded eyelids over the greenish eyes of her visitor answered the challenge. He stood small and black, peeping fixedly out of the window at the sunflecked laurels.

'Last night,' he said slowly, 'when I said good-bye to your husband, on the tip of my tongue were the words I have used, in season and out of season, for nearly forty-five years—"God knows best." Well, my dear lady, a sense of humour, a sense of reverence, or perhaps even a taint of scepticism—call it what you will—just intercepted them. Oh no, not any of these, my child; just pity, overwhelming pity. God does know best;

but in a matter like this it is not even my place to say so. It would be good for none of us to endanger our souls even with *verbal* cant. Now, if, do you think, I had just five minutes' talk—five minutes; would it disquiet him?'

Only by an almost undignified haste, for the vicar was remarkably agile, Sheila managed to unlock the bedroom door without apparently his perceiving it, and with a warning finger she preceded him into the great bedroom. 'Oh, yes, yes,' he was whispering to himself; 'alone—well, well!' He hung his hat on his umbrella and leaned it in a corner, and then he turned.

'I don't think, you know, an old friend does him any wrong; but last night I had no real oppor—' He firmly adjusted his spectacles, and looked long into the dark, dispassioned face.

'H'm!' he said, and fidgeted, and peered again. Mrs Lawford watched him keenly.

'Do you still—' she began.

But at the same moment he too broke silence, suddenly stepping back with the innocent remark, 'Has he—has he asked for anything?'

'Only for Quain.'

'"Quain"?'

'The medical Dictionary.'

'Oh, yes; bless me; of course.... A calm, complete sleep of utter prostration—utter nervous prostration. And can one wonder? Poor fellow, poor fellow!' He walked to the window and peered between the blinds. 'Sparrows, sunshine—yes, and here's the postman,' he said, as if to himself. Then he turned sharply round, with mind made up.

'Now, do you leave me here,' he said. 'Take half an hour's quiet rest. He will be glad of a dull old fellow like me when he wakes. And as for my pretty bride, if I miss the train, she must wait till the next. Good discipline, my dear. Oh, dear me! *I* don't change. What a precious experience now this would have been for a tottery, talkative, owlish old parochial creature like me. But there, there. Light words make heavy hearts, I see. I shall be quite comfortable. No, no, I breakfasted at home. There's hat and umbrella; at 9.3 I can fly.'

Mrs Lawford thanked him mutely. He smilingly but firmly bowed her out and closed the door.

But eyes and brain had been very busy. He had looked at the gutted candle; at the tinted bland portrait on the dressing-table; at the chair drawn-up; at the boots; and now again he turned almost with a groan towards the sleeper. Then he took out an envelope, on which he had jotted various memoranda, and waited awhile. Minutes passed and at last the sleeper faintly stirred, muttering.

Mr Bethany stooped quickly. 'What is it, what is it?' he whispered.

Lawford sighed. 'I was only dreaming, Sheila,' he said, and softly, peacefully opened his eyes. 'I dreamed I was in the—' His lids narrowed, his dark eyes fixed themselves on the anxious spectacled face bending over him. 'Mr Bethany! Where? What's wrong?'

His friend put out his hand. 'There, there,' he said soothingly, 'do not be disturbed; do not disquiet yourself.'

Lawford struggled up. Slowly, painfully consciousness returned to him. He glanced furtively round the room, at his clothes, slinkingly at the vicar; licked his lips; flushed with extraordinary rapidity; and suddenly burst into tears.

Mr Bethany sat without movement, waiting till he should have spent himself. 'Now, Lawford,' he said gently, 'compose yourself, old friend. We must face the music—like men.' He went to the window, drew up the blind, peeped out, and took off his spectacles.

'The first thing to be done,' he said, returning briskly to his chair, 'is to send for Simon. Now, does Simon know you *well?*' Lawford shook his head. 'Would he recognise you?... I mean...'

'I have only met him once—in the evening.'

'Good; let him come immediately, then. Tell him just the facts. If I am not mistaken, he will pooh-pooh the whole thing; tell you to keep quiet, not to worry, and so on. My dear fellow, if we realised, say, typhoid, who'd dare to face it? That will give us time; to wait a while, to recover our breath, to see what happens next. And if—as I don't believe for a moment—Why, in that case I heard the other day of a most excellent man—Grosser, of Wimpole Street; nerves. He would be absorbed. He'll bottle you in spirit, Lawford. We'll have him down quietly. You see? But there won't be any necessity. Oh no. By then light will have come. We shall remember. What I mean is this.' He crossed his legs and pushed out his lips. 'We are on quaky ground; and it's absolutely essential that you keep cool, and trust. I am yours, heart and soul—you know that. I own frankly, at first I was shaken. And I have, I confess, been very cunning. But first, faith, then evidence to bolster it up. The faith was absolute'—he placed one firm hand on Lawford's knee—'why, I cannot explain; but it was. The evidence is convincing. But there are others to think of. The shock, the incredibleness, the consequences; we must not scan too closely. Think *with*; never against: and bang go all the arguments. Your wife, poor dear, believes; but of course, of course, she is horribly—' he broke off; 'of course she is *shaken*, you old simpleton! Time will heal all that. Time will wear out the mask. Time will tire out this detestable physical witchcraft. The mind, the self's the thing. Old fogey though I may seem for saying it—that must be kept unsmirched. We won't go wearily over the painful subject again. You told me last night, dear old friend, that you were absolutely alone at Widderstone. That is enough. But here we have visible facts, tangible effects, and there must have been a definite reason and a cause for them. I believe in the devil, in the Powers of Darkness, Lawford, as firmly as I believe he and they are powerless—in the long run. They—what shall we say?—have surrendered their intrinsicality. You can just go through evil, as you can go through a sewer, and come out on the other side too. A loathsome process too. But there—we are not speaking of any such monstrosities, and even if we were, you and I with God's help would just tire them out. And that ally gone, our poor dear old Mrs Grundy will at once capitulate. Eh? Eh?'

Through all this long and arduous harangue, consciousness, like the gradual light of dawn, had been flooding that other brain. And the face that now confronted Mr Bethany, though with his feeble unaided sight he could only very obscurely discern it, was vigilant and keen, in every sharp-cut hungry feature.

A rather prolonged silence followed, the visitor peering mutely. The black eyes nearly closed, the face turned slowly towards the window, saw burnt-out candle, comprehensive glass.

'Yes, yes.' he said; 'I'll send for Simon at once.'

'Good,' said Mr Bethany, and more doubtfully repeated 'good.' 'Now there's only one thing left,' he went on cheerfully. 'I have jotted down a few test questions here; they are questions no one on this earth could answer but you, Lawford. They are merely for external proofs. You won't, you can't, mistake my motive. We cannot foretell or foresee what need may arise for just such jog-trot primitive evidence. I propose that you now answer them here, in writing.'

Lawford stood up and walked to the looking-glass, and paused. He put his hand to his head, 'Yes,' he said, 'of course; it's a rattling good move. I'm not quite awake; myself, I mean. I'll do it now.' He took out a pencil case and tore another leaf from his pocket-book. 'What are they?'

Mr Bethany rang the bell. Sheila herself answered it. She stood on the threshold and looked across through a shaft of autumnal sunshine at her husband, and her husband with a quiet strange smile looked across through the sunshine at his wife. Mr Bethany waited in vain.

'I am just going to put the arch-impostor through his credentials,' he said tartly. 'Now then, Lawford!' He read out the questions, one by one, from his crafty little list, pursing his lips between each; and one by one, Lawford, seated at the dressing-table, fluently scribbled his answers. Then question and answer were rigorously compared by Mr Bethany, with small white head bent close and spectacles poised upon the powerful nose, and signed and dated, and passed to Mrs Lawford without a word.

Mrs Lawford read question and answer where she stood, in complete silence. She looked up. 'Many of these questions I don't know the answers to myself,' she said.

'It is immaterial,' said Mr Bethany.

'One answer is—is inaccurate. 'Yes, yes, quite so: due to a mistake in a letter from myself.'

Mrs Lawford read quietly on, folded the papers, and held them out between finger and thumb. 'The—handwriting...' she remarked very softly.

'Wonderful, isn't it?' said Mr Bethany warmly; 'all the general look and run of the thing different, but every real essential feature unchanged. Now into the envelope. And now a little wax?'

Mrs Lawford stood waiting. 'There's a green piece of sealing-wax,' almost drawled the quiet voice, 'in the top right drawer of the nest in the study, which old James gave me the Christmas before last.' He glanced with lowered eyelids at his wife's flushed cheek. Their eyes met.

'Thank you,' she said.

When she returned the vicar was sitting in a chair, leaning his chin on the knobbed handle of his umbrella. He rose and lit a taper for her with a match from a little green pot on the table. And Mrs Lawford, with trembling fingers, sealed the letter, as he directed, with his own seal.

'There!' he said triumphantly, 'how many more such brilliant lawyers, I wonder, lie dormant in the Church? And who shall keep this?... Why, all three, of course.' He went on without pausing. 'Some little drawer now, secret and undetectable, with a lock.' Just such a little drawer that locked itself with a spring lay by chance in the looking-glass. There the letter was hidden. And Mr Bethany looked at his watch. 'Nineteen minutes,' he said. 'The next thing, my dear child—we're getting on swimmingly—and it's astonishing how things are simplified by mere use—the next thing is to send for Simon.'

Sheila took a deep breath, but did not look up. 'I am entirely in your hands,' she replied.

'So be it,' said he crisply. 'Get to bed, Lawford; it's better so. And I'll look in on my way back from Witchett. I came, my dear fellow, in gloomy disturbance of mind. It was getting up too early; it fogs old brains. Good-bye, good-bye.'

He squeezed Lawford's hand. Then, with umbrella under his arm, his hat on his head, his spectacles readjusted, he hurried out of the room. Mrs Lawford followed him. For a few minutes Lawford sat motionless, with head bent a little, and eyes restlessly scanning the door. Then he rose abruptly, and in a quarter of an hour was in bed, alone with his slow thoughts: while a basin of cornflour stood untasted on a little table at his bedside, and a cheerful fire burned in the best visitors' room's tiny grate.

At half-past eleven Dr Simon entered this soundless seclusion. He sat down beside Lawford, and took temperature and pulse. Then he half closed his lids, and scanned his patient out of an unusually dark, un-English face, with straight black hair, and listened attentively to his rather incoherent story. It was a story very much modified and rounded off. Nor did Lawford draw Dr Simon's attention to the portrait now smiling conventionally above their heads from the wall over the fireplace.

'It was rather bleak—the wind; and, I think, perhaps, I had had a touch of influenza. It was a silly thing to do. But still, Dr Simon, one doesn't expect—well, there, I don't feel the same man—physically. I really cannot explain how great a change has taken place. And yet I feel perfectly fit in myself. And if it were not for—for being laughed at, go back to town, to-day. Why my wife scarcely recognised me.'

Dr Simon continued his scrutiny. Try as he would, Lawford could not raise his downcast eyes to meet direct the doctor's polite attention.

'And what,' said Dr Simon, 'what precisely is the nature of the change? Have you any pain?'

'No, not the least pain,' said Lawford; 'I think, perhaps, or rather my face *is* a little shrunken—and yet lengthened; at least it feels so; and a faint twinge of rheumatism. But my hair—well, I don't know; it's difficult to say one's self.' He could get on so very much better, he thought, if only his mind would be at peace and these preposterous promptings and voices were still.

Dr Simon faced the window, and drew his hand softly over his head. 'We never can be too cautious at a certain age, and especially after influenza,' he said. 'It undermines the whole system, and in particular the nervous system; leaving the mind the prey of the most melancholy fancies. I should astound you, Mr Lawford, with the devil influenza plays.... A slight nervous shock and a chill; quite slight, I hope. A few days' rest and plenty of nourishment. There's nothing; temperature inconsiderable. All perfectly intelligible. Most certainly reassure yourself! And as for the change you speak of'—he looked steadily at the dark face on the pillow and smiled amiably—'I don't think we need worry much about that. It certainly was a bleak wind yesterday—and a cemetery, my dear sir! It was indiscreet—yes, very.' He held out his hand. 'You must not be alarmed,' he said, very distinctly with the merest trace of an accent; 'air, sunshine, quiet, nourishment; sleep—that is all. The little window might be a few inches open, and—and any light reading.'

He opened the door and joined Mrs Lawford on the staircase. He talked to her quietly over his shoulder all the way downstairs. 'It was, it was sporting with Providence—a wind, believe me, nearly due east, in spite of the warm sunshine.'

'But the change—the change!' Mrs Lawford managed to murmur tragically, as he strode to the door. Dr Simon smiled, and gracefully tapped his forehead with a red-gloved forefinger.

'Humour him, humour him,' he repeated indulgently. 'Rest and quiet will soon put that little trouble out of his head. Oh yes, I did notice it—the set drawn look, and the droop: quite so. Good morning.'

Mrs Lawford gently closed the door after him. A glimpse of Ada, crossing from room to room, suggested a precaution. She called out in her clearest notes. 'If Dr Ferguson should call while I am out, Ada, will you please tell him that Dr Simon regretted that he was unable to wait? Thank you.' She paused with hand on the balusters, then slowly ascended the stairs. Her husband's face was turned to the ceiling, his hands clasped above his head. She took up her stand by the fireplace, resting one silk-slippered foot on the fender. 'Dr Simon is reassuring,' she said, 'but I do hope, Arthur, you will follow his advice. He looks a fairly clever man.... But with a big practice.... Do you think, dear, he quite realised the extent of the—the change?'

'I told him what happened,' said her husband's voice out of the bed-clothes.

'Yes, yes, I know,' said Sheila soothingly; 'but we must remember he is comparatively a stranger. He would not detect—'

'What did he tell you?' asked the voice.

Mrs Lawford deliberately considered. If only he would always thus keep his face concealed, how much easier it would be to discuss matters rationally. 'You see, dear,' she said softly, 'I know, of course, nothing about the nerves; but personally, I think his suggestion absurd. No mere fancy, surely, can make a lasting alteration in one's face. And your hair—I don't want to say anything that may seem unkind—but isn't it really quite a distinct shade darker, Arthur?'

'Any great strain will change the colour of a man's hair,' said Lawford stolidly; 'at any rate, to white. Why, I read once of a fellow in India, a Hindoo, or something, who—'

'But have you *had* any intense strain, or anxiety?' broke in Sheila. 'You might, at least, have confided in me; that is, unless—But there, don't you think really, Arthur, it would be much more satisfactory in every way if we had further advice at once? Alice will be home next week. To-morrow is the Harvest Festival, and next week, of course, the Dedication; and, in any case, the Bazaar is out of the question. They will have to find another stall-holder. We must do our utmost to avoid comment or scandal. Every minute must help to—to fix a thing like that. I own even now I cannot realise what this awful calamity means. It's useless to brood on it. We must, as the poor dear old vicar said only last night, keep our heads clear. But I am sure Dr Simon was under a misapprehension. If, now, it was explained to him, a little more fully, Arthur—a photograph. Oh, anything on earth but this dreadful wearing uncertainty and suspense! Besides ...is Simon quite an English name?'

Lawford drew further into his pillow. 'Do as you think best, Sheila,' he said. 'For my own part, I believe it may be as he suggests—partly an illusion, a touch of nervous breakdown. It simply can't be as bad as I think it is. If it were, you would not be here talking like this; and Bethany wouldn't have believed a word I said. Whatever it is, it's no good crying it on the housetops. Give me time, just time. Besides, how do we know what he really thought? Doctors don't tell their patients everything. Give the poor chap a chance, and more so if he is a foreigner. He's'—his voice sank almost to a whisper—'he's no darker than this. And do, please, Sheila, take this infernal stuff away, and let me have something solid. I'm not ill—in that way. All I want is peace and quiet, time to think. Let me fight it out alone. It's been sprung on me. The worst's not over. But I'll win through; wait! And if not—well, you shall not suffer, Sheila. Don't be afraid. There are other ways out.'

Sheila broke down. 'Any one would think to hear you talk, that I was perfectly heartless. I told Ada to be most careful about the cornflour. And as for other ways out, it's a positively wicked thing to say to me when I'm nearly distracted with trouble and anxiety. What motive could you have had for loitering in an old cemetery? And in an east wind! It's useless for me to remain here, Arthur, to be accused of every horrible thing that comes into a morbid imagination. I will leave you, as you suggest, in peace.'

'One moment, Sheila,' answered the muffled voice. 'I have accused you of nothing. If you knew all; if you could read my thoughts, you would be surprised, perhaps, at my—But never mind that. On the other hand, I really do think it would be better for the present to discuss the thing no more. To-day is Friday. Give this miserable face a week. Talk it over with Bethany if you like. But I forbid'—he struggled up in bed, sallow and sinister—'I flatly forbid, please understand, any other interference till then. Afterwards you must do exactly as you please. Send round the Town Crier! But till then, silence!'

Sheila with raised head confronted him. 'This, then, is your gratitude. So be it. Silence, no doubt! Until it's too late to take action. Until you have wormed your way in, and think you are safe. To have believed! Where is my husband? that is what I am asking you now. When and how you have learned his secrets God only knows, and your conscience! But he always was a simpleton at heart. I warn you, then. Until next Thursday I consent to say nothing provided you remain quiet; make no disturbance, no scandal here. The servants and all who inquire shall simply be told that my husband is confined to his room with—with a nervous breakdown, as you have yourself so glibly suggested. I am at your mercy, I own it. The vicar believes your preposterous story—with his spectacles off. You would convince anybody with the wicked cunning with which you have cajoled and wheedled him, with which you have deceived and fooled a foreign doctor. But you will not convince me. You will not convince Alice. I have friends in the world, though you may not be aware of it, who will not be quite so apt to believe any cock-and-bull story you may see fit to invent. That is all I have to say. To-night I tell the vicar all that I have just told you. And from this moment, please, we are strangers. I shall come into the room no more than necessity dictates. On Friday we resume our real parts. My husband—Arthur—to—to connive at... Phh!'

Rage had transfigured her. She scarcely heard her own words. They poured out senselessly, monotonously, one calling up another, as if from the lips of a Cassandra. Lawford sank back into bed, clutching the sheets with both lean hands. He took a deep breath and shut his mouth.

'It reminds me, Sheila,' he began arduously, 'of our first quarrel before we were married, the evening after your aunt Rose died at

Llandudno—do you remember? You threw open the window, and I think—I saved your life.' A pause followed. Then a queer, almost inarticulate voice added, 'At least, I am afraid so.'

A cold and awful quietness fell on Sheila's heart. She stared fixedly at the tuft of dark hair, the only visible sign of her husband, on the pillow. Then, taking up the basin of cold cornflour, she left the room. In a quarter of an hour she reappeared carrying a tray, with ham and eggs and coffee and honey invitingly displayed. She laid it down.

'There is only one other question,' she said, with perfect composure—'that of money. Your signature as it appears on the—the document drawn up this morning, would, of course, be quite useless on a cheque. I have taken all the money I could find; it is in safety. You may, however, conceivably be in need of some yourself; here is five pounds. I have my own cheque-book, and shall therefore have no need to consider the question again for—for the present. So far as you are concerned, I shall be guided solely by Mr Bethany. He will, I do not doubt, take full responsibility.'

'And may the Lord have mercy on my soul!' uttered a stifled, unfamiliar voice from the bed. Mrs Lawford stooped. 'Arthur!' she cried faintly, 'Arthur!'

Lawford raised himself on his elbow with a sigh that was very near to being a sob. 'Oh, Sheila, if you'd only be your real self! What is the use of all this pretence? Just consider *my* position a little. The fear and horror are not all on your side. You called me Arthur even then. I'd willingly do anything you wish to save you pain; you know that. Can't we be friends even in this—this ghastly—Won't you, Sheila?'

Mrs Lawford drew back, struggling with a doubtful heart.

'I think,' she said, 'it would be better not to discuss that now.'

The rest of the morning Lawford remained in solitude.

CHAPTER SIX

There were three books in the room—Jeremy Taylor's 'Holy Living and Dying,' a volume of the *Quiver*, and a little gilded book on wildflowers. He read in vain. He lay and listened to the uproar of his thoughts on which an occasional sound—the droning of a fly, the cry of a milkman, the noise of a passing van—obtruded from the workaday world. The pale gold sunlight edged softly over the bed. He ate up everything on his tray. He even, on the shoals of nightmare, dreamed awhile. But by and by as the hours wheeled slowly on he grew less calm, less strenuously resolved on lying there inactive. Every sparrow that twittered cried reveille through his brain. He longed with an ardour strange to his temperament to be up and doing.

What if his misfortune was, as he had in the excitement of the moment suggested to Sheila, only a morbid delusion of mind; shared too in part by sheer force of his absurd confession? Even if he was going mad, who knows how peaceful a release that might not be? Could his shrewd old vicar have implicitly believed in him if the change were as complete as he supposed it? He flung off the bedclothes and locked the door. He dressed himself, noticing, he fancied, with a deadly revulsion of feeling, that his coat was a little too short in the sleeves, his waistcoat too loose. In the midst of his dressing came Sheila bringing his luncheon. 'I'm sorry,' he called out, stooping quickly beside the bed, 'I can't talk now. Please put the tray down.'

About half an hour afterwards he heard the outer door close, and peeping from behind the curtains saw his wife go out. All was drowsily quiet in the house. He devoured his lunch like a schoolboy. That finished to the last crumb, without a moment's delay he covered his face with a towel, locked the door behind him, put the key in his pocket, and ran lightly downstairs. He stuffed the towel into an ulster pocket, put on a soft, wide-brimmed hat, and noiselessly let himself out. Then he turned with an almost hysterical delight and ran—ran like the wind, without pausing, without thinking, straight on, up one turning, down another, until he reached a broad open common, thickly wooded, sprinkled with gorse and hazel and may, and faintly purple with fading heather. There he flung himself down in the beautiful sunlight, among the yellowing bracken, to recover his breath.

He lay there for many minutes, thinking almost with composure. Flight, it seemed, had for the moment quietened the demands of that other feebly struggling personality which was beginning to insinuate itself into his consciousness, which had so miraculously broken in and taken possession of his body. He would not think now. All he needed was a little quiet and patience before he threw off for good and all his right to be free, to be his own master, to call himself sane.

He scrambled up and turned his face towards the westering sun. What was there in the stillness of its beautiful splendour that seemed to sharpen his horror and difficulty, and yet to stir him to such a daring and devilry as he had never known since he was a boy? There was little sound of life; somewhere an unknown bird was singing, and a few late bees were droning in the bracken. All these years he had, like an old blind horse, stolidly plodded round and round in a dull self-set routine. And now, just when the spirit had come for rebellion, the mood for a harmless truancy, there had fallen with them too this hideous enigma. He sat there with the dusky silhouette of the face that was now drenched with sunlight in his mind's eye. He set off again up the stony incline.

Why not walk on and on? In time real wholesome weariness would come; he could sleep at ease in some pleasant wayside inn, without once meeting the eyes that stood as it were like a window between himself and a shrewd incredulous scoffing world that would turn him into a monstrosity and his story into a fable. And in a little while, perhaps in three days, he would awaken out of this engrossing nightmare, and know he was free, this black dog gone from his back, and (as the old saying expressed it without any one dreaming what it really meant) his own man again. How astonished Sheila would be; how warmly she would welcome him!... Oh yes, of course she would.

He came again to a standstill. No voice answered him out of that illimitable gold and blue. Nothing seemed aware of him. But as he stood there, doubtful as Cain on the outskirts of the unknown, he caught the sound of a footfall on the lonely and stone-strewn path.

The ground sloped steeply away to the left, and slowly mounting the hillside came mildly on an old lady he knew, a Miss Sinnet, an old friend of his mother's. There was just such a little seat as that other he knew so well, on the brow of the hill. He made his way to it, intending to sit quietly there until the little old lady had passed by. Up and up she came. Her large bonnet appeared, and then her mild white face, inclined a little towards him as she ascended. Evidently this very seat was her goal; and evasion was impossible. Evasion!... Memory rushed back and set his pulses beating. He turned boldly to the sun, and the old lady, with a brief glance into his face, composed herself at the other end of the little seat. She gazed out of a gentle reverie into the golden valley. And so they sat a while. And almost as if she had felt the bond of acquaintance between them, she presently sighed, and addressed him: 'A very, very, beautiful view, sir.'

Lawford paused, then turned a gloomy, earnest face, gilded with sunshine. 'Beautiful, indeed,' he said, 'but not for me. No, Miss Sinnet, not for me.'

The old lady gravely turned and examined the aquiline profile. 'Well, I confess,' she remarked urbanely, 'you have the advantage of me.'

Lawford smiled uneasily. 'Believe me, it is little advantage.'

'My sight,' said Miss Sinnet precisely, 'is not so good as I might wish; though better perhaps than I might have hoped; I fear I am not much wiser; your face is still unfamiliar to me.'

'It is not unfamiliar to me,' said Lawford. Whose trickery was this? he thought, putting such affected stuff into his mouth.

A faint lightening of pity came into the silvery and scrupulous countenance. 'Ah, dear me, yes,' she said courteously.

Lawford rested a lean hand on the seat. 'And have you,' he asked, 'not the least recollection in the world of my face?'

'Now really,' she said, smiling blandly, 'is that quite fair? Think of all the scores and scores of faces in seventy long years; and how very treacherous memory is. You shall do me the service of *reminding* me of one whose name has for the moment escaped me.'

'I am the son of a very old friend of yours, Miss Sinnet,' said Lawford quietly 'a friend that was once your schoolfellow at Brighton.'

'Well, now,' said the old lady, grasping her umbrella, 'that is undoubtedly a clue; but then, you see, all but one of the friends of my girlhood are dead; and if I have never had the pleasure of meeting her son, unless there is a decided resemblance, how am I to recollect *her* by looking at *him?*'

'There is, I believe, a likeness,' said Lawford.

She nodded her great bonnet at him with gentle amusement. 'You are insistent in your fancy. Well, let me think again. The last to leave me was Fanny Urquhart, that was—let me see—last October. Now you are certainly not Fanny Urquhart's son,' she stooped austerely, 'for she never had one. Last year, too, I heard that my dear, dear Mrs Jameson was dead. *Her* I hadn't met for many, many years. But, if I may venture to say so, yours is not a Scottish face; and she not only married a Scottish husband, but was herself a Dunbar. No, I am still at a loss.'

A miserable strife was in her chance companion's mind, a strife of anger and recrimination. He turned his eyes wearily to the fast declining sun. 'You will forgive my persistency, but I assure you it is a matter of life or death to me. Is there no one my face recalls? My voice?'

Miss Sinnet drew her long lips together, her eyebrows lifted with the faintest perturbation. 'But he certainly knows my name,' she said to herself. She turned once more, and in the still autumnal beauty, beneath that pale blue arch of evening, these two human beings confronted one another again. She eyed him blandly, yet with a certain grave directness.

'I don't really think,' she said, 'you *can* be Mary Lawford's son. I could scarcely have mistaken *him*.'

Lawford gulped and turned away. He hardly knew what this surge of feeling meant. Was it hope, despair, resentment; had he caught even the echo of an unholy joy? His mind for a moment became confused as if in the tumult of a struggle. He heard himself expostulate, 'Ah, Miss Bennett, I fear I set you too difficult a task.'

The old lady drew abruptly in, like a trustful and gentle snail into its shocked house. 'Bennett, sir; but my name is not Bennett.'

And again Lawford accepted the miserable prompting. 'Not Bennett!... How can I ever then apologise for so frantic a mistake?'

The little old lady took firm hold of her umbrella. She did not answer him. 'The likeness, the likeness!' he began unctuously, and stopped, for the glance that dwelt fleetingly on him was cold with the formidable dignity and displeasure of age. He raised his hat and turned miserably home. He strode on out of the last gold into the blue twilight. What fantastic foolery of mind was mastering him? He cast a hurried look over his shoulder at the kindly and offended old figure sitting there, solitary, on the little seat, in her great bonnet, with back turned resolutely upon him—the friend of his dead mother who might have proved in his need a friend indeed to him. And he had by this insane caprice hopelessly estranged her.

She would remember this face well enough now, he thought bitterly, and would take her place among his quiet enemies, if ever the day of reckoning should come. It was scandalous, it was banal to have abused her trust and courtesy. Oh, it was hopeless to struggle any more! The fates were against him. They had played him a trick. He was to be their transitory sport, as many a better man he could himself recollect had been before him. He would go home and give in; let Sheila do with him what she pleased. No one but a lunatic could have acted as he had, with just that frantic hint of method so remarkable in the insane.

He left the common. A lamplighter was lighting the lamps. A thin evening haze was on the air. If only he had stayed at home that fateful afternoon! Who, what had induced him, enticed him to venture out? And even with the thought welled up into his mind an intense desire to go to the old green time-worn churchyard again; to sit there contentedly alone, where none heeded the completest metamorphosis, down beside the yew-trees. What a fool he had been. There alone, of course, lay his only possible chance of recovery. He would go to-morrow. Perhaps Sheila had not yet discovered his absence; and there would be no difficulty in repeating so successful a stratagem.

Remembrance of his miserable mistake, of Miss Sinnet, faintly returned to him as he swiftly mounted the steps to his porch. Poor old lady. He would make amends for his discourtesy when he was quite himself again. She should some day hear, perhaps, his infinitely tragic, infinitely comic experience from his own lips. He would take her some flowers, some old keepsake of his mother's. What would he not do when the old moods and brains of the stupid Arthur Lawford, whom he had appreciated so little and so superficially, came back to him.

He ran up the steps and stopped dead, his hand in his pocket, chilled and aghast. Sheila had taken his keys. He stood there, dazed and still, beneath the dim yellow of his own fanlight; and once again that inward spring flew back. 'Brazen it out; brazen it out! Knock and ring!'

He knocked flamboyantly, and rang.

There came a quiet step and the door opened. 'Dr Simon, of course, has called?' he inquired suavely.

'Yes, sir.'

'Ah, and gone'—as I feared. And Mrs Lawford?'

'I think Mrs Lawford is in, sir.'

Lawford put out a detaining hand. 'We will not disturb her; we will not disturb her. I can find my way up; oh yes, thank you!'

But Ada still palely barred the way. 'I think, sir,' she said, 'Mrs Lawford would prefer to see you herself; she told me most particularly "all callers." And Mr Lawford was not to be disturbed on any account.'

'Disturbed? God forbid!' said Lawford, but his dark eyes failed to move these lightest hazel. 'Well,' he continued nonchalantly, 'perhaps—perhaps it—*would* be as well if Mrs Lawford should know that I am here. No, thank you, I won't come in. Please go and tell—' But even as the maid turned to obey, Sheila herself appeared at the dining-room door in hat and veil.

Lawford hesitated an immeasurable moment. In one swift glance he perceived the lamplit mystery of evening, beckoning, calling, pleading—Fly, fly! Home's here for you. Begin again, begin again. And there before him in quiet and hostile decorum stood maid and mistress. He took off his hat and stepped quickly in.

'So late, so very late, I fear,' he began glibly. 'A sudden call, a perfectly impossible distance. Shall we disturb him, do you think?'

'Wouldn't it,' began Sheila softly, 'be rather a pity perhaps? Dr Simon seemed to think.... But, of course, you must decide that.'

Ada turned quiet small eyes.

'No, no, by no means,' he almost mumbled.

And a hard, slow smile passed over Sheila's face. 'Excuse me one moment,' she said; 'I will see if he is awake.' She swept swiftly forward, superb and triumphant, beneath the gaze of those dark, restless eyes. But so still was home and street that quite distinctly a clear and youthful laughter was heard, and light footsteps approaching. Sheila paused. Ada, in the act of closing the door, peered out. 'Miss Alice, ma'am,' she said.

And in this infinitesimal advantage of time Dr Ferguson had seized his vanishing opportunity, and was already swiftly mounting the stairs. Mrs Lawford stood with veil half raised and coldly smiling lips and, as if it were by pre-arrangement, her daughter's laughing greeting from the garden, and from the landing above her, a faint 'Ah, and how are we now?' broke out simultaneously. And Ada, silent and discreet, had thrown open the door again to the twilight and to the young people ascending the steps.

Lawford was still sitting on his bed before a cold and ashy hearth when Sheila knocked at the door.

'Yes?' he said; 'who's there?' No answer followed. He rose with a shuddering sigh and turned the key. His wife entered.

'That little exhibition of finesse was part of our agreement, I suppose?'

'I say—' began Lawford.

'To creep out in my absence like a thief, and to return like a mountebank; that was part of our compact?'

'I say,' he stubbornly began again, 'did you *wire* for Alice?'

'Will you please answer my question? Am I to be a mere catspaw in your intrigues, in this miserable masquerade before the servants? To set the whole place ringing with the name of a doctor that doesn't exist, and a bedridden patient that slips out of the house with his bedroom key in his pocket! Are you aware that Ada has been hammering at your door every half-hour of your absence? Are you aware of that? How much,' she continued in a low, bitter voice, 'how much should I offer for her discretion?'

'Who was that with Alice?' inquired the same toneless voice.

'I refuse to be ignored. I refuse to be made a child of. Will you please answer me?'

Lawford turned. 'Look here, Sheila,' he began heavily, 'what about Alice? If you wired: well, it's useless to say anything more. But if you didn't, I ask you just this one thing. Don't tell her!'

'Oh, I perfectly appreciate a father's natural anxiety.'

Her husband drew up his shoulders as if to receive a blow. 'Yes, yes,' he said, 'but you won't?'

The sound of a young laughing voice came faintly up from below. 'How did Jimmie Fortescue know she was coming home to-day?'

'Will you not inquire of Jimmie Fortescue for yourself?'

'Oh, what is the use of sneering?' began the dull voice again. 'I am horribly tired, Sheila. And try how you will, you can't convince me that you believe for a moment that I am not myself, that you are as hard as you pretend. An acquaintance, even a friend might be deceived; but husband and wife—oh no! It isn't only a man's face that's himself—or even his hands.' He looked at them, straightened them slowly out, and buried them in his pockets. 'All I care about now is Alice. Is she, or is she not going to be told? I am simply asking you to give her just a chance.'

'"Simply asking me to give Alice a chance"; now isn't that really just a little...?'

Lawford slowly shook his head. 'You know in your heart it isn't, Sheila; you understand me quite well, although you persistently pretend not to. I can't argue now. I can't speak up for myself. I am just about as far down as I can go. It's only Alice.'

'I see; a lucid interval?' suggested his wife in a low, trembling voice.

'Yes, yes, if you like,' said her husband patiently, '"a lucid interval." Don't please look at my face like that, Sheila. Think—think that it's just lupus, just some horrible disfigurement.'

Not much light was in the large room, and there was something so extraordinarily characteristic of her husband in those stooping shoulders, in the head hung a little forward, and in the preternaturally solemn voice, that Sheila had to bend a little over the bed to catch a glimpse of the sallow and keener face again. She sighed; and even on her own strained ear her sigh sounded almost like one of relief.

'It's useless, I know, to ask you anything while you are in this mood,' continued Lawford dully; 'I know that of old.'

The white, ringed hands clenched, '"Of old!"'

'I didn't mean anything. Don't listen to what I say. It's only—it's just Alice knowing, that was all; I mean at once.'

'Don't for a moment suppose I am not perfectly aware that it is only Alice you think of. You were particularly anxious about my feelings, weren't you? You broke the news to me with the tenderest solicitude. I am glad our—our daughter shares my husband's love.'

'Look here,' said Lawford densely, 'you know that I love you as much as ever; but with this—as I am; what would be the good of my saying so?' Mrs Lawford took a deep breath.

And a voice called softly at the door, 'Mother, are you there? Is father awake? May I come in?'

In a flash the memory returned to her; twenty-four hours ago she was asking that very question of this unspeakable figure that sat hunched-up before her.

'One moment, dear,' she called. And added in a very low voice, 'Come here!'

Lawford looked up. 'What?' he said.

'Perhaps, perhaps,' she whispered, 'it isn't quite so bad.'

'For mercy's sake, Sheila,' he said, 'don't torture me; tell the poor child to go away.'

She paused. 'Are you there, Alice? Would you mind, father says, waiting a little? He is so very tired.'

'Too tired to.... Oh, very well, mother.'

Mrs Lawford opened the door, and called after her, 'Is Jimmie gone?'

'Oh, yes, hours.'

'Where did you meet?'

'I couldn't get a carriage at the station. He carried my dressing-bag; I begged him not to. The other's coming on. You know what Jimmie is. How very, very lucky I *did* come home. I don't know what made me; just an impulse; they did laugh at me so. Father dear—do speak to me; how are you now?'

Lawford opened his mouth, gulped, and shook his head.

'Ssh, dear!' whispered Sheila, 'I think he has fallen asleep. I will be down in a minute.' Mrs Lawford was about to close the door when Ada appeared.

'If you please, ma'am,' she said, 'I have been waiting, as you told me, to let Dr Ferguson out, but it's nearly seven now; and the table's not laid yet.'

'I really should have thought, Ada,' Sheila began, then caught back the angry words, and turned and looked over her shoulder into the room. 'Do you think you will need anything more, Dr Ferguson?' she asked in a sepulchral voice.

Again Lawford's lips moved; again he shook his head.

'One moment, Ada,' she said closing the door. 'Some more medicine—what medicine? Quick! She mustn't suspect.'

'"What medicine?"' repeated Lawford stolidly.

'Oh, vexing, vexing; don't you *see* we must send her out? Don't you see? What was it you sent to Critchett's for last night? Tell him that's gone: we want more of *that*.'

Lawford stared heavily. Oh, yes, yes,' he said thickly, 'more of that....'

Sheila, with a shrug of extreme distaste and vexation, hastily opened the door. 'Dr Ferguson wants a further supply of the drug which Mr Critchett made up for Mr Lawford yesterday evening. You had better go at once, Ada, and please make as much haste as you possibly can.'

'I say, I say,' began Lawford; but it was too late, the door was shut.

'How I detest this wretched falsehood and subterfuge. What could have induced you....?'

'Yes,' said her husband, 'what! I think I'll be getting to bed again, Sheila; I forgot I had been ill. And now I do really feel very tired. But I should like to feel—in spite of this hideous—I should like to feel we are friends, Sheila.'

Sheila almost imperceptibly shuddered, crossed the room, and faced the still, almost lifeless mask. 'I spoke,' she said, in a low, cold, difficult voice—'I spoke in a temper this morning. You must try to understand what a shock it has been to me. Now, I own it frankly, I know you are—Arthur. But God only knows how it frightens me, and—and—horrifies me.' She shut her eyes beneath her veil. They waited on in silence a while.

'Poor boy!' she said at last, lightly touching the loose sleeve; 'be brave; it will all come right, soon. Meanwhile, for Alice's sake, if not for mine, don't give way to—to caprices, and all that. Keep quietly here, Arthur. And—and forgive my impatience.'

He put out his hand as if to touch her. 'Forgive you!' he said humbly, pushing it stubbornly back into his pocket again. 'Oh, Sheila, the forgiveness is all on your side. You know *I* have nothing to forgive.' A long silence fell between them.

'Then, to-night,' at last began Sheila wearily, drawing back, 'we say nothing to Alice, except that you are too tired—just nervous prostration—to see her. What we should do without this influenza, I cannot conceive. Mr Bethany will probably look in on his way home; and then we can talk it over—we can talk it over again. So long as you are like this, yourself, in mind, why I—What is it now?' she broke off querulously.

'If you please, ma'am, Mr Critchett says he doesn't know Dr Ferguson, his name's not in the Directory, and there must be something wrong with the message, and he's sorry, but he must have it in writing because there was more even in the first packet than he ought by rights to send. What shall I do, if you please?'

Still looking at her husband. Sheila listened quietly to the end, and then, as if in inarticulate disdain, she deliberately shrugged her shoulders, and went out to play her part unaided.

CHAPTER SEVEN

Her husband turned wearily once more, and drawing up a chair sat down in front of the cold grate. He realised that Sheila thought him as much of a fool now as she had for the moment thought him an impostor, or something worse, the night before. That was at least something gained. He realised, too, in a vague way that the exuberance of mind that had practically invented Dr Ferguson, and outraged Miss Sinnet, had quite suddenly flickered out. It was astonishing, he thought, with gaze fixed innocently on the black coals, that he should ever have done such things. He detested that kind of 'rot'; that jaunty theatrical pose so many men prided their jackdaw brains on.

And he sat quite still, like a cat at a cranny, listening, as it were, for the faintest remotest stir that might hint at any return of this—activity. It was the first really sane moment he had had since the 'change.' Whatever it was that had happened at Widderstone was now distinctly weakening in effect. Why, now, perhaps? He stole a thievish look over his shoulder at the glass, and cautiously drew finger and thumb down that beaked nose. Then he really quietly smiled, a smile he felt this abominable facial caricature was quite unused to, the superior Lawford smile of guileless contempt for the fanatical, the fantastic, and the bizarre: *He* wouldn't have sat with his feet on the fender before a burnt-out fire.

And the animosity of that 'he,' uttered only just under his breath, surprised even himself. It actually did seem as if there were a chance; if only he kept cool and collected. If the whole mind of a man was bent on being one thing, surely no power on earth, certainly not on earth, could for long compel him to look another, any more (followed the resplendent thought) than vice versa.

That, in fact, was the trick that had been in fitful fashion played him since yesterday. Obviously, and apart altogether from his promise to Sheila, the best possible thing he could do would be to walk quietly over to Widderstone to-morrow and like a child that has lost a penny, just make the attempt to reverse the process: look at the graves, read the inscriptions on the weather-beaten stones, compose himself once more to sleep on the little seat.

Magic, witchcraft, possession, and all that—well, Mr Bethany might prefer to take it on the authority of the Bible if it was his duty. But it was at least mainly Old Testament stuff, like polygamy, Joshua, and the 'unclean beasts.' The 'unclean beasts.' It was simply, as Simon had said, mainly an affair of the nerves, like Indian jugglery. He had heard of dozens of such cases, or similar cases. And it was hardly likely that cases even remotely like his own would be much bragged about, or advertised. All those mysterious 'disappearances,' too, which one reads about so repeatedly? What of them? Even now, he felt (and glanced swiftly behind him at the fancy), it would be better to think as softly as possible, not to hope too openly, certainly not to triumph in the least degree, just in case of—well—listeners.

He would wrap up too. And he wouldn't tell Sheila of the project till he had come safely back. What an excellent joke it would be to confess meekly to his escapade, and to be scolded, and then suddenly to reveal himself. He sat back and gazed with an almost malignant animosity at the face in the portrait, comely and plump.

An inarticulate, unfathomable depression rolled back on him, like a mist out of the sea. He hastily undressed, put watch and door-key and Critchett's powder under his pillow, paused, vacantly ruminated, and then replaced the powder in his waistcoat pocket, said his prayers, and got shivering to bed. He did not feel hurt at Sheila's leaving him like this. So long as she really believed in him. And now—Alice was home. He listened, trying not to shiver, for her voice; and sometimes heard, he fancied, the clear note. It was this beastly influenza that made him feel so cold and lifeless. But all would soon come right—that is, if only that face, luminous against the floating darkness within, would not appear the instant he closed his eyes.

But legions of dreams are Influenza's allies. He fell into a chill doze, heard voices innumerable, and one above the rest, shouting them down, until there fell a lull. And another, as it were, from afar said quite clearly and distinctly, 'But surely, my dear, you have heard the story of the poor old charwoman who talked Greek in her delirium? A little school French need not alarm us.' And Lawford opened his eyes again on Mr Bethany standing at his bed.

'Tt, tt! There, I've been and waked him. And yet they say men make such excellent nurses in time of war. But you see, Lawford, what did I tell you? Wasn't I now an infallible prophet? Your wife has been giving me a most glowing account. Quite your old self, she tells me, except for just this—this touch of facial paralysis. And I think, do you know' (the kind old creature stooped over the bed, but still, Lawford noticed bitterly, still without his spectacles)—'yes, I really think there is a decided improvement. Not quite so—drawn. We must make haste slowly. Wedderburn, you know, believes profoundly in Simon; he pulled his wife through a dangerous confinement. And here's pills and tonics and liniments—a whole chemist's shop. Oh, we are getting on swimmingly.'

Flamelight was flickering in the candled dusk. Lawford turned his head and saw Sheila's coiled, beautiful hair in the firelight.

'You haven't told Alice?' he asked.

'My dear good man,' said Mr Bethany, 'of course we haven't. You shall tell her yourself on Monday. What an incredible tradition it will be! But you mustn't worry; you mustn't even think. And no more of these jaunts, eh? That Ferguson business—that was too bad. What are we going to do with the fellow now we have created him? He will come home to roost—mark my words. And as likely as not down the Vicarage chimney. I wouldn't have believed it of you, my dear fellow.' He beamed, but looked, none the less, very lean and fagged and depressed.

'How did the wedding go off?' Lawford managed to think of inquiring.

'Oh, A1,' said Mr Bethany. 'I've just been describing it to Alice—the bride, her bridegroom, mother, aunts, cake, presents, finery, blushes, tears, and everything that was hers. We've been in fits, haven't we, Mrs Lawford? And Alice says I'm a Worth in a clerical collar—didn't she? And that it's only Art that has kept me out of an apron. Now look here; quiet, quiet, quiet; no excitement, no pranks. What is there to worry about, pray? And now Little Dorrit's down with influenza too. And Craik and I will have double work to do. Well, well; good-bye, my dear. God bless you, Lawford. I can't tell you how relieved, how unspeakably relieved I am to find you so much—so much better. Feed him up, my other dear; body and mind and soul and spirit. And there goes the bell. I must have a biscuit. I've swallowed nothing but a Cupid in plaster of Paris since breakfast. Goodnight; we shall miss you both—both.'

But when Sheila returned, her husband was sunk again into a quiet sleep, from which not even the many questions she fretted to put to him seemed weighty enough to warrant his disturbance.

So when Lawford again opened his eyes he found himself lying wide awake, clear and refreshed, and eager to get up. But upon the air lay the still hush of early morning. He tried in vain to catch back sleep again. A distant shred of dream still floated in his mind, like a cloud at evening. He rarely dreamed, but certainly something immensely interesting had but a moment ago eluded him. He sat up and looked at the clear red cinders and their maze of grottoes. He got out of bed and peeped through the blinds. To the east and opposite to him gardens and an apple-orchard lay, and there in strange liquid tranquillity hung the morning star, and rose, rifling into the dusk of night, the first grey of dawn. The street beneath its autumn leaves was vacant, charmed, deserted.

Hardly since childhood had Lawford seen the dawn unless over his winter breakfast-table. Very much like a child now he stood gazing out of his bow-window—the child whom Time's busy robins had long ago covered over with the leaves of numberless hours. A vague exultation fumed up into his brain. Still on the borders of sleep, he unlocked the great wardrobe and took out an old faded purple and crimson dressing-gown that had belonged to his grandfather, the chief glory of every Christmas charade. He pulled the cowl-like hood over his head and strode majestically over to the looking-glass.

He looked in there a moment on the strange face, like a child dismayed at its own excitement, and a fit of sobbing that was half uncontrollable laughter swept over him. He threw off the hood and turned once more to the window. Consciousness had flooded back indeed. What would Sheila have said to see him there? The unearthly beauty and stillness, and man's small labours, garden and wall and roof-tree idle and smokeless in the light of daybreak—there seemed to be some half-told secret between them. What had life done with him to leave a reality so clouded? He put on his slippers, and, gently opening the door, crept with extreme caution up the stairs. At a long, narrow landing window he confronted a panorama of starry night-gardens, sloping orchards; and beyond them fields, hills, Orion, the Dogs, in the clear and cloudless darkness.

'My God, how beautiful!' a voice whispered. And a cock crowed mistily afar. He stood staring like a child into the wintry brightness of a pastry-cook's. Then once more he crept stealthily on. He stooped and listened at a closed door, until he fancied that above the beating of his own heart he could hear the breathing of the sleeper within. Then, taking firm hold of the handle with both hands, he slowly noiselessly turned it, and peeped in on Alice.

The moon was long past her faint shining here. The blind was down. And yet it was not pitch dark. He stood with eyes fixed, waiting. Then he edged softly forward and knelt down beside the bed. He could hear her breathing now: long, low, quiet, unhastening—the miracle of life. He could just dimly discern the darkness of her hair against the pillow. Some long-sealed spring of tenderness seemed to rise in his heart with a grief and an ache he had never known before. Here at least he could find a little peace, a brief pause, however futile and stupid all his hopes of the night had been. He leant his head on his hands on the counterpane and refused to think. He felt a quick tremor, a startled movement, and knew that eyes wide open with fear were striving to pierce the gloom between them.

'There, there, dearest,' he said in a low whisper, 'it's only me, only me.' He stroked the narrow hand and gazed into the shadowiness. Her fingers lay quiet and passive in his, with that strange sense of immateriality that sleep brings to the body.

'You, you!' she answered with a deep sigh. 'Oh, dearest, how you frightened me. What is wrong? why have you come? Are you worse, dearest, dearest?'

He kissed her hand. 'No, Alice, not worse. I couldn't sleep, that was all.'

'Oh, and I came so utterly miserable to bed because you would not see me. And Mother would tell me only so very little. I didn't even know you had been ill.' She pressed his hand between her own. 'But this, you know, is very, very naughty—you will catch cold, you bad thing. What *would* Mother say?'

'I think we mustn't tell her, dear. I couldn't help it; I felt much I wanted to see you. I have been rather miserable.'

'Why?' she said, stroking his hand from wrist to fingertips with one soft finger. 'You mustn't be miserable. You and me have never done such a thing before; have we? Was it that wretched old Flu?'

It was too dark in the little fragrant room even to see her face so close to his own. And yet he feared. 'Dr Simon,' she went on softly, 'said it was. But isn't your voice a little hoarse, and it sounds so melancholy in the dark. And oh'—she squeezed his wrist—'you have grown so thin! You do frighten me. Whatever should I do if you were really ill? And it was so odd, dear. When first I woke I seemed to be still straining my eyes in a dream, at such a curious, haunting face—not very nice. I am glad, I am glad you were here.'

'What was the dream-face like?' came the muttered question.

'Dark and sharp, and rather dwelling eyes; you know those long faces one sees in dreams: like a hawk, like a conjuror's.'

Like a conjuror's!—it was the first unguarded and ungarbled criticism. 'Perhaps, dear, if you find my voice different, and my hand shrunk up, you will find my face changed, too—like a conjuror's.... What then?'

She laughed gaily and tenderly. 'You silly silly; I should love you more than ever. Your hands are icy cold. I can't warm them nohow.'

Lawford held tight his daughter's hand. 'You do love me, Alice? You would not turn against me, whatever happened? Ah, you shall see, you shall see.' A sudden burning hope sprang up in him. Surely when all was well again, these last few hours would not have been spent in vain. Like the shadow of death they had been, against whose darkness the green familiar earth seems beautiful as the plains of paradise. Had he but realized before how much he loved her—what years of life had been wasted in leaving it all unsaid! He came back from his reverie to find his hand wet with her tears. He stroked her hair, and touched gently her eyelids without speaking.

'You will let me come in to-morrow?' she pleaded; 'you won't keep me out?'

'Ah, but, dear, you must remember your mother. She gets so anxious, and every word the doctor says is law. How would you like me to come again like this, perhaps?—like Santa Claus?'

'You know how I love having you,' she said, and stopped. 'But—but...' He leaned closer. 'Yes, yes, come,' she said, clutching his hand and hiding her eyes; 'it is only my dream—that horrible, dwelling face in the dream; it frightened me so.'

Lawford rose very slowly from his knees. He could feel in the dark his brows drawn down; there came a low, sullen beating on his ear; he saw his face as it were in dim outline against the dark. Rage and rebellion surged up in him; even his love could be turned to bitterness. Well, two could play at any game! Alice sprang up in bed and caught his sleeve. 'Dearest, dearest, you must not be angry with me now!'

He flung himself down beside the bed. Anger, resentment died away. 'You are all I have left,' he said.

He stole back, as he had come, in the clear dawn to his bedroom.

It was not five yet. He put a few more coals on his fire and blew out the night-light, and lay down. But it was impossible to rest, to remain inactive. He would go down and search for that first volume of Quain. Hallucination, Influenza, Insanity—why, Sheila must have purposely mislaid it. A rather formidable figure he looked, descending the stairs in the grey dusk of daybreak. The breakfast-room was at the back of the house. He tilted the blind, and a faint light flowed in from the changing colours of the sky. He opened the glass door of the little bookcase to the right of the window, and ran eye and finger over the few rows of books. But as he stood there with his back to the room, just as the shadow of a bird's wing floats across the moonlight of a pool, he became suddenly conscious that something, somebody had passed across the doorway, and in passing had looked in on him.

He stood motionless, listening; but no sound broke the morning slumbrousness, except the faraway warbling of a thrush in the first light. So sudden and transitory had been the experience that it seemed now to be illusory; yet it had so caught him up, it had with so furtive and sinister a quietness broken in on his solitude, that for a moment he dared not move. A cold, indefinite sensation stole over him that he was being watched; that some dim, evil presence was behind him biding its time, patient and stealthy, with eyes fixed unmovingly on him where he stood. But, watch and wait as silently as he might, only the day broadened at the window, and at last a narrow ray of sunlight stole trembling up into the dusky bowl of the sky.

At any rate Quain was found, with all the ills of life, from A to I; and Lawford turned back to his bondage with the book under his arm.

CHAPTER EIGHT

The Sabbath, pale with September sunshine, and monotonous with chiming bells, had passed languidly away. Dr Simon had come and gone, optimistic and urbane, yet with a faint inward dissatisfaction over a patient behind whose taciturnity a hint of mockery and subterfuge seemed to lurk. Even Mrs Lawford had appeared to share her husband's reticence. But Dr Simon had happened on other cases in his experience where tact was required rather than skill, and time than medicine.

The voices and footsteps, even the *frou-frou* of worshippers going to church, the voices and footsteps of worshippers returning from church, had floated up to the patient's open window. Sunlight had drawn across his room in one pale beam, and vanished. A few callers had called. Hothouse flowers, waxen and pale, had been left with messages of sympathy. Even Dr Critchett had respectfully and discreetly made inquiries on his way home from chapel.

Lawford had spent most of his time in pacing to and fro in his soft slippers. The very monotony had eased his mind. Now and again he had lain motionless, with his face to the ceiling. He had dozed and had awakened, cold and torpid with dream. He had hardly been aware of the process, but every hour had done something, it seemed, towards clarifying his point of view. A consciousness had begun to stir in him that was neither that of the old, easy Lawford, whom he had never been fully aware of before, nor of this strange ghostly intelligence that haunted the hawklike, restless face, and plucked so insistently at his distracted nerves. He had begun in a vague fashion to be aware of them both, could in a fashion discriminate between them, almost as if there really were two spirits in stubborn conflict within him. It would, of course, wear him down in time. There could be only one end to such a struggle—*the* end.

All day he had longed for freedom, on and on, with craving for the open sky, for solitude, for green silence, beyond these maddening walls. This heedful silken coming and going, these Sunday voices, this reiterant yelp of a single peevish bell—would they never cease? And above all, betwixt dread and an almost physical greed, he hungered for night. He sat down with elbows on knees and head on his hands, thinking of night, its secrecy, its immeasurable solitude.

His eyelids twitched; the fire before him had for an instant gone black out. He seemed to see slow-gesturing branches, grass stooping beneath a grey and wind-swept sky. He started up; and the remembrance of the morning returned to him—the glassy light, the changing rays, the beaming gilt upon the useless books. Now, at last, at the windows; afternoon had begun to wane. And when Sheila brought up his tea, as if Chance had heard his cry, she entered in hat and stole. She put down the tray, and paused at the glass, looking across it out of the window.

'Alice says you are to eat every one of those delicious sandwiches, and especially the tiny omelette. You have scarcely touched anything to-day, Arthur. I am a poor one to preach, I am afraid; but you know what that will mean—a worse breakdown still. You really must try to think of—of us all.'

'Are you going to church?' he asked in a low voice.

'Not, of course, if you would prefer not. But Dr Simon advised me most particularly to go out at least once a day. We must remember, this is not the beginning of your illness. Long-continued anxiety, I suppose, does tell on one in time. Anyhow, he said that I looked worried and run-down. I *am* worried. Let us both try for each other's sakes, or even if only for Alice's, to—to do all we can. I must not harass you; but is there any—do you see the slightest change of any kind?'

'You always look pretty, Sheila; to-night you look prettier: *that* is the only change, I think.'

Mrs Lawford's attitude intensified in its stillness. 'Now, speaking quite frankly, what is it in you suggests these remarks at such a time? That's what baffles me. It seems so childish, so needlessly blind.'

'I am very sorry, Sheila, to be so childish. But I'm not, say what you like, blind. You *are* pretty: I'd repeat it if I was burning at the stake.'

Sheila lowered her eyes softly on to the rich-toned picture in the glass. 'Supposing,' she said, watching her lips move, 'supposing—of course, I know you are getting better and all that—but supposing you don't change back as Mr Bethany thinks, what will you do? Honestly, Arthur, when I think over it calmly, the whole tragedy comes back on me with such a force it sweeps me off my feet; I am for the moment scarcely my own mistress. What would you do?'

'I think, Sheila,' replied a low, infinitely weary voice, 'I think I should marry again.' It was the same wavering, faintly ironical voice that had slightly discomposed Dr Simon that same morning.

'"Marry again"!' exclaimed incredulously the full lips in the looking-glass. 'Who?'

'*You*, dear!'

Sheila turned softly round, conscious in a most humiliating manner that she had ever so little flushed.

Her husband was pouring out his tea, unaware, apparently, of her change of position. She watched him curiously. In spite of all her reason, of her absolute certainty, she wondered even again for a moment if this really could be Arthur. And for the first time she realised the power and mastery of that eager and far too hungry face. Her mind seemed to pause, fluttering in air, like a bird in the wind. She hastened rather unsteadily to the door.

'Will you want anything more, do you think, for an hour?' she asked.

Her husband looked up over his little table. 'Is Alice going with you?'

'Oh yes; poor child, she looks so pale and miserable. We are going to Mrs Sherwin's, and then on to Church. You will lock your door?'

'Yes, I will lock my door.'

'And I do hope Arthur—nothing rash!'

A change, that seemed almost the effect of actual shadow, came over his face. 'I wish you could stay with me,' he said slowly. 'I don't think you have any idea what—what I go through.'

It was as if a child had asked on the verge of terror for a candle in the dark. But an hour's terror is better than a lifetime of timidity. Sheila sighed.

'I think,' she said, 'I too might say that. But there; giving way will do nothing for either of us. I shall be gone only for an hour, or two at the most. And I told Mr Bethany I should have to come out before the sermon: it's only Mr Craik.'

'But why Mrs Sherwin? She'd worm a secret out of one's grave.'

'It's useless to discuss that, Arthur; you have always consistently disliked my friends. It's scarcely likely that you would find any improvement in them now.'

'Oh, well—' he began. But the door was already closed.

'Sheila!' he called in a burst of anger.

'Well, Arthur?'

'You have taken my latchkey.'

Sheila came hastily in again. 'Your latchkey?'

'I am going out.'

'"Going out!"—you will not be so mad, so criminal; and after your promise!'

He stood up. 'It is useless to argue. If I do not go out, I shall certainly go mad. As for criminal—why, that's a woman's word. Who on earth is to know me?'

'It is of no consequence, then, that the servants are already gossiping about this impossible Dr Ferguson; that you are certain to be seen either going or returning; that Alice is bound to discover that you are well enough to go out, and yet not even enough to say good-night to your own daughter—oh, it's monstrous, it's a frantic, a heartless thing to do!' Her voice vaguely suggested tears.

Lawford eyed her coldly and stubbornly—thinking of the empty room he would leave awaiting his return, its lamp burning, its fire-flames shining. It was almost a physical discomfort, this longing unspeakable for the twilight, the green secrecy and the silence of the graves. 'Keep them out of the way,' he said in a low voice; 'it will be dark when I come in.' His hardened face lit up. 'It's useless to attempt to dissuade me.'

'Why must you always be hurting me? why do you seem to delight in trying to estrange me?' Husband and wife faced each other across the clear-lit room. He did not answer.

'For the last time,' she said in a quiet, hard voice, 'I ask you not to go.'

He shrugged his shoulders. 'Ask me not to come back,' he said; 'that's nearer your hope.' He turned his face to the fire. Without moving he heard her go out, return, pause, and go out again. And when he deliberately wheeled round in his chair the little key lay conspicuous there on the counterpane.

CHAPTER NINE

The last light of sunset lay in the west; and a sullen wrack of cloud was mounting into the windless sky when Lawford entered the country graveyard again by its dark weather-worn lych-gate. The old stone church with its square tower stood amid trees, its eastern window faintly aglow with crimson and purple. He could hear a steady, rather nasal voice through its open lattices. But the stooping stones and the cypresses were out of sight of its porch. He would not be seen down there. He paused a moment, however; his hat was drawn down over his eyes; he was shivering. Far over the harvest fields showed a growing pallor in the sky. He would have the moon to go home by.

'Home!'—these trees, this tongueless companionship, this heavy winelike air, this soundless turf—these in some obscure desolate fashion seemed far rather really home. His eyes wandered towards the fading crimson. And with that on his right hand he began softly, almost on tiptoe, descending the hill. It seemed to him that the steady eyes of the dead were watching him in his slow progress. The air was echoing with little faint, clear calls. He turned and snapped his fingers at a robin that was stalking him with its stony twittering from bush to bush.

But when after some little time he actually came out of the narrow avenue and looked down, his heart misgave him, for some one was already sitting there on his low and solitary seat beneath the cypresses. He stood hesitating, gazing steadily and yet half vacantly at the motionless figure, and in a while a face was lifted in his direction, and undisconcerted eyes calmly surveyed him.

'I am afraid,' called Lawford rather nervously—'I hope I am not intruding?'

'Not at all, not at all,' said the stranger. 'I have no privileges here; at least as yet.'

Lawford again hesitated, then slowly advanced. 'It's astonishingly quiet and beautiful,' he said.

The stranger turned his head to glance over the fields. 'Yes, it is, very,' he replied. There was the faintest accent, a little drawl of unfriendliness in the remark.

'You often sit here?' Lawford persisted.

The stranger raised his eyebrows. 'Oh yes, often.' He smiled. 'It is my own modest fashion of attending divine service. The congregation is rapt.'

'*My* visits,' said Lawford, 'have been very few—in fact, so far as I know, I have only once been here before.'

'I envy you the novelty.' There was again the same faint unmistakable antagonism in voice and attitude; and yet so deep was the relief in talking to a fellow creature who hadn't the least suspicion of anything unusual in his appearance that Lawford was extremely disinclined to turn back. He made another effort—for conversation with strangers had always been a difficulty to him—and advanced towards the seat. 'You mustn't please let me intrude upon you,' he said, 'but really I am very interested in this queer old place. Perhaps you would tell me something of its history?' He sat down. His companion moved slowly to the other side of the broken gravestone.

'To tell you the truth,' he replied, picking his way as it were from word to word, 'it's "history," as people call it, does not interest me in the least. After all, it's not *when* a thing is, but *what* it is, that much matters. What this is'—he glanced, with head bent, across the shadowy stones, 'is pretty evident. Of course, age has its charms.'

'And is this very old?'

'Oh yes, it's old right enough, as things go; but even age, perhaps, is mainly an affair of the imagination. There's a tombstone near that little old hawthorn, and there are two others side by side under the wall, still even legibly late seventeenth century. That's pretty good weathering.' He smiled faintly. 'Of course, the church itself is centuries older, drenched with age. But she's still sleep-walking while these old tombstones dream. Glow-worms and crickets are not such bad bedfellows.'

'What interested me most, I think,' said Lawford haltingly, 'was this.' He pointed with his stick to the grave at his feet.

'Ah, yes, Sabathier's,' said the stranger; 'I know his peculiar history almost by heart.'

Lawford found himself staring with unusual concentration into the rather long and pale face. 'Not, I suppose,' he resumed faintly—'not, I suppose, beyond what's there.'

His companion leant his hand on the old stooping tombstone. 'Well, you know, there's a good deal there'—he stooped over—'if you read between the lines. Even if you don't.'

'A suicide,' said Lawford, under his breath.

'Yes, a suicide; that's why our Christian countrymen have buried him outside of the fold. Dead or alive, they try to keep the wolf out.'

'Is this, then, unconsecrated ground?' said Lawford.

'Haven't you noticed,' drawled the other, 'how green the grass grows down here, and how very sharp are poor old Sabathier's thorns? Besides, he was a stranger, and they—kept him out.'

'But, surely,' said Lawford, 'was it so entirely a matter of choice—the laws of the Church? If he did kill himself, he did.'

The stranger turned with a little shrug. 'I don't suppose it's a matter of much consequence to *him*. I fancied I was his only friend. May I venture to ask why you are interested in the poor old thing?'

Lawford's mind was as calm and shallow as a millpond. 'Oh, a rather unusual thing happened to me here,' he said. 'You say you often come?'

'Often,' said the stranger rather curtly.

'Has anything—ever—occurred?'

'"Occurred?"' He raised his eyebrows. 'I wish it had. I come here simply, as I have said, because it's quiet; because I prefer the company of those who never answer me back, and who do not so much as condescend to pay me the least attention.' He smiled and turned his face towards the quiet fields.

Lawford, after a long pause, lifted his eyes. 'Do you think,' he said softly, 'it is possible one ever could?'

'"One ever could?"'

'Answer back?'

There was a low rotting wall of stone encompassing Sabathier's grave; on this the stranger sat down. He glanced up rather curiously at his companion. 'Seldom the time and the place and the *revenant* altogether. The thought has occurred to others,' he ventured to add.

'Of course, of course,' said Lawford eagerly. 'But it is an absolutely new one to me. I don't mean that I have never had such an idea, just in one's own superficial way; but'—he paused and glanced swiftly into the fast-thickening twilight—'I wonder: are they, do you think, really, all quite dead?'

'Call and see!' taunted the stranger softly.

'Ah, yes, I know,' said Lawford. 'But I believe in the resurrection of the body; that is what we say; and supposing, when a man dies—supposing it was most frightfully against one's will; that one hated the awful inaction that death brings, shutting a poor devil up like a child kicking against the door in a dark cupboard; one might surely one might—just quietly, you know, try to get out? wouldn't you?' he added.

'And, surely,' he found himself beginning gently to argue again, 'surely, what about, say, him?' He nodded towards the old and broken grave that lay between them.

'What, Sabathier?' the other echoed, laying his hand upon the stone.

And a sheer enormous abyss of silence seemed to follow the unanswerable question.

'He was a stranger; it says so. Good God!' said Lawford, 'how he must have wanted to get home! He killed himself, poor wretch, think of the fret and fever he must have been in—just before. Imagine it.'

'But it might, you know,' suggested the other with a smile—'might have been sheer indifference.'

'"Nicholas Sabathier, Stranger to this parish"—no, no,' said Lawford, his heart beating as if it would choke him, 'I don't fancy it was indifference.'

It was almost too dark now to distinguish the stranger's features but there seemed a faint suggestion of irony in his voice. 'And how do you suppose your angry naughty child would set about it? It's narrow quarters; how would he begin?'

Lawford sat quite still. 'You say—I hope I am not detaining you—you say you have come here, sat here often, on this very seat; have you ever had—have you ever fallen asleep here?'

'Why do you ask?' inquired the other curiously.

'I was only wondering,' said Lawford. He was cold and shivering. He felt instinctively it was madness to sit on here in the thin gliding mist that had gathered in swathes above the grass, milk-pale in the rising moon. The stranger turned away from him.

'"For in that sleep of death what dreams may come must give us pause,"' he said slowly, with a little satirical catch on the last word. 'What did *you* dream?'

Lawford glanced helplessly about him. The moon cast lean grey beams of light between the cypresses. But to his wide and wandering eyes it seemed that a radiance other than hers haunted these mounds and leaning stones. 'Have you ever noticed it?' he said, putting out his hand towards his unknown companion; 'this stone is cracked from head to foot?... But there'—he rose stiff and chilled—'I am afraid I have bored you with my company. You came here for solitude, and I have been trying to convince you that we are surrounded with witnesses. You will forgive my intrusion?' There was a kind of old-fashioned courtesy in his manner that he himself was dimly aware of. He held out his hand.

'I hope you will think nothing of the kind,' said the other earnestly; 'how could it be in any sense an intrusion? It's the old story of Bluebeard. And I confess I too should very much like a peep into his cupboard. Who wouldn't? But there, it's merely a matter of time, I suppose.' He paused, and together they slowly ascended the path already glimmering with a heavy dew. At the porch they paused once more. And now it was the stranger that held out his hand.

'Perhaps,' he said, 'you will give me the pleasure of some day continuing our talk. As for our friend below, it so happens that I *have* managed to pick up a little more of his history than the sexton seems to have heard of—if you would care some time or other to share it. I live only at the foot of the hill, not half a mile distant. Perhaps you could spare the time now?'

Lawford took out his watch, 'You are really very kind,' he said. 'But, perhaps—well, whatever that history may be, I think you would agree that mine is even—but, there, I've talked too much about myself already. Perhaps to-morrow?'

'Why, to-morrow, then,' said his companion. 'It's a flat wooden house, on the left-hand side. Come at any time of the evening'; he paused again and smiled—'the third house after the Rectory, which is marked up on the gate. My name is Herbert—Herbert Herbert to be precise.'

Lawford took out his pocket-book and a card. 'Mine,' he said, handing it gravely to his companion. 'is Lawford—at least...' It was really the first time that either had seen the other's face at close quarters and clear-lit; and on Lawford's a moon almost at the full shone dazzlingly. He saw an expression—dismay, incredulity, overwhelming astonishment—start suddenly into the dark, rather indifferent eyes.

'What is it?' he cried, hastily stooping close.

'Why,' said the other, laughing and turning away, 'I think the moon must have bewitched me too.'

CHAPTER TEN

Lawford listened awhile before opening his door. He heard voices in the dining-room. A light shone faintly between the blinds of his bedroom. He very gently let himself in, and unheard, unseen, mounted the stairs. He sat down in front of the fire, tired out and bitterly cold in spite of his long walk home. But his mind was wearier even than his body. He tried in vain to catch up the thread of his thoughts. He only knew for certain that so far as his first hope and motives had gone his errand had proved entirely futile. 'How could I possibly fall asleep with that fellow talking there?' he had said to himself angrily; yet knew in his heart that their talk had driven every other idea out of his mind. He had not yet even glanced into the glass. His every thought was vainly wandering round and round the one curious hint that had drifted in, but which he had not yet been able to put into words.

Supposing, though, that he had really fallen into a deep sleep, with none to watch or spy—what then? However ridiculous that idea, it was not more ridiculous, more incredible than the actual fact. If he had remained there, he might, it was just possible that he would by now, have actually awakened just his own familiar every-day self again. And the thought of that—though he hardly realised its full import—actually did send him on tip-toe for a glance that more or less effectually set the question at rest. And there looked out at him, it seemed, the same dark sallow face that had so much appalled him only two nights ago—expressionless, cadaverous, with shadowy hollows beneath the glittering eyes. And even as he watched it, its lips, of their own volition, drew together and questioned him—'Whose?'

He was not to be given much leisure, however, for fantastic reveries like this. As he leaned his head on his hands, gladly conscious that he could not possibly bear this incessant strain for long, Sheila opened the door. He started up.

'I wish you would knock,' he said angrily; 'you talk of quiet; you tell me to rest, and think; and here you come creeping and spying on me as if I was a child in a nursery. I refuse to be watched and guarded and peeped on like this.' He knew that his hands were trembling, that he could not keep his eyes fixed, that his voice was nearly inarticulate.

Sheila drew in her lips. 'I have merely come to tell you, Arthur, that Mr Bethany has brought Mr Danton in to supper. He agrees with me it really would be advisable to take such a very old and prudent and practical friend into our confidence. You do nothing I ask of you. I simply cannot bear the burden of this incessant anxiety. Look, now, what your night walk has done for you! You look positively at death's door.'

'What—what an instinct you have for the right word,' said Lawford softly. 'And Danton, of all people in the world! It was surely rather a curious, a thoughtless choice. Has he had supper?'

'Why do you ask?'

'He won't believe: too—bloated.'

'I think,' said Sheila indignantly, 'it is hardly fair to speak of a very old and a very true friend of mine in such—well, vulgar terms as that. Besides, Arthur, as for believing—without in the least desiring to hurt your feelings—I must candidly warn you, some people won't.'

'Come along,' said Lawford, with a faint gust of laughter; 'let's see.'

They went quickly downstairs, Sheila with less dignity, perhaps, than she had been surprised into since she had left a slimmer girlhood behind. She swept into the gaze of the two gentlemen standing together on the hearthrug; and so was caught, as it were, between a rain of conflicting glances, for her husband had followed instantly, and stood now behind her, stooping a little, and with something between contempt and defiance confronting an old fat friend, whom that one brief challenging instant had congealed into a condition of passive and immovable hostility.

Mr Danton composed his chin in his collar, and deliberately turned himself towards his companion. His small eyes wandered, and instantaneously met and rested on those of Mrs Lawford.

'Arthur thought he would prefer to come down and see you himself.'

'You take such formidable risks, Lawford,' said Mr Bethany in a dry, difficult voice.

'Am I really to believe,' Danton began huskily. 'I am sure, Bethany, you will—My dear Mrs Lawford!' said he, stirring vaguely, glancing restlessly.

'It was not my wish, Vicar, to come at all,' said a voice from the doorway. 'To tell you the truth, I am too tired to care a jot either way. And'—he lifted a long arm—'I must positively refuse to produce the least, the remotest proof that I am not, so far as I am personally aware, even the Man in the Moon. Danton at heart was always an incorrigible sceptic. Aren't you, T. D.? You pride your dear old brawn on it in secret?'

'I really—' began Danton in a rich still voice.

'Oh, but you know you are,' drawled on the slightly hesitating long-drawn syllables; 'it's your parochial *métier*. Firm, unctuous, subtle, scepticism; and to that end your body flourishes. You were born fat; you became fat; and fat, my dear Danton, has been deliberately thrust on you—in layers! Lampreys! You'll perish of surfeit some day, of sheer Dantonism. And fat, postmortem, Danton. Oh, what a basting's there!'

Mr Bethany, with a convulsive effort, woke. He turned swiftly on Mrs Lawford. 'Why, why, could you not have seen?' he cried.

'It's no good, Vicar. She's all sheer Laodicean. Blow hot, blow cold. North, south, east, west—to have a weathercock for a wife is to marry the wind. There's nothing to be got from poor Sheila but...'

'Lawford!' the little man's voice was as sharp as the crack of a whip; 'I forbid it. Do you hear me? I forbid it. Some self-command; my dear good fellow, remember, remember it's only the will, the will that keeps us breathing.'

Lawford peered as if out of a gathering dusk, that thickened and flickered with shadows before his eyes. 'What's he mean, then,' he muttered huskily, 'coming here with his black, still carcase—peeping, peeping—what's he mean, I say?' There was a moment's silence. Then with lifted brows and wide eyes that to every one of his three witnesses left an indelible memory of clear and wolfish light within their glassy pupils, he turned heavily, and climbed back to his solitude.

'I suppose,' began Danton, with an obvious effort to disentangle himself from the humiliation of the moment, 'I suppose he was—wandering?'

'Bless me, yes,' said Mr Bethany cordially—'fever. We all know what that means.'

'Yes,' said Danton, taking refuge in Mrs Lawford's white and intent gaze.

'Just think, think, Danton—the awful, incessant strain of such an ordeal. Think for an instant what such a thing *means*!'

Danton inserted a plump, white finger between collar and chin. 'Oh yes. But—eh?—needlessly abusive? I never *said* I disbelieved him.'

'Do you?' said Mrs Lawford's voice.

He poised himself, as if it were, on the monolithic stability of his legs. 'Eh?' he said.

Mr Bethany sat down at the table. 'I rather feared some such temporary breakdown as this, Danton. I think I foresaw it. And now, just while we are all three alone here together in friendly conclave, wouldn't it be as well, don't you think, to confront ourselves with the difficulties? I know—we all know, that that poor half-demented creature *is* Arthur Lawford. This morning he was as sane, as lucid as I hope I am now. An awful calamity has suddenly fallen upon him—this change. I own frankly at the first sheer shock it staggered me as I think for the moment it has staggered you. But when I had seen the poor fellow face to face, heard him talk, and watched him there upstairs in the silence stir and awake and come up again to his trouble out of his sleep. I had no more doubt in my own mind and heart that he was he than I have in my mind that I—am I. We do in some mysterious way, you'll own at once, grow so accustomed, so inured, if you like, to each other's faces (masks though they be) that we hardly realise we see them when we are speaking together. And yet the slightest, the most infinitesimal change is instantly apparent.'

'Oh yes, Vicar; but you see—'

Mr Bethany raised a small lean hand: 'One moment, please. I have heard Lawford's own account. Conscious or unconscious, he has been through some terrific strain, some such awful conflict with the unseen powers that we—thank God!—have only read about, and never perhaps, until death is upon us, shall witness for ourselves. What more likely, more inevitable than that such a thing should leave its scar, its cloud, its masking shadow?—call it what you will. A smile can turn a face we dread into a face we'd die for. Some experience, which would be nothing but a hideous cruelty and outrage to ask too closely about—one, perhaps, which he could, even if he would, poor fellow, give no account of—has put him temporarily at the world's mercy. They made him a nine days' wonder, a byword. And that, my dear Danton, is just where we come in. We know the man himself; and it is to be our privilege to act as a buffer-state, to be intermediaries between him and the rest of this deadly, craving, sheepish world—for the time being; oh yes, just for the time being. Other and keener and more knowledgeable minds than mine or yours will some day bring him back to us again. We don't attempt to explain; we can't. We simply believe.'

But Danton merely continued to stare, as if into the quiet of an aquarium.

'My dear good Danton,' persisted Mr Bethany with cherubic patience, 'how old are you?'

'I don't see quite...' smiled Danton with recovered ease, and rapidly mobilising forces. 'Excuse the confidence, Mrs Lawford, I'm forty-three.'

'Good,' said Mr Bethany; 'and I'm seventy-one, and this child here'—he pointed an accusing finger at Sheila—is youth perpetual. So,' he briskly brightened, 'say, between us we're six score all told. Are we—can *we*, deliberately, with this mere pinch of years at our command out of the wheeling millions that have gone—can we say, "This is impossible," to any single phenomenon? *Can* we?'

'No, we can't, of course,' said Danton formidably. 'Not finally. That's all very well, but'—he paused, and nodded, nodding his round head upward as if towards the inaudible overhead, 'I suppose he can't *hear?*'

Mr Bethany rose cheerfully. 'All right, Danton; I am afraid you are exactly what the poor fellow in his delirium solemnly asseverated. And, jesting apart, it is in delirium that we tell our sheer, plain, unadulterated truth: you're a nicely covered sceptic. Personally, I refuse to discuss the matter. Mere dull, stubborn prejudice; bigotry, if you like. I will only remark just this—that Mrs Lawford and I, in our inmost hearts, *know*. You, my dear Danton, forgive the freedom, merely incredulously grope. Faith versus Reason—that prehistoric Armageddon. Some day, and a day not far distant either, Lawford will come back to us. This—this shutter will be taken down as abruptly as by some inconceivably drowsy heedlessness of common Nature it has been put up. He'll win through; and of his own sheer will and courage. But now, because I ask it, and this poor child here entreats it, you will say nothing to a living soul about the matter, say, till Friday? What step-by-step creatures we are, to be sure! I say Friday because it will be exactly a week then. And what's a week?—to Nature scarcely the unfolding of a rose. But still, Friday be it. Then, if nothing has occurred, we will, we shall *have* to call a friendly gathering, we shall be compelled to have a friendly consultation.'

'I'm not, I hope, a brute, Bethany,' said Danton apologetically; 'but, honestly, speaking for myself, simply as a man of the world, it's a big risk to be taking on—what shall we call it?—on mere intuition. Personally, and even in a court of law—though Heaven forbid it ever reaches that stage—personally, I could swear that the fellow that stood abusing me there, in that revolting fashion, was not Lawford. It would be easier even to believe in him, if there were not that—that glaze, that shocking simulation of the man himself, the very man. But then, I am a sceptic; I own it. And 'pon my word, Mrs Lawford, there's plenty of room for sceptics in a world like this.'

'Very well,' said Mr Bethany crisply, 'that's settled, then. With your permission, my dear,' he added, turning untarnishably clear childlike eyes on Sheila, 'I will take all risks—even to the foot of the gibbet: accessory, Danton, *after* the fact.' And so direct and cloudless was his gaze that Sheila tried in vain to evade it and to catch a glimpse of Danton's small agate-like eyes, now completely under mastery, and awaiting confidently the meeting with her own.

'Of course,' she said, 'I am entirely in your hands, dear Mr Bethany.'

CHAPTER ELEVEN

Lawford slept far into the cloudy Monday morning, to wake steeped in sleep, lethargic, and fretfully haunted by inconclusive remembrances of the night before. When Sheila, with obvious and capacious composure, brought him his breakfast tray, he watched her face for some time without speaking.

'Sheila,' he began, as she was about to leave the room again.

She paused, smiling.

'Did anything happen last night? Would you mind telling me, Sheila? Who was it was here?'

Her lids the least bit narrowed. 'Certainly, Arthur; Mr Danton was here.'

'Then it was not a dream?'

'Oh no,' said Sheila.

'What did I say? What did *he* say? It was hopeless, anyhow.'

'I don't quite understand what you mean by "hopeless," Arthur. And must I answer the other questions?'

Lawford drew his hand over his face, like a tired child. 'He didn't—believe?'

'No, dear,' said Sheila softly.

'And you, Sheila?' came the subdued voice.

Sheila crossed slowly to the window. 'Well, quite honestly, Arthur, I was not very much surprised. Whatever we are agreed about on the whole, you were scarcely yourself last night.'

Lawford shut his eyes, and re-opened them full on his wife's calm scrutiny, who had in that moment turned in the light of the one drawn blind to face him again.

'Who is? Always?'

'No,' said Sheila; 'but—it was at least unfortunate. We can't, I suppose, rely on Dr Bethany alone.'

Lawford crouched over his food. 'Will he blab?'

'Blab! Mr Danton is a gentleman, Arthur.'

Lawford rolled his eyes as if in temporary vertigo. 'Yes,' he said. And Sheila once more prepared to make a reposeful exit.

'I don't think I can see Simon this morning.'

'Oh. Who, then?'

'I mean I would prefer to be left alone.'

'Believe me, I had no intention to intrude.' And this time the door really closed.

'He is in a quiet, soothing sleep,' said Sheila a few minutes later.

'Nothing could be better,' said Dr Simon; and Lawford, to his inexpressible relief, heard the fevered throbbing of the doctor's car reverse, and turned over and shut his eyes, dulled and exhausted in the still unfriendliness of the vacant room. His spirits had sunk, he thought, to their lowest ebb. He scarcely heeded the fragments of dreams—clear, green landscapes, amazing gleams of peace, the sudden broken voices, the rustling and calling shadowiness of subconsciousness—in this quiet sunlight of reality. The clouds had broken, or had been withdrawn like a veil from the October skies. One thought alone was his refuge; one face alone haunted him with its peace; one remembrance soothed him—Alice. Through all his scattered and purposeless arguments he strove to remember her voice, the loving-kindness of her eyes, her untroubled confidence.

In the afternoon he got up and dressed himself. He could not bring himself to stand before the glass and deliberately shave. He even smiled at the thought of playing the barber to that lean chin. He dressed by the fireplace.

'I couldn't rest,' he told Sheila, when she presently came in on one of her quiet, cautious, heedful visits; 'and one tires of reading even Quain in bed.'

'Have you found anything?' she inquired politely.

'Oh yes,' said Lawford wearily; 'I have discovered that infinitely worse things are infinitely commoner. But that there's nothing quite so picturesque.'

'Tell me,' said Sheila, with refreshing naivete. 'How does it feel? does it even in the slightest degree affect your mind?'

He turned his back and looked up at his broad gilt portrait for inspiration. 'Practically, not at all,' he said hollowly. 'Of course, one's nerves—that fellow Danton—when one's overtired. You have'—his voice, in spite of every effort, faintly quavered—'*you* haven't noticed anything? My mind?'

'Me? Oh dear, no! I never was the least bit observant; you know that, Arthur. But apart from that, and I hope you will not think me unsympathetic—but don't you think we must sooner or later be thinking of what's to be done? At present, though I fully agree with Mr Bethany as to the wisdom of hushing this unhappy business up as long as possible, at least from the gossiping outside world, still we are only standing still. And your malady, dear, I suppose, isn't. You *will* help me, Arthur? You will try and think? Poor Alice!'

'What about Alice?'

'She mopes, dear, rather. She cannot, of course, quite understand why she must not see her father, and yet his not being, or, for the matter of that, even if he was, at death's door.'

'At death's door,' murmured Lawford under his breath; 'who was it was saying that? Have you ever, Sheila, in a dream, or just as one's thoughts go sometimes, seen that door?...its ruinous stone lintel carved into lichenous stone heads...stonily silent in the last thin sunlight, hanging in peace unlatched. Heated, hunted, in agony—in that cold, green-clad shadowed porch is haven and sanctuary....But beyond—O God, beyond!'

Sheila stood listening with startled eyes. 'And was all that in Quain?' she inquired rather flutteringly.

Lawford turned a sidelong head, and looked steadily at his wife.

She shook herself, with a slight shiver. 'Very well, then,' she said and paused in the silence.

Her husband yawned, and smiled, and almost as if lit with that thin last sunshine seemed the smile that passed for an instant across the reverie of his shadowy face. He drew a hand wearily over his eyes. 'What has he been saying now?' he inquired like a fretful child.

Sheila stood very quiet and still, as if in fear of scaring some rare, wild, timid creature by the least stir. 'Who?' she merely breathed.

Lawford paused on the hearth-rug with his comb in his hand. 'It's just the last rags of that beastly influenza,' he said, and began vigorously combing his hair. And yet, simple and frank though the action was, it moved Sheila, perhaps, more than any other of the congested occurrences of the last few days. Her forehead grew suddenly cold, the palms of her hands began to ache, she had to hasten out of the room to avoid revealing the sheer physical repulsion she had experienced.

But Lawford, quite unmindful of the shock, continued in a kind of heedless reverie to watch, as he combed, the still visionary thoughts that passed in tranced stillness before his eyes. He longed beyond measure for freedom that until yesterday he had not even dreamed existed outside the covers of some old impossible romance—the magic of the darkening sky, the invisible flocking presences of the dead, the shock of imaginations that had no words, of quixotic emotions which the stranger had stirred in that low, mocking, furtive talk beside the broken stones of the Huguenot. Was the 'change' quite so monstrous, so meaningless? How often, indeed, he remembered curiously had he seemed to be standing outside these fast-shut gates of thought, that now had been freely opened to him.

He drew ajar the door, and leant his ear to listen. From far away came a rich, long-continued chuckle of laughter, followed by the clatter of a falling plate, and then, still more uncontrollable laughter. There was a faint smell of toast on the air. Lawford ventured out on to the landing and into a little room that had once, in years gone by, been Alice's nursery. He stood far back from the strip of open window that showed beneath the green blind, craning forward to see into the garden—the trees, their knotted trunks, and then, as he stole nearer, a flower-bed, late roses, geraniums, calceolarias, the lawn and—yes, three wicker chairs, a footstool, a work-basket, a little table on the smooth grass in the honey-coloured sunshine; and Sheila sitting there in the autumnal sunlight, her hands resting on the arms of her chair, her head bent, evidently deeply engrossed in her thoughts. He crept an inch or two forward, and stooped. There was a hat on the grass—Alice's big garden hat—and beside it lay Flitters, nose on paws, long ears sagging. He had forgotten Flitters. Had Flitters forgotten him? Would he bark at the strange, distasteful scent of a—Dr Ferguson? The coast was clear, then. He turned even softlier yet, to confront, rapt, still, and hovering betwixt astonishment and dread, the blue calm eyes of his daughter, looking in at the door. It seemed to Lawford as if they had both been suddenly swept by some unseen power into a still, unearthly silence.

'We thought,' he began at last, 'we thought just to beckon Mrs Lawford from the window. He—he is asleep.'

Alice nodded. Her whole face was in a moment flooded with red. It ebbed and left her pale. 'I will go down and tell mother you want to see her. It was very silly of me. I did not quite recognise at first...I suppose, thinking of my father—' The words faltered, and the eyes were lifted to his face again with a desolate, incredulous appeal. Lawford turned away heartsick and trembling.

'Certainly, certainly, by no means,' he began, listening vaguely to the glib patter that seemed to come from another mouth. 'Your father, my dear young lady, I venture to think is now really on the road to recovery. Dr Simon makes excellent progress. But, of course—two heads, we know, are so much better than one when there's the least—the least difficulty. The great thing is quiet, rest, isolation, no possibility of a shock, else—' His voice fell away, his eloquence failed.

For Alice stood gazing stirlessly on and on into this infinitely strange, infinitely familiar shadowy, phantasmal face. 'Oh yes,' she replied, 'I quite understand, of course; but if I might just peep even, it would—I should be so much, much happier. Do let me just see him, Dr Ferguson, if only his head on the pillow! I wouldn't even breathe. Couldn't it possibly help—even a faith-cure?' She leant forward impulsively, her voice trembling, and her eyes still shining beneath their faint, melancholy smile.

'I fear, my dear...it cannot be. He longs to see you. But with his mind, you know, in this state, it might—?'

'But mother never told me,' broke in the girl desperately, 'there was anything wrong with his *mind*. Oh, but that was quite unfair. You don't mean, you don't mean—that—?'

Lawford scanned swiftly the little square beloved and memoried room that fate had suddenly converted for him into a cage of unspeakable pain and longing. 'Oh no; believe me, no! Not his brain, not that, not even wandering; really: but always thinking, always longing on and on for you, dear, only. Quite, quite master of himself, but—'

'You talk,' she broke in again angrily, 'only in pretence! You are treating me like a child; and so does mother, and so it has been ever since I came home. Why, if mother can, and you can, why may not I? Why, if he can walk and talk in the night....'

'But who—who "can walk and talk in the night?"' inquired a low stealthy voice out of the quietness behind her.

Alice turned swiftly. Her mother was standing at a little distance, with all the calm and moveless concentration of a waxwork figure, looking up at her from the staircase.

'I was—I was talking to Dr Ferguson, mother.'

'But as I came up the stairs I understood you to be inquiring something of Dr Ferguson, "if," you were saying, "he can walk and talk in the night": you surely were not referring to your father, child? That could not possibly be, in his state. Dr Ferguson, I know, will bear me out in that at least. And besides, I really must insist on following out medical directions to the letter. Dr Ferguson I know, will fully concur. Do, pray, Dr Ferguson,' continued Sheila, raising her voice even now scarcely above a rapid murmur—'do pray assure my daughter that she must have patience; that however much even he himself may desire it, it is impossible that she should see her father yet. And now, my dear child, come down, I want to have a moment's talk with Dr Ferguson. I feared from his beckoning at the window that something was amiss.'

Alice turned, dismayed, and looked steadily, almost with hostility, at the stranger, so curiously transfixed and isolated in her small old play-room. And in this scornful yet pleading confrontation her eye fell suddenly on the pin in his scarf—the claw and the pearl she had known all her life. From that her gaze flitted, like some wild demented thing's, over face, hair, hands, clothes, attitude, expression, and her heart stood still in an awful, inarticulate dread of the unknown. She turned slowly towards her mother, groped forward a few steps, turned once more, stretching out her hands towards the vague still figure whose eyes had called so piteously to her out of their depths, and fell fainting in the doorway. Lawford stood motionless, vacantly watching Sheila, who knelt, chafing the cold hands. 'She has fainted?' he said; 'oh, Sheila, tell me—only fainted?'

Sheila made no answer; did not even raise her eyes.

'Some day, Sheila' he began in a dull voice, and broke off, and without another word, without even another glance at the still face and blue, twitching lids, he passed her rapidly by, and in another instant Sheila heard the house-door shut. She got up quickly, and after a glance into the vacant bedroom turned the key; then she hastened upstairs for sal volatile and eau de cologne....

It was yet clear daylight when Lawford appeared beneath the portico of his house. With a glance of circumspection that almost seemed to suggest a fear of pursuit, he descended the steps, only to be made aware in so doing that Ada was with a kind of furtive eagerness pointing out the mysterious Dr Ferguson to a steadily gazing cook. One or two well-known and many a well-remembered face he encountered in the thin stream of City men treading blackly along the pavement. It was a still, high evening, and something very like a forlorn compassion rose in his mind at sight of their grave, rather pretentious, rather dull, respectable faces.

He found himself walking with an affectation of effrontery, and smiling with a faint contempt on all alike, as if to keep himself from slinking, and the wolf out of his eyes. He felt restless, and watchful, and suspicious, as if he had suddenly come down in the world. His, then, was a disguise as effectual as a shabby coat and a glazing eye. His heart sickened. Was it even worth while living on a crust of social respectability so thin and so exquisitely treacherous? He challenged no one. One or two actual acquaintances raised and lowered a faintly inquiring eyebrow in his direction. One even recalled in his confusion a smile of recognition just a moment too late. There was, it seemed, a peculiar aura in Lawford's presence, a shadow of a something in his demeanour that proved him alien.

None the less green Widderstone kept calling him, much as a bell in the imagination tolls on and on, the echo of reality. If the worst should come to the worst, why—there is pasture in the solitary by-ways for the beast that strays. He quickened his pace along lonelier streets, and soon strode freely through the little flagged and cobbled village of shops, past the same small jutting window whose clock had told him the hour on that first dark hurried night. All was pale and faint with dying colours now; and decay was in the leaf, and the last swallows filled the gold air with their clashing stillness. No one heeded him here. He looked from side to side, exulting in the strangeness. Shops were left behind, the last milestone passed, and in a little while he was descending the hill beneath the elm boughs, which he remembered had stood like a turreted wall against the sunset when first he had wandered down into the churchyard.

At the foot of the hill he passed by the green and white Rectory, and there was the parson, a short fat, pursy man with wrists protruding from his jacket sleeves as he stood on tip-toe tying up a rambling rose-shoot on his trim cedared lawn. The next house barely showed its old red chimney-tops, above its bowers; the next was empty, with windows vacantly gazing, its paths peopled with great bearded weeds that stood mutely watching and guarding the seldom-opened gate. Then came more lofty grandmotherly elms, a dense hedge of every leaf that pricks, and then Lawford found himself standing at the small canopied gate of the queer old wooden house that the stranger of his talk had in part described.

It stood square and high and dark in a small amphitheatre of verdure. Roses here and there sprang from the grass, and a narrow box-edged path led to a small door in a low green-mantled wing, with its one square window above the porch. And while, with vacant mind, Lawford stood waiting, as one stands forebodingly upon the eve of a new experience he heard as if at a distance the sound of falling water. He still paused on the country roadside, scrutinising this strange, still, wooden presence; but at last with an effort he pushed open the gate, followed the winding path, and pulled the old iron hanging bell. There came presently a quiet tread, and Herbert himself opened the door which led into a little square wood-panelled hall, hung with queer old prints and obscure portraits in dark frames.

'Ah, yes, come in, Mr Lawford,' he drawled; 'I was beginning to be afraid you were not coming.'

Lawford laid hat and walking-stick on an oak bench, and followed his churchyard companion up a slightly inclined corridor and a staircase into a high room, covered far up the yellowish walls with old books on shelves and in cases, between which hung in little black frames, mezzo tints, etchings, and antiquated maps. A large table stood a few paces from the deep alcove of the window, which was surrounded by a low, faded, green seat, and was screened from the sunshine by wooden shutters. And here the tranquil surge of falling water shook incessantly on the air, for the three lower casements stood open to the fading sunset. On a smaller table were spread cups, old earthenware dishes of fruit, and a big bowl of damask roses.

'Please sit down; I shan't be a moment; I am not sure that my sister is in; but if so, I will tell her we are ready for tea.' Left to himself in this quiet, strange old room, Lawford forgot for a while everything else, he was for the moment so taken up with his surroundings.

What seized on his fancy and strangely affected his mind was this incessant changing roar of falling water. It must be the Widder, he said to himself, flowing close to the walls. But not until he had had the boldness to lean head and shoulders out of the nearest window did he fully realize how close indeed the Widder was. It came sweeping dark and deep and begreened and full with the early autumnal rains, actually against the lower walls of the house itself, and in the middle suddenly swerved in a black, smooth arch, and tumbled headlong into a great pool, nodding with tall slender water-weeds, and charged in its bubbled blackness here and there with the last crimson of the setting sun. To the left of the house, where the waters floated free again, stood vast, still trees above the clustering rushes; and in glimpses between their spreading boughs lay the far-stretching countryside, now dimmed with the first mists of approaching evening. So absorbed he became as he stood leaning over the wooden sill above the falling water, that eye and ear became enslaved by the roar and stillness. And in the faint atmosphere of age that seemed like a veil to hang about the odd old house and these prodigious branches, he fell into a kind of waking dream.

When at last he did draw back into the room it was perceptibly darker, and a thin keen shaft of recollection struck across his mind—the recollection of what he was, and of how he came to be there, his reasons for coming and of that dark indefinable presence which like a raven had begun to build its dwelling in his mind. He sat on, his eyes restlessly wandering, his face leaning on his hands; and in a while the door opened and Herbert returned, carrying an old crimson and green teapot and a dish of hot cakes.

'They're all out,' he said; 'sister, Sallie, and boy; but these were in the oven, so we won't wait. I hope you haven't been very much bored.'

Lawford dropped his hands from his face and smiled. 'I have been looking at the water,' he said.

'My sister's favorite occupation; she sits for hours and hours, with not even a book for an apology, staring down into the black old roaring pot. It has a sort of hypnotic effect after a time. And you'd be surprised how quickly one gets used to the noise. To me it's even less distracting than sheer silence. You don't know, after all, what on earth sheer silence means—even at Widderstone. But one can just realize a water-nymph. They chatter; but, thank Heaven, it's not articulate.' He handed Lawford a cup with a certain niceness and self-consciousness, lifting his eyebrows slightly as he turned.

Lawford found himself listening out of a peculiar stillness of mind to the voice of this suave and rather inscrutable acquaintance. 'The curious thing is, do you know,' he began rather nervously, 'that though I must have passed your gate at least twice in the last few months, I have never noticed it before, never even caught the sound of the water.'

'No, that's the best of it; nobody ever does. We are just buried alive. We have lived here for years, and scarcely know a soul—not even our own, perhaps. Why on earth should one? Acquaintances, after all, are little else than a bad habit.'

'But then, what about me?' said Lawford.

'But that's just it,' said Herbert. 'I said *acquaintances*; that's just exactly what I'm going to prove—what very old friends we are. You've no idea! It really is rather queer.' He took up his cup and sauntered over to the window.

Lawford eyed him vacantly for a moment, and, following rather his own curious thoughts than seeking any light on this somewhat vague explanation, again broke the silence. 'It's odd, I suppose, but this house affects me much in the same way as Widderstone does. I'm not particularly fanciful—at least, I used not to be. But sitting here I seem, I hope it isn't a very frantic remark, it seems as though, if only my ears would let me, I should hear—well, voices. It's just what you said about the silence. I suppose it's the age of the place; it *is* very old?'

'Pretty old, I suppose; it's worm-eaten and rat-eaten and tindery enough in all conscience; and the damp doesn't exactly foster it. It's a queer old shanty. There are two or three accounts of it in some old local stuff I have. And of course there's a ghost.'

'A ghost?' echoed Lawford, looking up.

CHAPTER TWELVE

'What's in a name?' laughed Herbert. 'But it really is a queer show-up of human oddity. A fellow comes in here, searching; that's all.' His back was turned, as he stood staring absently out, sipping his tea between his sentences. 'He comes in—oh, it's a positive fact, for I've seen him myself, just sitting back in my chair here, you know, watching him as one would a tramp in one's orchard.' He cast a candid glance over his shoulder. 'First he looks round, like a prying servant. Then he comes cautiously on—a kind of grizzled, fawn-coloured face, middle-size, with big hands; and then just like some quiet, groping, nocturnal creature, he begins his precious search—shelves, drawers that are not here, cupboards gone years ago, questing and nosing no end, and quite methodically too, until he reaches the window. Then he stops, looks back, narrows his foxy lids, listens—quite perceptibly, you know, a kind of gingerish blur; then he seems to open this corner bookcase here, as if it were a door and goes out along what I suppose might at some time have been an outside gallery or balcony, unless, as I rather fancy, the house extended once beyond these windows. Anyhow, out he goes quite deliberately, treading the air as lightly as Botticelli's angels, until, however far you lean out of the window, you can't follow him any further. And then—and this is the bit that takes one's fancy—when you have contentedly noddled down again to whatever you may have been doing when the wretch appeared, or are sitting in a cold sweat, with bolting eyes awaiting developments, just according to your school of thought, or of nerves, the creature comes back—comes back; and with what looks uncommonly like a lighted candle in his hand. That really is a thrill, I assure you.'

'But you've seen this—you've really seen this yourself?'

'Oh yes, twice,' replied Herbert cheerfully. 'And my sister, quite by haphazard, once saw him from the garden. She was shelling peas one evening for Sallie, and she distinctly saw him shamble out of the window here, and go shuffling along, mid-air, across the roaring washpot down below, turn sharp round the high corner of the house, sheer against the stars, in a kind of frightened hurry. And then, after five minutes' concentrated watching over the shucks, she saw him come shuffling back again—the same distraction, the same nebulous snuff colour, and a candle trailing its smoke behind him as he whisked in home.'

'And then?'

'Ah, then,' said Herbert, lagging along the bookshelves, and scanning the book-backs with eyes partially closed: he turned with lifted teapot, and refilled his visitor's cup; 'then, wherever you are—I mean,' he added, cutting up a little cake into six neat slices, 'wherever the chance inmate of the room happens to be, he comes straight for you, at a quite alarming velocity, and fades, vanishes, melts, or, as it were, silts inside.'

Lawford listened in a curious hush that had suddenly fallen over his mind. '"Fades inside? silts?"—I'm awfully stupid, but what on earth do you mean?' The room had slowly emptied itself of daylight; its own darkness, it seemed, had met that of the narrowing night, and Herbert deliberately lit a cigarette before replying. His clear pale face, with its smooth outline and thin mouth and rather long dark eyes, turned with a kind of serene good-humour towards his questioner.

'Why,' he said, 'I mean frankly just that. Besides, it's Grisel's own phrase; and an old nurse we used to have said much the same. He comes, or *it* comes towards you, first just walking, then with a kind of gradually accelerated slide or glide, and sweeps straight into you,' he tapped his chest, 'me, whoever it may be is here. In a kind of panic, I suppose, to hide, or perhaps simply to get back again.'

'Get back where?'

'Be resumed, as it were, via you. You see, I suppose he is compelled to regain his circle, or Purgatory, or Styx, whatever you like to call it, via consciousness. No one present, then no revenant or spook, or astral body, or hallucination: what's in a name? And of course even an hallucination is mind-stuff, and on its own, as it were. What I mean is that the poor devil must have some kind of human personality to get back through in order to make his exit from our sphere of consciousness into his. And naturally, of course to make his entrance too. If like a tenuous smoke he can get in, the probability is that he gets out in precisely the same fashion. For really, if you weren't consciously expecting the customary impact (you actually jerk forward in the act of resistance unresisted), you would not notice his going. I am afraid I must be horribly boring you with all these tangled theories. All I mean is, that if you were really absorbed in what you happened to be doing at the time, the thing might come and go, with your mind for entrance and exit, as it were, without your being conscious of it at all.' There was a longish pause, in which Herbert slowly inhaled and softly breathed out his smoke.

'And what—what is the poor wretch searching *for?* And what—why, what becomes of him when he does go?'

'Ah, there you have me! One merely surmises just as one's temperament or convictions lean. Grisel says it's some poor derelict soul in search of peace—that the poor beggar wants finally to die, in fact, and can't. Sallie smells crime. After all, what is every man?' he talked on; 'a horde of ghosts—like a Chinese nest of boxes—oaks that were acorns that were oaks. Death lies behind us, not in front—in our ancestors, back and back, until—'

'"Until?"' Lawford managed to remark.

'Ah, that settles me again. Don't they call it an amoeba? But really I am abjectly ignorant of all that kind of stuff. We are *all* we are, and all in a sense we care to dream we are. And for that matter, anything outlandish, bizarre, is a godsend in this rather stodgy life. It is after all just what the old boy said—it's only the impossible that's credible; whatever credible may mean....'

It seemed to Lawford as if the last remark had wafted him bodily into the presence of his kind, blinking, intensely anxious old friend, Mr Bethany. And what leagues asunder the two men were who had happened on much the same words to express their convictions.

He drew his hand gropingly over his face, half rose, and again seated himself. 'Whatever it may be,' he said, 'the whole thing reminds me, you know—it is in a way so curiously like my own—my own case.'

Herbert sat on, a little drawn up in his chair, quietly smoking. The crash of the falling water, after seeming to increase in volume with the fading of evening, had again died down in the darkness to a low multitudinous tumult as of countless inarticulate, echoing voices.

'"Bizarre," you said; God knows *I* am.' But Herbert still remained obdurately silent. 'You remember, perhaps,' Lawford faintly began again, 'our talk the other night?'

'Oh, rather,' replied the cordial voice out of the dusk.

'I suppose you thought I was insane?'

'Insane!' There was a genuinely amused astonishment in the echo. 'You were lucidity itself. Besides—well, honestly, if I may venture, I don't put very much truck in what one calls one's sanity: except, of course, as a bond of respectability and a means of livelihood.'

'But did you realise in the least from what I said how I really stand? That I went down into that old shadowy hollow one man, and came back—well—this?'

'I gathered vaguely something like that. I thought at first it was merely an affectation—that what you said was an affectation, I mean—until—well, to be frank, it was the "this" that so immensely interested me. Especially,' he added almost with a touch of gaiety, 'especially the last glimpse. But if it's really not a forbidden question, what precisely *was* the other? What precise manner of man, I mean, came down into Widderstone?'

'It is my face that is changed, Mr Herbert. If you'll try to understand me—my *face*. What you see now is not what I really am, not what I was. Oh, it is all quite different. I know perfectly well how absurd it must sound. And you won't press me further. But that's the truth: that's what they have done for me.'

It seemed to Lawford as if a remote tiny shout of laughter had been suddenly caught back in the silence that had followed this confession. He peered in vain in the direction of his companion. Even his cigarette revealed no sign of him. 'I know, I know,' he went gropingly on; 'I felt it would sound to you like nothing but frantic incredible nonsense. *You* can't see it. *You* can't feel it. *You* can't hear these hooting voices. It's no use at all blinking the fact; I am simply on the verge, if not over it, of insanity.'

'As to that, Mr Lawford,' came the still voice out of the darkness; 'the very fact of your being able to say so seems to me all but proof positive that you're not. Insanity is on another plane, isn't it? in which one can't compare one's states. As for what you say being credible, take our precious noodle of a spook here! Ninety-nine hundredths of this amiable world of ours would have guffawed the poor creature into imperceptibility ages ago. To such poor credulous creatures as my sister and I he is no more and no less a fact, a personality, an amusing reality than—well, this teacup. Here we are, amazing mysteries both of us in any case; and all round us are scores of books, dealing just with life, pure, candid, and unexpurgated; and there's not a single one among them but reads like a taradiddle. Yet grope between the lines of any autobiography, it's pretty clear what one has got—a feeble, timid, creeping attempt to describe the indescribable. As for what you say *your* case is, the bizarre—that kind very seldom gets into print at all. In all our make-believe, all our pretence, how, honestly, could it? But there, this is immaterial. The real question is, may I, can I help? What I gather is this:

You just trundled down into Widderstone all among the dead men, and—but one moment, I'll light up.'

A light flickered up in the dark. Shading it in his hand from the night air straying through the open window, Herbert lit the two candles that stood upon the little chimneypiece behind Lawford's head. Then sauntering over to the window again, almost as if with an affectation of nonchalance, he drew one of the shutters, and sat down. 'Nothing much struck me,' he went on, leaning back on his hands, 'I mean on Sunday evening, until you said good-bye. It was then that I caught in the moon a distinct glimpse of your face.'

'This,' said Lawford, with a sudden horrible sinking of the heart.

Herbert nodded. 'The fact is, I have a print of it,' he said.

'A print of it?'

'A miserable little dingy engraving.'

'Of this?' Herbert nodded, with eyes fixed. 'Where?'

'That's the nuisance. I searched high and low for it the instant I got home. For the moment it has been mislaid; but it must be somewhere in the house and it will turn up all in good time. It's the frontispiece of one of a queer old hotchpotch of pamphlets, sewn up together by some amateur enthusiast in a marbled paper cover—confessions, travels, trials and so on. All eighteenth century, and all in French.'

'And mine?' said Lawford, gazing stonily across the candlelight.

Herbert, from a head slightly stooping, gazed back in an almost birdlike fashion across the room at his visitor.

'Sabathier's,' he said.

'Sabathier's!'

'A really curious resemblance. Of course, I am speaking only from memory; and perhaps it's not quite so vivid in this light; but still astonishingly clear.'

Lawford sat drawn up, staring at his companion's face in an intense and helpless silence. His mouth opened but no words came.

'Of course,' began Herbert again, 'I don't say there's anything in it—except the—the mere coincidence,' he paused and glanced out of the open casement beside him. 'But there's just one obvious question. Do you happen to know of any strain of French blood in your family?'

Lawford shut his eyes, even memory seemed to be forsaking him at last. 'No,' he said, after a long pause, 'there's a little Dutch, I think, on my mother's side, but no French.'

'No Sabathier, then?' said Herbert, smiling. 'And then there's another question—this change; is it really as complete as you suppose?

Has it—please just warn me off if I am in the least intruding—has it been noticed?'

Lawford hesitated. 'Oh, yes,' he said slowly, 'it has been noticed—my wife, a few friends.'

'Do you mind this infernal clatter?' said Herbert, laying his fingers on the open casement.

'No, no. And you think?'

'My dear fellow, I don't think anything. It's all the craziest conjecture. Stranger things even than this have happened. There are dozens here—in print. What are we human beings after all? Clay in the hands of the potter. Our bodies are merely an inheritance, packed tight and corded up. We have practically no control over their main functions. We can't even replace a little finger-nail. And look at the faces of us—what atrocious mockeries most of them are of *any* kind of image! But we know our bodies change—age, sickness, thought, passion, fatality. It proves they are amazingly plastic. And merely even as a theory it is not in the least untenable that by force of some violent convulsive effort from outside one's body *might* change. It answers with odd voluntariness to friend or foe, smile or snarl. As for what we call the laws of Nature, they are pure assumptions to-day, and may be nothing better than scrap-iron tomorrow. Good Heavens, Lawford, consider man's abysmal impudence.' He smoked on in silence for a moment. 'You say you fell asleep down there?'

Lawford nodded. Herbert tapped his cigarette on the sill. 'Just following up our ludicrous conjecture, you know,' he remarked musingly, 'it wasn't such a bad opportunity for the poor chap.'

'But surely,' said Lawford, speaking as it were out of a dream of candlelight and reverberating sound and clearest darkness, towards this strange deliberate phantom with the unruffled clear-cut features—'surely then, in that case, he is here now? And yet, on my word of honour, though every friend I ever had in the world should deny it, I am the same. Memory stretches back clear and sound to my childhood. I can see myself with extraordinary lucidity, how I think, my motives and all that; and in spite of these voices that I seem to hear, and this peculiar kind of longing to break away, as it were, just to press on—it is I,—I myself, that am speaking to you now out of this—this mask.'

Herbert glanced reflectively at his companion. 'You mustn't let me tire you,' he said; 'but even on our theory it would not necessarily follow that you yourself would be much affected. It's true this fellow Sabathier really was something of a personality. He had a rather unusual itch for life, for trying on and on to squeeze something out of experience that isn't there; and he seemed never to weary of a magnificent attempt to find in his fellow-creatures, especially in the women he met, what even—if they have it—they cannot give. The little book I wanted to show you is partly autobiographical and really does manage to set the fellow on his feet. Even there he does absolutely take one's imagination. I shall never forget the thrill of picking him up in the Charing Cross Road. You see, I had known the queer old tombstone for years. He's enormously vivid—quite beyond my feebleness to describe, with a kind of French verve and rapture. Unluckily we can't get nearer than two years to his death. I shouldn't mind guessing some last devastating dream swept over him, held him the breath of an instant too long beneath the wave, and he caved in. We know he killed himself; and perhaps lived to regret it ever after.

'After all, what is this precious dying we talk so much about?' Herbert continued after a while, his eyes restlessly wandering from shelf to shelf. 'You remember our talk in the churchyard? We all know that the body fades quick enough when its occupant is gone. Supposing even in the sleep of the living it lies very feebly guarded. And supposing in that state some infernally potent thing outside it, wandering disembodied, just happens on it—like some hungry sexton beetle on the carcase of a mouse. Supposing—I know it's the most outrageous theorising—but supposing all these years of sun and dark, Sabathier's emanation, or whatever you like to call it, horribly restless, by some fatality longing on and on just for life, or even for the face, the voice, of some "impossible she" whom he couldn't get in this muddled world, simply loathing all else; supposing he has been lingering in ambush down beside those poor old dusty bones that had poured out for him such marrowy hospitality—oh, I know it; the dead do. And then, by a chance, one quiet autumn evening, a veritable godsend of a little Miss Muffet comes wandering down under the shade of his immortal cypresses, half asleep, fagged out, depressed in mind and body, perhaps: imagine yourself in his place, and he in yours!' Herbert stood up in his eagerness, his sleek hair shining. 'The one clinching chance of a century! Wouldn't you have made a fight for it? Wouldn't you have risked the raid? I can just conceive it—the amazing struggle in that darkness within a darkness; like some dazed alien bee bursting through the sentinels of a hive; one mad impetuous clutch at victory; then the appalling stirring on the other side; the groping back to a house dismantled, rearranged, not, mind you, disorganised or disintegrated....' He broke off with a smile, as if of apology for his long, fantastic harangue.

Lawford sat listening, his eyes fixed on Herbert's colourless face. There was not a sound else, it seemed, than that slightly drawling scrupulous voice poking its way amid a maze of enticing, baffling thoughts. Herbert turned away with a shrug. 'It's tempting stuff,' he said, choosing another cigarette. 'But anyhow, the poor beggar failed.'

'Failed?'

'Why, surely; if he had succeeded I should not now be talking to a mere imperfect simulacrum, to the outward illusion of a passing likeness to the man, but to Sabathier himself!' His eyes moved slowly round and dwelt for a moment with a dark, quiet scrutiny on his visitor.

'You say a passing likeness; do you *mean* that?'

Herbert smiled indulgently. 'If one *can* mean what is purely a speculation. I am only trying to look at the thing dispassionately, you see. We are so much the slaves of mere repetition. Here is life—yours and mine—a kind of *plenum in vacuo*. It is only when we begin to play the eavesdropper; when something goes askew; when one of the sentries on the frontier of the unexpected shouts a hoarse "*Qui vive?*"—it is only then we begin to question; to prick our aldermen and pinch the calves of our kings. Why, who is there can answer to anybody's but his own satisfaction just that one fundamental question—Are we the prisoners, the slaves, the inheritors, the creatures, or the creators of our bodies? Fallen angels or horrific dust? As for identity or likeness or personality, we have only our neighbours' nod for them, and just a fading memory. No, the old fairy tales knew better; and witchcraft's witchcraft to the end of the chapter. Honestly, and just of course on that one theory, Lawford, I can't help thinking that Sabathier's raid only just so far succeeded as to leave his impression in the wax. It doesn't, of course, follow that it will necessarily end there. It might—it may be even now just gradually fading away. It may, you know, need driving out—with whips and scorpions. It might, perhaps, work in.'

Lawford sat cold and still. 'It's no good, no good,' he said, 'I don't understand; I can't follow you. I was always stupid, always bigoted and cocksure. These things have never seemed anything but old women's tales to me. And now I must pay for it. And this Nicholas Sabathier; you say he was a blackguard?'

'Well,' said Herbert with a faint smile, 'that depends on your definition of the word. He wasn't a flunkey, a fool, or a prig, if that's what you mean. He wasn't perhaps on Mrs Grundy's visiting list. He wasn't exactly gregarious. And yet in a sense that kind of temperament is so rare that Sappho, Nelson, and Shelley shared it. To the stodgy, suety world of course it's little else than sheer moonshine, midsummer madness. Naturally, in its own charming and stodgy way the world kept flickering cold water in his direction. Naturally it hissed.... I shall find the book. You shall have the book; oh yes.'

'There's only one more question,' said Lawford in a dull, slow voice, stooping and covering his face with his hands. 'I know it's impossible for you to realise—but to me time seems like that water there, to be heaping up about me. I wait, just as one waits when the conductor of an orchestra lifts his hand and in a moment the whole surge of brass and wood, cymbal and drum will crash out—and sweep me under. I can't tell you Herbert, how it all is, with just these groping stirrings of that mole in my mind's dark. You say it may be this face, working in! God knows. I find it easy to speak to you—this cold, clear sense, you know. The others feel too much, or are afraid, or—Let me think—yes, I was going to ask you a question. But no one can answer it.' He peered darkly, with white face suddenly revealed between his hands. 'What remains now? Where do *I* come in? What is there left for *me* to do?'

And at that moment there sounded, even above the monotonous roar of the water beyond the window—there fell the sound of a light footfall approaching along the corridor.

'Listen,' said Herbert; 'here's my sister coming; we'll ask her.'

CHAPTER THIRTEEN

The door opened. Lawford rose, and into the further rays of the candlelight entered a rather slim figure in a light summer gown.

'Just home?' said Herbert.

'We've been for a walk—'

'My sister always forgets everything,' said Herbert, turning to Lawford; 'even tea-time. This is Mr Lawford, Grisel. We've been arguing no end. And we want you to give a decision. It's just this: Supposing if by some impossible trick you had come in now, not the charming familiar sister you are, but shorter, fatter, fair and round-faced, quite different, physically, you know—what would you do?'

'What nonsense you talk, Herbert!'

'Yes, but supposing: a complete transmogrification—by some unimaginable ingression or enchantment, by nibbling a bunch of roses, or whatever you like to call it?'

'*Only* physically?'

'Well, yes, actually; but potentially, why—that's another matter.'

The dark eyes passed slowly from her brother's face and rested gravely on their visitor's.

'Is he making fun of me?'

Lawford almost imperceptibly shook his head.

'But what a question! And I've had no tea.' She drew her gloves slowly through her hand. 'The thing, of course, isn't possible, I know. But shouldn't I go mad, don't you think?'

Lawford gazed quietly back into the clear, grave, deliberate eyes. 'Suppose, suppose, just for the sake of argument—*not*,' he suggested.

She turned her head and reflected, glancing from one to the other of the pure, steady candle-flames.

'And what was *your* answer?' she said, looking over her shoulder at her brother.

'My dear child, you know what *my* answers are like!'

'And yours?'

Lawford took a deep breath, gazing mutely, forlornly, into the lovely untroubled peace of her eyes, and without the least warning tears swept up into his own. With an immense effort he turned, and choking back every sound, beating back every thought, groped his way towards the square black darkness of the open door.

'I must think, I must think,' he managed to whisper, lifting his hand and steadying himself. He caught over his shoulder the glimpse of a curiously distorted vision, a lifted candle, and a still face gazing after him with infinitely grieved eyes, then found himself groping and stumbling down the steep, uneven staircase into the darkness of the queer old wooden and hushed and lonely house. The night air cold on his face calmed his mind. He turned and held out his hand.

'You'll come again?' Herbert was saying, with a hint of anxiety, even of apology in his voice.

Lawford nodded, with eyes fixed blankly on the candle, and turning once more, made his way slowly down the narrow green-bordered path upon which the stars rained a scattered light so feeble it seemed but as a haze that blurred the darkness. He pushed open the little white wicket and turned his face towards the soundless, leaf-crowned hill. He had advanced hardly a score of steps in the thick dust when almost as if its very silence had struck upon his ear he remembered the black broken grave with its sightless heads that lay beyond the leaves. And fear, vast and menacing, fear such as only children know, broke like a sea of darkness on his heart. He stopped dead—cold, helpless, trembling. And, in the silence he heard a faint cry behind him and light footsteps pursuing him. He turned again. In the thick close gloom beneath the enormous elm-boughs the grey eyes shone clearly visible in the face upturned to him. 'My brother,' she began breathlessly—'the little French book. It was I who—who mislaid it.'

The set, stricken face listened unmoved.

'You are ill. Come back! I am afraid you are very ill.'

'It's not that, not that,' Lawford muttered; 'don't leave me; I am alone. Don't question me,' he said strangely, looking down into her face, clutching her hand; 'only understand that I can't, I can't go on.' He swept a lean arm towards the unseen churchyard. 'I am afraid.'

The cold hand clasped his closer. 'Hush, don't speak! Come back; come back. I am with you, a friend, you see; come back.'

Lawford clutched her hand as a blind man in sudden peril might clutch the hand of a child. He saw nothing clearly; spoke almost without understanding his words.

'Oh, but it's *must*,' he said; 'I *must* go on. You see—why, everything depends on struggling through: the future! But if you only knew—

There!' Again his arm swept out, and the lean terrified face turned shuddering from the dark.

'I do know; believe me, believe me! I can guess. See, I am coming with you; we will go together. As if, as if I did not know what it is to be afraid. Oh, believe me; no one is near; we go on; and see! it gradually, gradually lightens. How thankful I am I came.'

She had turned and they were steadily ascending as if pushing their way, battling on through some obstacle of the mind rather than of the senses beneath the star-powdered callous vault of night. And it seemed to Lawford as if, as they pressed on together, some obscure detestable presence as slowly, as doggedly had drawn worsted aside. He could see again the peaceful outspread branches of the trees, the lych-gate standing in clear-cut silhouette against the liquid dusk of the sky. A strange calm stole over his mind. The very meaning and memory of his fear faded out and vanished, as the passed-away clouds of a storm that leave a purer, serener sky.

They stopped and stood together on the brow of the little hill, and Lawford, still trembling from head to foot, looked back across the hushed and lightless countryside. 'It's all gone now,' he said wearily, 'and now there's nothing left. You see, I cannot even ask your forgiveness—and a stranger!'

'Please don't say that—unless—unless—a "pilgrim" too. I think, surely, you must own we did have the best of it that time. Yes—and I don't care *who* may be listening—but we *did* win through.'

'What can I say? How shall I explain? How shall I make you understand?'

The clear grey eyes showed not the faintest perturbation. 'But I do; I do indeed, in part; I do understand, ever so faintly.'

'And now I will come back with *you*.'

They paused in the darkness face to face, the silence of the sky, arched in its vastness above the little hill, the only witness of their triumph.

She turned unquestioningly. And laughing softly almost as children do, the stalking shadows of a twilight wood behind them—they trod in silence back to the house. They said good-bye at the gate, and Lawford started once more for home. He walked slowly, conscious of an almost intolerable weariness, as if his strength had suddenly been wrested away from him. And at some distance beyond the top of the hill he sat down on the bank beside a nettled ditch, and with his book pressed down upon the wayside grass struck a match, and holding it low in the scented, windless air turned slowly the cockled leaf.

Few of them were alike except for the dinginess of the print and the sinister smudge of the portraits. All were sewn roughly together into a mould-stained, marbled cover. He lit a second match, and as he did so glanced as if inquiringly over his shoulder. And a score or so of pages before the end he came at last upon the name he was seeking, and turned the page.

It was a likeness even more striking in its crudeness of ink and line and paper than the most finished of portraits could have been. It repelled, and yet it fascinated him. He had not for a moment doubted Herbert's calm conviction. And yet as he stooped in the grass, closely scrutinising the blurred obscure features, he felt the faintest surprise not so much at the significant resemblance but at his own composure, his own steady, unflinching confrontation with this sinister and intangible adversary. The match burned down to his fingers. It hissed faintly in the grass.

He stuffed the book into his pocket, and stared into the pale dial of his watch. It was a few minutes after eleven. Midnight, then, would just see him in. He rose stiffly and yawned in sheer exhaustion. Then, hesitating, he turned his head and looked back towards the hollow. But a vague foreboding held him back. A sour and vacuous incredulity swept over him. What was the use of all this struggling and vexation. What gain in living on? Once dead *his* sluggish spirit at least would find its rest. Dust to dust it would indeed be for him. What else, in sober earnest, had he been all his daily stolid life but half dead, scarce conscious, without a living thought, or desire, in head or heart?

And while he was still gloomily debating within himself he had turned towards home, and soon was walking in a kind of reverie, even his extreme tiredness in part forgotten, and only a far-away dogged recollection in his mind that in spite of shame, in spite of all his miserable weakness, the words had been uttered once for all, and in all sincerity, 'We *did* win through.'

Yet a desolate and odd air of strangeness seemed to drape his unlighted house as he stood looking up in a kind of furtive communion with its windows. It affected him with that discomforting air of extreme and meaningless novelty that things very familiar sometimes take upon themselves. In this leaden tiredness no impression could be trustworthy. His lids shut of themselves as he softly mounted the steps. It seemed a needlessly wide door that soundlessly admitted him. But however hard he pressed the key his bedroom door remained stubbornly shut until he found that it was already unlocked and he had only to turn the handle. A night-light burned in a little basin on the washstand. The room was hung, as it were, with the stillness of night. And half lying on the bed in her dressing-gown, her head leaning on the rail at the foot, was Alice, just as sleep had overtaken her.

Lawford returned to the door and listened. It seemed he heard a voice talking downstairs, and yet not talking, for it ran on and on in an incessant slightly argumentative monotony that had neither break nor interruption. He closed the door, and stooping laid his hand softly on Alice's narrow, still childish hand that lay half-folded on her knee. Her eyes opened instantly and gazed widely into his face. A slow vacant smile of sleep came and went and her fingers tightened gently over his as again her lids drooped down over the drowsy blue eyes.

'At last, at last, dear,' she said; 'I have been waiting such a time. But we mustn't talk much. Mother is waiting up, reading.'

Faintly through the close-shut door came the sound of that distant expressionless voice monotonously rising and falling.

'Why didn't you tell me, dear?' Alice still sleepily whispered. 'Would I have asked a single question? How could I? Oh, if you had only trusted me!'

'But the change—the change, Alice! You must have seen that. You spoke to me, you did think I was only a stranger; and even when you knew, it was only fear on your face, dearest, and aversion; and you turned to your mother first. Don't think, Alice, that I am...God only knows—I'm not complaining. But truth is best whatever it is. I do feel that. You mustn't be afraid of hurting me, my dear.'

Her very hands seemed to quicken in his as now, with sleep quite gone, the fret of memory returned, and she must reassure both herself and him. 'But you see, dear, mother had told me that you—besides, I did know you at once, really; quite inside, you know, deep down. I know I was perplexed; I didn't understand; but that was all. Why, even when you came up in the dark, and we talked—if you only knew how miserable I had been—though I knew even then there was something different, still I was not a bit afraid. Was I? And shouldn't I have been afraid, horribly afraid, if *you* had not been *you?*' She repressed a little shudder, and clasped his hand more closely. 'Don't let us say anything more about it, she implored him; 'we are just together again, you and I; that is all that matters.' But her words were like brave soldiers who have fought their way through an ambuscade but have left all confidence behind them.

Lawford listened; and that was enough just now—that she still, in spite of doubt, believed in him, and thought and cared for him. He was too tired to have refused the least kindness. He made no answer, but leant his head on the cool, slender fingers in gratitude and peace. And, just as he was, he almost instantly fell asleep. He woke in the darkness to find himself alone. He groped his way heavily to the door and turned the handle. But now it was really locked. Energy failed him. 'I suppose—Sheila...' he muttered.

CHAPTER FOURTEEN

Sheila, calm, alert, reserved, was sitting at the open window when he awoke again. His breakfast tray stood on a little table beside the bed. He raised himself on his elbow and looked at his wife. The morning light shone full on her features as she turned quickly at sound of his stirring.

'You have slept late,' she said, in a low, mellow voice.

'Have I, Sheila? I suppose I was tired out. It is very kind of you to have got everything ready like this.'

'I am afraid, Arthur, I was thinking rather of the maids. I like to inconvenience them as little as possible; in their usual routine, I mean. How are you feeling, do you think, this morning?'

'I—I haven't seen the glass, Sheila.'

She paused to place a little pencil tick at the foot of the page of her butcher's book. 'And did you—did you try?'

'Did I try? Try what?'

'I understood,' she said, turning slowly in her chair, 'you gave me to understand that you went out with the specific intention of trying to regain.... But there, forgive me, Arthur; I think I must be getting a little bit hardened to the position, so far at least as any hope is in my mind of rather amateurish experiments being of much help. I may seem unsympathetic in saying frankly what I feel. But amateurish or no, you are curiously erratic. Why, if you really were the Dr Ferguson whose part you play so admirably you could scarcely spend a more active life.'

'All you mean, Sheila, I suppose, is that I have failed.'

'"Failed" did not enter my mind. I thought, looking at you just now in your clothes on the bed, one might for the moment be deceived into thinking there was a slight—quite the slightest improvement. There was not quite that'—she hovered for the right word—'that tenseness. Whether or not, whether you desired any such change or didn't, I should have supposed in any case it would have been better to act as far as possible like any ordinary person. You were certainly in an extraordinarily sound sleep. I was almost alarmed; until I remembered that it was a little after two when I looked up from reading aloud to keep myself awake and discovered that you had only just come home. I had no fire. You know how easily late hours bring on my headaches; a little thought might possibly have suggested that I should be anxious to hear.

But no; it seems I cannot profit by experience, Arthur. And even now you have not answered surely a very natural question. You do not recollect, perhaps, exactly what did happen last night? Did you go in the direction even of Widderstone?'

'Yes, Sheila, I went to Widderstone.'

'It was of course absurd to suppose that sitting on a seat beside the broken-down grave of a suicide would have the slightest effect on one's—one's physical condition; though possibly it might affect one's brain. It would mine; I am at least certain of that. It was your own prescription, however; and it merely occurred to me to inquire whether the actual experience has not brought you round to my own opinion.'

'Yes, I think it has,' Lawford answered calmly. 'But I don't quite see what suicide has got to do with it; unless—You know Widderstone, then, Sheila?'

'I drove there last Saturday afternoon.'

'For prayer or praise?' Although Lawford had not actually raised his head, he became conscious rather of the wonderfully adjusted mass of hair than of the pained dignity in the face that was now closely regarding him.

'I went,' came the rigidly controlled retort, 'simply to test an inconceivable story.'

'And returned?'

'Convinced, Arthur, of its inconceivability. But if you would kindly inform me what precise formula you followed at Widderstone last night, I would tell you why I think the explanation, or rather your first account of the matter, is not an explanation of the facts.'

Lawford shot a rather doglike glance over his toast. 'Danton?' he said.

'Candidly, Arthur, Mr Danton doubts the whole story. Your very conduct—well, it would serve no useful purpose to go into that. Candidly, on the other hand, Mr. Danton did make some extremely helpful suggestions—basing them, of course, on the *truth* of your account. He has seen a good deal of life; and certainly very mysterious things do occur to quite innocent and well-meaning people without the faintest shadow of warning, and as Mr. Bethany himself said, evil birds do come home to roost, and often out of a clear sky, as it were. But there, every fresh solution that occurs to me only makes the thing more preposterous, more, I was going to say, disreputable—I mean, of course, to the outside world. And we have our duties to perform to them too, I suppose. Why, what can we say? What plausible account of ourselves have we? We shall never be able to look anybody in the face again. I can only—I am compelled to believe that God has been pleased to make this precise visitation upon us—an eye for an eye, I suppose, *somewhere*. And to that conviction I shall hold until actual circumstances convince me that it's false. What, however, and this is all that I have to say now, what I cannot understand are your amazing indiscretions.'

'Do you understand your own, Sheila?'

'My indiscretions, Arthur?'

'Well,' said Lawford, 'wasn't it indiscreet, don't you think, to risk divine retribution by marrying me? Shouldn't you have inquired? Wasn't it indiscreet to allow me to remain here in—in my "visitation?" Wasn't it indiscreet to risk the moral stigma this unhappy face of mine must cast on its surroundings? I am not sure whether such a change as this constitutes cruelty.... Oh, what is the use of fretting and babbling on like this?'

'Am I to understand, then, that you refuse positively to discuss this horrible business any more? You are doing your best to drive me away, Arthur; you must see that. Will you be very disappointed if I refuse to go?'

Lawford rose from the bed. 'Listen just this once,' he said, seating himself on the corner of the dressing-table. 'Imagine all this—whatever you like to call it—obliterated. Take this,' he nodded towards the glass, 'entirely for itself, on its own merits, as it were. Let the dead past bury its dead. Which, now, precisely, *really* do you prefer—him,' he jerked his head in the direction of the dispassionate youthful picture on the wall, 'him or me?'

He was so close to her now that he could see the faintest tremor on the face that had suddenly become grey and still in the thin clear sunshine.

'I own it, I own it,' he went on, slowly; 'the change is more than skin-deep now. One can't go through what I have gone through these last few terrifying days, Sheila, unchanged. They have played the devil with my body; now begins the tampering with my mind. Not even Danton knows how it will end. But shall I tell you why you won't, why you can't answer me that one question—him or me? Shall I tell you?'

Sheila slowly raised her eyes.

'It is because, my dear, you don't care the ghost of a straw for either. That one—he was worn out long ago, and we never knew it. I know it now. Time and the sheer going-on of day by day, without either of us guessing at it, wore that down till it had no more meaning for you or me than any other faded remembrance in this interminable footling with truth that we call life. And this one—the whole abject meaning of it lies simply in the fact that it has pierced down and shown us up. I had no courage. I couldn't see how feeble a hold I had on life—just one's friends' opinions. It was all at second hand. What I want to know now is—leave me out; don't think, or care, or regard my living-on one shadow of an iota—all I ask is, What am I to do for you?' He turned away and stood staring down at the cinders in the fireless grate.

'I answer that mad wicked outburst with one plain question,' said a low, trembling voice; 'did you or did you not go to Widderstone yesterday?'

'I did go.'

'You sat there, just as you said you sat before; and with all your heart and soul strove to regain—yourself?'

Lawford lifted a still, colourless face into the sunlight. 'No,' he said; 'I spent the evening at the house of a friend.'

'Then I say it is infamous. You cast all this on me. You have brought me into contempt and poisoned Alice's whole life. You dream and idle on just as you used to do, without the least care or thought or consideration for others; and go out in this condition—go out absolutely unashamed—to spend the evening at a friend's. Peculiar friends they must be. Why, really, Arthur, you must be mad!'

Lawford paused. Like a flock of sheep streaming helter-skelter before the onset of a wolf were the thoughts that a moment before had seemed so orderly and sober.

'Not mad—possessed,' he said softly.

'And I add this,' cried Sheila, as it were out of a tragic mask, 'somewhere in the past, whether of your own life, or of the lives of those who brought you into the world—the world which you pretend so conveniently to despise—somewhere is hidden some miserable secret. God visits all sins. On you has fallen at last the payment. *That* I believe. You can't run away, any more than a child can run away from the cupboard it has been locked into for a punishment. Who's going to hear you now? You have deliberately refused to make a friend of me. Fight it out alone, then!'

Lawford heard the door close, and the dying away of the sound that had been the unceasing accompaniment of all these later years—the rustling of his wife's skirts, her crisp, authoritative footstep. And he turned towards the flooding sunlight that streamed in on the upturned surface of the looking-glass. No clear decisive thought came into his mind, only a vague recognition that so far as Sheila was concerned this was the end. No regret, no remorse visited him. He was just alone again, that was all—alone, as in reality he had always been alone, without having the sense or power to see or to acknowledge it. All he had said had been the mere flotsam of the moment, and now it stood stark and irrevocable between himself and the past.

He sat down dazed and stupid. Again and again a struggling recollection tried to obtrude itself; again and again he beat it back. And rather for something to distract his attention than for any real interest or enlightenment he might find in its pages, he took out the grimy dog's-eared book that Herbert had given him, and turned slowly over the leaves till he came to Sabathier once more. Snatches of remembrance of their long talk returned to him, but just as that dark, water-haunted house had seemed to banish remembrance and the reality of the room in which he now sat, and of the old familiar life; so now the house, the faces of yesterday seemed in their turn unreal, almost spectral, and the thick print on the smudgy page no more significant than a story one reads and throws away.

But a moment's comparison in the glass of the two faces side by side suddenly sharpened his attention—the resemblance was so oddly arresting, and yet, and yet, so curiously inconclusive. There was then something of the stolid old Saxon left, he thought. Or had it been regained? Which was it? Not merely the complexity of the question, but a half-conscious distaste of attempting to face it, set him reading very slowly and laboriously, for his French was little more than fragmentary recollection, the first few pages of the life of this buried Sabathier. But with a disinclination almost amounting to aversion he made very slow progress. Many of the words were meaningless to him, and every other moment he found himself listening with intense concentration for the least hint of what Sheila was doing, of what was going on in the house beneath him. He had not very long to wait. He was sitting with his head leaning on his hand, the book unheeded beneath the other on the table, when the door opened again behind him, and Sheila entered. She stood for a moment, calm and dignified, looking down on him through her veil.

'Please understand, Arthur, that I am not taking this step in pique, or even in anger. It would serve no purpose to go on like this—this incessant heedlessness and recrimination. There have been mistakes, misconceptions, perhaps, on both sides. To me naturally yours are most conspicuous. That need not, however, blind me to my own.'

She paused in vain for an answer.

'Think the whole thing over candidly and quietly,' she began again in a quiet rapid voice. 'Have you really shown the slightest regard, I won't say for me, or even for Alice, but for just the obvious difficulties and—and proprieties of our position? I have given up as far as I can brooding on and on over the same horrible impossible thoughts. I withdraw unreservedly what I said just now about punishment. Whatever the evidence, it is not even a wife's place to judge like that. You will forgive me that?'

Lawford did not turn his head. 'Of course,' he said, looking rather vacantly out of the window, 'it was only in the heat of the moment, Sheila; though, who knows? it may be true.'

'Well,' she took hold of the great brass knob at the foot of the bed with one gloved hand—'well, I feel it is my duty to withdraw it. Apart from it, I see only too clearly that even though all that has happened in these last few days was in reality nothing but a horrible nightmare, I see that even then what you have said about our married life together can never be recalled. You have told me quite deliberately that for years past your life has been nothing but a pretence—a sham. You implied that mine had been too. Honestly, I was not aware of it, Arthur. But supposing all that has happened to you had been merely what might happen at any moment to anybody, some actual defacement (you will forgive me suggesting such a horrible thing)—why, if what you say is true, even in that case my sympathy would have been only a continual fret and annoyance to you. And this—this change, I own, is infinitely harder to bear. It would be an outrage on common sense and on all that we hold seemly and—and sacred in life, even in some trumpery story. You do, you must see all that, Arthur?'

'Oh yes,' said Lawford, narrowing his eyes to pierce through the sunlight, 'I see all that.'

'Then we need not go over it all again. Whatever others may say, or think, I shall still, at least so long as nothing occurs to the contrary, keep firmly to my present convictions. Mr Bethany has assured me repeatedly that he has no—no misgivings; that he understands. And even if I still doubted, which I don't, Arthur, though it would be rather trying to have to accept one's husband at second-hand, as it were, I should have to be satisfied. I dare say even such an unheard-of thing as what we are discussing now, or something equally ghastly, does occur occasionally. In foreign countries, perhaps. I have not studied such things enough to say. We were all very much restricted in our reading as children, and I honestly think, not unwisely. It is enough for the present to repeat that I do believe, and that whatever may happen—and I know absolutely nothing about the procedure in such cases—but whatever may happen, I shall still be loyal; I shall always have your interests at heart.' Her words faltered and she turned her head away. 'You did love me once, Arthur, I can't forget that.' The contralto voice trembled ever so little, and the gloved hand smoothed gently the brass knob beneath.

'If,' said Lawford, resting his face on his hands, and curiously watching the while his moving reflection in the looking-glass before him—'if I said I still loved you, what then?

'But you have already denied it, Arthur.'

'Yes; but if I said that that too was said only in haste, that brooding over the trouble this—this metamorphosis was bringing on us all had driven me almost beyond endurance: supposing that I withdrew all that, and instead said now that I do still love you, just as I—' he turned a little, and turned back again, 'like this?'

Sheila paused. 'Could *any* woman answer such a question?' she almost sighed at last.

'Yes, but,' Lawford pressed on, in a voice almost naive and stubborn as a child's, 'If I tried to—to make you? I did once, Sheila.'

'I can't, I can't conceive such a position. Surely that alone is almost as frantic as it is heartless! Is it, is it even right?'

'Well, I have not actually asked it. I own,' he added moodily, almost under his breath, 'it would be—dangerous.... But there, Sheila, this poor old mask of mine is wearing out. I am somehow convinced of that. What will be left, God only knows. You were saying—' He rose abruptly. 'Please, please sit down,' he said; 'I did not notice you were standing.'

'I shall not keep you a moment,' she answered hurriedly; 'I will sit here. The truth is, Arthur,' she began again almost solemnly, 'apart from all sentiment and—and good intentions, my presence here only harasses you and keeps you back. I am not so bound up in myself that I cannot realise *that*. The consequence is that after calmly—and I hope considerately—thinking the whole thing over, I have come to the conclusion that it would arouse very little comment, the least possible perhaps in the circumstances, if I just went away for a few days. You are not in any sense ill. In fact, I have never known you so—so robust, so energetic. You will be alone: Mr Bethany, perhaps.... You could go out and come in just as you pleased. Possibly,' Sheila smiled frankly beneath her veil, 'even this Dr Ferguson you have invented will be a help. It's only the servants that remain to be considered.'

'I should prefer to be quite alone.'

'Then do not worry about *them*. I can easily explain. And if you would not mind letting her in, Mrs Gull can come in every other day or so just to keep things in order. She's entirely trustworthy and discreet. Or perhaps, if you would prefer—'

'Mrs Gull will do nicely, Sheila. It's very good of you to have given me so much thought.' A long and rather arduous pause followed.

'Oh, one other thing, Arthur. You sent out to Mr Critchett—do you remember?—the night you first came home. I think, too, after the first awful shock, when we were sitting in our bedroom, you actually referred to—to violent measures. You will promise me, I may perhaps at least ask that, you will promise me on your word of honour, for Alice's sake, if not for mine, to do nothing rash.'

'Yes, yes,' said Lawford, sinking lower even than he had supposed possible into the thin and lightless chill of ennui—'nothing rash.'

Sheila rose with a sigh only in part suppressed. 'I have not seen Mr Bethany again. I think, however, it would be better to let Harry know; I mean, dear, of your derangement. After all, he is one of the family—at least, of mine. He will not interfere. He would, perhaps quite naturally, be hurt if we did not take him into our confidence. Otherwise there is no pressing cause for haste, at least for another week or so. After that, I suppose, something will have to be done. Then there's Mr Wedderburn; wouldn't it be as well to let him know that at least for the present you are quite unable to think of returning to town? That, too, in time will have to be arranged, I suppose, if nothing happens meanwhile; I mean if things don't come right. And I do hope, Arthur, you will not set your mind too closely on what may only prove false hopes. This is all intensely painful to me; of course, to us both.'

Again Lawford, even though he did not turn to confront it, became conscious of the black veil turned towards him tentatively, speculatively, impenetrably.

'Yes,' he said, 'I'll write to Wedderburn; he's had his ups and downs too.'

'I always rather fancied so,' said Sheila reflectively, 'he looks rather a—a restless man. Oh, and then again,' she broke off quickly, 'there's the question of money. I suppose—it is only a conjecture—I suppose it would be better to do nothing in that direction just for the present. Ada has now gone to the Bank. Fifty pounds, Arthur; it is out of my own private account—do you think that will be enough, just, of course, for your *present* needs?'

'As a bribe, hush-money, or a thank-offering, Sheila?' murmured her husband wearily.

'I don't follow you,' replied the discreet voice from beneath the veil.

He did actually turn this time and glance steadily over his shoulder. 'How long are you going for? and where?'

'I proposed to go to my cousin's, Bettie Lovat's; that is, of course, if you have no objection. It's near; it will be a long-deferred visit; and she need know very little. And, of course, if for the least thing in the world you should want me, there I am within call, as it were. And you will write? We *are* acting for the best, Arthur?'

'So long as it is your best, Sheila.'

Sheila pondered. 'You think, you mean, they'll all say I ought to have stayed. Candidly, I can't see it in that light. Surely every experience of life proves that in intimate domestic matters, and especially in those between husband and wife, only the parties concerned have any means of judging what is best for them? It has been our experience at any rate: though I must in fairness confess that, outwardly at least, I haven't had much of that kind of thing to complain of.' Sheila paused again for a reply.

'What kind of thing?'

'Domestic experience, dear.'

The house was quiet. There was not a sound stirring in the still sunny road of orchards and discreet and drowsy villas. A long silence followed, immensely active and alert on the one side, almost morbidly lethargic so far as the stooping figure in front of the looking-glass was concerned. At last the last haunting question came in a kind of croak, as if only by a supreme effort could it be compelled to produce itself for consideration.

'And Alice, Sheila?'

'Alice, dear, of course goes with *me*.'

'You realise,' he stirred uneasily, 'you realise it may be final.'

'My dear Arthur,' cried Sheila, 'it is surely, apart from mere delicacy, a parental obligation to screen the poor child from the shock. Could she be at such a time in any better keeping than her mother's? At present she only vaguely guesses. To know definitely that her father, infinitely worse than death, had—had—Oh, is it possible to realise anything in this awful cloud? It would kill her outright.'

Lawford made no stir. The quietest of raps came at the door. 'The money from the Bank, ma'am,' said a faint voice.

Sheila carefully opened the door a few inches. She laid the blue envelope on the dressing-table at her husband's elbow. 'You had better perhaps count it,' she said in a low voice—'forty in notes, the rest in gold,' and narrowed her eyes beneath her veil upon her husband's very peculiar method of forgetting his responsibilities.

'French?' she said with a nod. 'How very quaint.'

Lawford's eyes fell and rested gravely on the dingy page of Herbert's mean-looking bundle of print. A queer feeling of cold crept over him. 'Yes,' he said vaguely, 'French,' and hopelessly failed to fill in the silence that seemed like some rather sleek nocturnal creature quietly waiting to be fed.

Sheila swept softly towards the door. 'Well, Arthur, I think that is all. The servants will have gone by this evening. I have ordered a carriage for half-past twelve. Perhaps you would first write down anything that occurs to you to be necessary? Perhaps, too, it would be better if Dr Simon were told that we shall not need him any more, that you are thinking of a complete change of scene, a voyage. He is obviously useless. Besides, Mr Bethany, I think, is going to discuss a specialist with you. I have written him a little note, just briefly explaining. Shall I write to Dr Simon too?'

'You remember everything,' said Lawford, and it seemed to him it was a remark he had heard ages and ages ago. 'It's only this money, Sheila; will you please take that away?'

'Take it away?'

'I think, Sheila, if I do take a voyage I should almost prefer to work my passage. As for a mere "change of scene," that's quite uncostly.'

'It is only your face, Arthur,' said Sheila solemnly, 'that suggest these wicked stabs. Some day you will perhaps repent of every one.'

'It is possible, Sheila; we none of us stand still, you know. One rips open a lid sometimes and the wax face rots before one's eyes. Take back your blue envelope; and thank you for thinking of me. It's always the woman of the house that has the head.'

'I wish,' said Sheila almost pathetically, and yet with a faint quaver of resignation, 'I wish it could be said that the man of the house sometimes has the heart. Think it over, Arthur!'

Sheila, with her husband's luncheon tray, brought also her farewells. Lawford surveyed, not without a faint, shy stirring of incredulity, the superbly restrained presence. He stood before her dry-lipped, inarticulate, a schoolboy caught redhanded in the shabbiest of offences.

'It is your wish then that I go, Arthur?' she said pleadingly.

He handed her her money without a word.

'Very well, Arthur; if you won't take it,' she said. 'I should scarcely have thought this the occasion for mere pride.'

'The tenth,' she continued, as she squeezed the envelope into her purse, with only the least hardening of voice, 'although I daresay you have not troubled to remember it—the tenth will be the eighteenth anniversary of our wedding-day. It makes parting, however advisable, and though only for the few days we should think nothing of in happier circumstances, a little harder to bear. But there, all will come right. You will see things in a different light, perhaps. Words may wound, but time will heal.' But even as she now looked closely into his colourless sunken face some distant memory seemed to well up irresistibly—the memory of eyes just as ingenuous, and as unassuming that even in claiming her love had expressed only their stolid unworthiness.

'Did you know it? have you seen it?' she said, stooping forward a little. 'I believe in spite of all....' He gazed on solemnly, almost owlishly, out of his fading mask.

'Wait till Mr Bethany tells you; you will believe it perhaps from him.' He saw the grey-gloved hand a little reluctantly lifted towards him.

'Good-bye, Sheila,' he said, and turned mechanically back to the window.

She hesitated, listening to a small far-away voice that kept urging her with an almost frog-like pertinacity to do, to say something, and yet as stubbornly would not say what; and she was gone.

CHAPTER FIFTEEN

Raying and gleaming in the sunlight the hired landau drove up to the gate. Lawford, peeping between the blinds, looked down on the coachman, with reins hanging loosely from his red squat-thumbed hand, seated in his tight livery and indescribable hat on the faded cushions. One thing only was in his mind; and it was almost with an audible cry that he turned towards the figure that edged, white and trembling, into the chill room, to fling herself into his arms. 'Don't look at me,' he begged her, 'only remember, dearest, I would rather have died down there and been never seen again than have given you pain. Run—run, your mother's calling. Write to me, think of me; good-bye!'

He threw himself on the bed and lay there till evening—till the door had shut gently behind the last rat to leave the sinking ship. All the clearness, the calmness were gone again. Round and round in dizzy sickening flare and clatter his thoughts whirled. Contempt, fear, loathing, blasphemy, laughter, longing: there was no end. Death was no end. There was no meaning, no refuge, no hope, no possible peace. To give up was to go to perdition: to go forward was to go mad. And even madness—he sat up with trembling lips in the twilight—madness itself was only a state, only a state. You might be bereaved, and the pain and hopelessness of that would pass. You might be cast out, betrayed, deserted, and still be you, still find solitude lovely and in a brave face a friend. But madness!—it surged in on him with all the clearness and emptiness of a dream. And he sat quite still, his hand clutching the bedclothes, his head askew, waiting for the sound of footsteps, for the presences and the voices that have their thin-walled dwelling beneath the shallow crust of consciousness.

Inky blackness drifted up in wisps, in smoke before his eyes; he was powerless to move, to cry out. There was no room to turn; no air to breathe. And yet there was a low, continuous, never-varying stir as of an enormous wheel whirling in the gloom. Countless infinitesimal faces arched like glimmering pebbles the huge dim-coloured vault above his head. He heard a voice above the monstrous rustling of the wheel, clamouring, calling him back. He was hastening headlong, muttering to himself his own flat meaningless name, like a child repeating as he runs his errand. And then as if in a charmed cold pool he awoke and opened his eyes again on the gathering darkness of the great bedroom, and heard a quick, importunate, long-continued knocking on the door below, as of some one who had already knocked in vain.

Cramped and heavy-limbed, he felt his way across the room and lit a candle. He stood listening awhile: his eyes fixed on the door that hung a little open. All in the room seemed acutely fantastically still. The flame burned dim, enisled in the sluggish air. He stole slowly to the door, looked out, and again listened. Again the knocking broke out, more impetuously and yet with a certain restraint and caution. Shielding the flame of his candle in the shell of his left hand, Lawford moved slowly, with chin uplifted, to the stairs. He bent forward a little, and stood motionless and drawn up, the pupils of his eyes slowly contracting and expanding as he gazed down into the carpeted vacant gloom; past the dim louring presence that had fallen back before him.

His mouth opened. 'Who's there?' at last he called.

'Thank God, thank God!' he heard Mr Bethany mutter. 'I mustn't call, Lawford,' came a hurried whisper as if the old gentleman were pressing his lips to speak through the letter-box. 'Come down and open the door; there's a good fellow! I've been knocking no end of a time.'

'Yes, I am coming,' said Lawford. He shut his mouth and held his breath, and stair by stair he descended, driving steadily before him the crouching, gloating menacing shape, darkly lifted up before him against the darkness, contending the way with him.

'Are you ill? Are you hurt? Has anything happened, Lawford?' came the anxious old voice again, striving in vain to be restrained.

'No, no,' muttered Lawford. 'I am coming; coming slowly.' He paused to breathe, his hands trembling, his hair lank with sweat, and still with eyes wide open he descended against the phantom lurking in the darkness—an adversary that, if he should but for one moment close his lids, he felt would master sanity and imagination with its evil. 'So long as you don't get in,' he heard himself muttering, 'so long as you don't get *in*, my friend!'

'What's that you're saying?' came up the muffled, querulous voice; 'I can't for the life of me hear, my boy.'

'Nothing, nothing,' came softly the answer from the foot of the stairs. 'I was only speaking to myself.'

Deliberately, with candle held rigidly on a level with his eyes, Lawford pushed forward a pace or two into the airless, empty drawing-room, and grasped the handle of the door. He gazed in awhile, a black oblique shadow flung across his face, his eyes fixed like an animal's, then drew the door steadily towards him. And suddenly some power that had held him tense seemed to fail. He thrust out his head, and, his face quivering with fear and loathing, spat defiance as if in a passion of triumph into the gloom.

Still muttering, he shut the door and turned the key. In another moment his light was gleaming out on the grey perturbed face and black narrow shoulders of his visitor.

'You gave me quite a fright,' said the old man almost angrily; 'have you hurt your foot, or something?'

'It was very dark,' said Lawford, 'down the stairs.'

'What!' said Mr Bethany still more angrily, blinking out of his unspectacled eyes; 'has she cut off the gas, then?'

'You got the note?' said Lawford, unmoved.

'Yes, yes; I got the note.... Gone?'

'Oh, yes; all gone. It was my choice. I preferred it so.'

Mr Bethany sat down on one of the hard old wooden chairs that stood on either side of the lofty hall, and breathing rather thickly, rested his hands on his knees. 'What's happened?' he inquired, looking up into the candle. 'I forgot my glasses, old fool that I am, and can't, my dear fellow, see you very plainly. But your voice—'

'I think,' said Lawford, 'I think it's beginning to come back.'

'What, the whole thing! Oh no, my dear, dear man; be frank with me; not the whole thing?'

'Yes,' said Lawford, 'the whole thing—very, very gradually, imperceptibly. I think even Sheila noticed. But I rather feel it than see it; that is all.... I'm cornering him.'

'Him?'

Lawford jerked his candle as if towards some definite goal. 'In time,' he said.

The two faces with the candle between them seemed as it were to gain light each from the other.

'Well, well,' said Mr Bethany, 'every man for himself, Lawford; it's the only way. But what's going to be done? We must be cautious; must think of—of the others?'

'Oh, that,' said Lawford; 'she's going to squeeze me out.'

'You've—squabbled? Oh, but my dear, honest old, *honest* old idiot, there are scores of families here in this parish, within a stone's throw, that squabble, wrangle, all but politely tear each other's eyes out, every day of their earthly lives. It's perfectly natural. Where should we poor old busybodies be else. Peace on earth we bring, and it's mainly between husband and wife.'

'Yes,' said Lawford, 'but you see, this was not our earthly life. It was between *us*.'

'Listen, listen to the dear mystic!' exclaimed the old creature scoffingly. 'What depths we're touching. Here's the first serious break of his lifetime, and he's gone stark staring transcendental. Ah well.' He paused and glanced quickly about him, with his curious bird-like poise of head. 'But you're not alone here?' he inquired suddenly; 'not absolutely alone?'

'Yes,' said Lawford. 'But there's plenty to think about—and read. I haven't thought or read for years.'

'No, nor I; after thirty, my dear boy, one merely annotates, and the book's called Life. Bless me, his solemn old voice is grinding epigrams out of even this poor old parochial barrel-organ. You don't suppose, you cannot be supposing you are the only serious person in the world? What's more, it's only skin deep.'

Lawford smiled. 'Skin deep. But think quietly over it; you'll see I'm done.'

'Come here,' said Mr Bethany. 'Where's the whiskey, where's the cigars? You shall smoke and drink, and I'll watch. If it weren't for a pitiful old stomach, I'd join you. Come on!' He led the way into the dining-room.

He looked sparer, more wizened and sinewy than ever as he stooped to open the sideboard. 'Where on earth do they keep everything?' he was muttering to himself.

Lawford put the candlestick down on the table. 'There's only one thing,' he said, watching his visitor's rummaging; 'what precisely do you think they will do with me?'

'Look here, Lawford,' snapped Mr Bethany; 'I've come round here, hooting through your letter-box, to talk sense, not sentiment. Why has your wife deserted you? Without a servant, without a single—It's perfectly monstrous.'

'On my word of honour, I prefer it so. I couldn't have gone on. Alone I all but forget this—this lupus. Every turn of her little finger reminded me of it. We are all of us alone, whether we know it or not; you said so yourself. And it's better to realize it stark and unconfused. Besides, you have no idea what—what odd things.... There may be; there *is* something on the other side. I'll win through to that.'

Mr Bethany had been listening attentively. He scrambled up from his knees with a half-empty syphon of sodawater. 'See here, Lawford,' he said; 'if you really want to know what's your most insidious and most dangerous symptom just now, it is spiritual pride. You've won what you think a domestic victory; and you can scarcely bear the splendour. Oh, you may shrug! Pray, what *is* this "other side" which the superior double-faced creature's going to win through to now?' He rapped it out almost bitterly, almost contemptuously.

Lawford hardly heard the question. Before his eyes had suddenly arisen the peace, the friendly unquestioning stillness, the thunderous lullaby old as the grave. 'It's only a fancy. It seemed I could begin again.'

'Well, look here,' said Mr Bethany, his whole face suddenly lined and grey with age. 'You can't. It's the one solitary thing I've got to say, as I've said it to myself morn, noon, and night these scores of years. You can't begin again; it's all a delusion and a snare. You say we're alone. So we are. The world's a dream, a stage, a mirage, a rack, call it what you will—but *you* don't change, *you're* no illusion. There's no crying off for *you* no ravelling out, no clean leaves. You've got this—this trouble, this affliction—my dear, dear fellow what shall I say to tell you how I grieve and groan for you oh yes, and actually laughed, I confess it, a vile hysterical laughter, to think of it. You've got this almost intolerable burden to bear; it's come like a thief in the night; but bear it you must, and *alone!* They say death's a going to bed; I doubt it; but anyhow life's a long undressing. We came in puling and naked, and every stitch must come off before we get out again. We must stand on our feet in all our Rabelaisian nakedness, and watch the world fade. Well then, and not another word of sense shall you worm out of my worn-out old brains after today—all I say is, don't give in! Why, if you stood here now, freed from this devilish disguise, the old, fat, sluggish fellow that sat and yawned his head off under my eyes in his pew the Sunday before last, if I know anything about human nature I'd say it to your face, and a fig for your vanity and resignation—your last state would be worse than the first. There!'

He bunched up a big white handkerchief and mopped it over his head. 'That's done,' he said, 'and we won't go back. What I want to know now is what are you going to do? Where are you sleeping? What are you going to think about? I'll stay—yes, yes, that's what it must be: I must stay. And I detest strange beds. I'll stay, you *sha'n't* be alone. Do you hear me, Lawford?—you *sha'n't* be alone!'

Lawford gazed gravely. 'There is just one little thing I want to ask you before you go. I've wormed out an extraordinary old French book; and—just as you say—to pass the time, I've been having a shot at translating it. But I'm frightfully rusty; it's old French; would you mind having a look?'

Mr Bethany blinked and listened. He tried for the twentieth time to judge his friend's eyes, to gain as best he could some sustained and unobserved glance at this baffling face. 'Where is your precious French book?' he said irritably.

'It's upstairs.'

'Fire away, then!' Lawford rose and glanced about the room. 'What, no light there either?' snapped Mr Bethany. 'Take this; *I* don't mind the dark. There'll be plenty of that for me soon.'

Lawford hesitated at the door, looking rather strangely back. 'No,' he said, 'there are matches upstairs.' He shut the door after him. The darkness seemed cold and still as water. He went slowly up, with eyes fixed wide on the floating luminous gloom, and out of memory seemed to gather, as faintly as in the darkness which they had exorcised for him, the strange pitiful eyes of the night before. And as he mounted a chill, terrible, physical peace seemed to steal over him.

Mr Bethany was sitting as he had left him, looking steadily on the floor, when Lawford returned. He flattened out the book on the table with a sniff of impatience. And dragging the candle nearer, and stooping his nose close to the fusty print, he began to read.

'Was this in the house?' he inquired presently.

'No,' said Lawford; 'it was lent to me by a friend—Herbert.'

'H'm! don't know him. Anyhow, precious poor stuff this is. This Sabathier, whoever he is, seems to be a kind of clap-trap eighteenth-century adventurer who thought the world would be better off, apparently, for a long account of all his sentimental amours. Rousseau, with a touch of Don Quixote in his composition, and an echo of that prince of bogies, Poe! What, in the name of wonder, induced you to fix on this for your holiday reading?'

'Sabathier's alive, isn't he?'

'I never said he wasn't. He's a good deal too much alive for my old wits, with his Mam'selle This and Madame the Other; interesting enough, perhaps, for the professional literary nose with a taste for patchouli.'

'Yet I suppose even that is not a very rare character?' Mr Bethany peered up from the dingy book at his ingenuous questioner. 'I should say decidedly that the fellow was a *very* rare character, so long as by rare you don't mean good. It's one of the dullest stupidities of the present day, my dear fellow, to dote on a man simply because he's different from the rest of us. Once a man strays out of the common herd, he's more likely to meet wolves in the thickets than angels. From what I can gather in just these few pages this Sabathier appears to have been an amorous, adventurous, emotional Frenchman, who went to the dogs as easily and as rapidly as his own nature and his period allowed. And I should say, Lawford, that he made precious bad reading for a poor old troubled hermit like yourself at the present moment.'

'There's a portrait of him a few pages back.'

Mr Bethany, with some little impatience, turned back to the engraving. '"Nicholas de Sabathier,"'s he muttered. '"De," indeed!' He poked in at the foxy print with narrowed eyes. 'I don't deny it's a striking, even perhaps, a rather taking face. I don't deny it.' He gazed on with an even more acute concentration, and looked up sharply. 'Look here, Lawford, what in the name of wonder—what trick are you playing on me now?'

'Trick?' said Lawford; and the world fell with the tiniest plash in the silence, like a vivid little float upon the surface of a shadowy pool.

The old face flushed. 'What conceivable bearing, I say, has this dead and gone old roué on us now?'

'You don't think, then, you see any resemblance—*any* resemblance at all?'

'Resemblance?' repeated Mr Bethany in a flat voice, and without raising his face again to meet Lawford's direct scrutiny. 'Resemblance to whom?'

'To me? To me, as I am?'

'But even, my dear fellow (forgive my dull old brains!), even if there was just the faintest superficial suggestion of—of that; what then?'

'Why,' said Lawford, 'he's buried in Widderstone.'

'Buried in Widderstone?' The keen childlike blue eyes looked almost stealthily up across the book; the old man sat without speaking, so still that it might even be supposed he himself was listening for a quiet distant footfall.

'He is buried in the grave beside which I fell asleep,' said Lawford; 'all green and still and broken,' he added faintly. 'You remember,' he went on in a repressed voice—'you remember you asked me if there was anybody else in sight, any eavesdropper? You don't think—him?'

Mr. Bethany pushed the book a few inches away from him. 'Who, did you say—who was it you said put the thing into your head? A queer friend surely?' he paused helplessly. 'And how, pray, do you know,' he began again more firmly, 'even if there is a Sabathier buried at Widderstone, how do you know it is this Sabathier? It's not, I think,' he added boldly, 'a very uncommon name; with two *b*'s at any rate. Whereabouts is the grave?'

'Quite down at the bottom, under the trees. And the little seat I told you of is there, too, where I fell asleep. You see,' he explained, 'the grave's almost isolated; I suppose because he killed himself.'

Mr Bethany clasped his knuckled fingers on the tablecloth. 'It's no good,' he concluded after a long pause; 'the fellow's got up into my head. I can't think him out. We must thrash it out quietly in the morning with the blessed sun at the window; not this farthing dip. To me the whole idea is as revolting as it is incredible. Why, above a century—no, no! And on the other hand, how easily one's fancy builds! A few straws and there's a nest and squawking fledglings, all complete. Is that why—is that why that good, practical wife of yours and all your faithful household have absconded? Does it'—he threw up his head as if towards the house above them—'does it *reek* with him?'

Lawford shook his head. 'She hasn't seen him: not—not apart. I haven't told her.'

Mr Bethany tossed the hugger-mugger of pamphlets across the table. 'Then, for simple sanity's sake, don't. Hide it; burn it; put the thing completely out of your mind. A friend! Who, where is this wonderful friend?'

'Not very far from Widderstone. He lives—practically alone.'

'And all that stumbling and muttering on the stairs?' he leant forward almost threateningly. 'There isn't anybody here, Lawford?'

'Oh, no,' said Lawford. 'We are practically alone with this, you know,' he pointed to the book, and smiled frankly, however faintly.

Again Mr Bethany sank into a fixed yet uneasy reverie, and again shook himself and raised his eyes.

'Well then,' he said, in a voice all but morose in its fretfullness, 'what I suggest is that first you keep quiet here; and next, that you write and get your wife back. You say you are better. I think you said she herself noticed a slight improvement. Isn't it just exactly as I foresaw? And yet she's gone! But that's not our business. Get her back. And don't for a single instant waste a thought on the other; not for a single instant, I implore you, Lawford. And in a week the whole thing will be no more than a dreary, preposterous dream.... You don't *answer* me!' he cried impulsively.

'But can one so easily forget a dream like this?'

'You don't speak out, Lawford; you mean *she* won't.'

'It must at least seem to have been in part of my own seeking, or contriving; or at any rate—she said it—of my own hereditary or unconscious deserving.'

'She said that!' Mr Bethany sat back. 'I see, I see,' he said. 'I'm nothing but a fumbling old meddler. And there was I, not ten minutes ago, preaching for all I was worth on a text I knew nothing about. God bless me, Lawford, how long we take a-learning. I'll say no more. But what an illusion. To think this—this—he laid a long lean hand at arm's length flat upon the table towards his friend—'to think this is our old jog-trot Arthur Lawford! From henceforth I throw you over, you old wolf in sheep's wool. I wash my hands of you. And now where am I going to sleep?'

He covered up his age and weariness for an instant with a small crooked hand.

Lawford took a deep breath. 'You're going, old friend, to sleep at home. And I—I'm going to give you my arm to the Vicarage gate. Here I am, immeasurably relieved, fitter than I've been since I was a dolt of a schoolboy. On my word of honour: I can't say why, but I am. I don't care *that*, vicar, honestly—puffed up with spiritual pride. If a man can't sleep with pride for a bed-fellow, well, he'd better try elsewhere. It's no good; I'm as stubborn as a mule; that's at least a relic of the old Adam. I care no more,' he raised his voice firmly and gravely—'I don't care a jot for solitude, not a jot for all the ghosts of all the catacombs!'

Mr. Bethany listened, grimly pursed up his lips. 'Not a jot for all the ghosts of all the catechisms!' he muttered. 'Nor the devil himself, I suppose?' He turned once more to glance sharply in the direction of the face he could so dimly—and of set purpose—discern; and without a word trotted off into the hall. Lawford followed with the candle.

''Pon my word, you haven't had a mouthful of supper. Let me forage; just a quarter of an hour, eh?'

'Not me,' said Mr Bethany; 'if you won't have me, home I go. I refuse to encourage this miserable grass-widowering. What *would* they say? What would the busybodies say? Ghouls and graves and shocking mysteries—Selina! Sister Anne! Come on.'

He shuffled on his hat and caught firm hold of his knobbed umbrella. 'Better not leave a candle,' he said.

Lawford blew out the candle.

'What? What?' called the old man suddenly. But no voice had spoken.

A thin trickle of light from the lamp in the street stuck up through the fanlight as, with a smile that could be described neither as mischievous, saturnine, nor vindictive, and was yet faintly suggestive of all three, Lawford quietly opened the drawing-room door and put down the candlestick on the floor within.

'What on earth, my good man, are you fumbling after now?' came the almost fretful question from under the echoing porch.

'Coming, coming,' said Lawford, and slammed the door behind them.

CHAPTER SIXTEEN

The first faint streaks of dawn were silvering across the stars when Lawford again let himself into his deserted house. He stumbled down to the pantry and cut himself a crust of bread and cheese, and ate it, sitting on the table, watching the leafy eastern sky through the painted bars of the area window. He munched on, hungry and tired. His night walk had cooled head and heart. Having obstinately refused Mr Bethany's invitation to sleep at the Vicarage, he had sat down on an old low wall, and watched until his light had shone out at his bedroom window. Then he had simply wandered on, past rustling glimmering gardens, under the great timbers of yellowing elms, hardly thinking, hardly aware of himself except as in a far-away vision of a sluggish insignificant creature struggling across the tossed-up crust of an old, incomprehensible world.

The secret of his content in that long leisurely ramble had been that repeatedly by a scarcely realised effort it had not lain in the direction of Widderstone. And now, as he sat hungrily devouring his breakfast on the table in the kitchen, with the daybreak comforting his eyes, he thought with a positive mockery of that poor old night-thing he had given inch by inch into the safe keeping of his pink and white drawing-room. Don Quixote, Poe, Rousseau—they were familiar but not very significant labels to a mind that had found very poor entertainment in reading. But they were at least representative enough to set him wondering which of their influences it was that had inflated with such a gaseous heroism the Lawford of the night before. He thought of Sheila with a not unkindly smile, and of the rest. 'I wonder what they'll do?' had been a question almost as much in his mind during these last few hours as had 'What am I to do?' in the first bout of his 'visitation.'

But the 'they' was not very precisely visualised. He saw Sheila, and Harry, and dainty pale-blue Bettie Lovat, and cautious old Wedderburn, and Danton, and Craik, and cheery, gossipy Dr Sutherland, and the verger, Mr Dutton, and Critchett, and the gardener, and Ada, and the whole vague populous host that keep one as definitely in one's place in the world's economy as a firm-set pin the camphored moth. What his place was to be only time could show. Meanwhile there was in this loneliness at least a respite.

Solitude!—he bathed his weary bones in it. He laved his eyelids in it, as in a woodland brook after the heat of noon. He sat on in calmest reverie till his hunger was satisfied. Then, scattering out his last crumbs to the birds from the barred window, he climbed upstairs again, past his usual bedroom, past his detested guest room, up into the narrow sweetness of Alice's, and flinging himself on her bed fell into a long and dreamless sleep.

By ten next morning Lawford had bathed and dressed. And at half-past ten he got up from Sheila's fat little French dictionary and his Memoirs to answer Mrs Gull's summons on the area bell. The little woman stood with arms folded over an empty and capacious bag, with an air of sustained melancholy on her friendly face. She wished him a very nervous 'Good morning,' and dived down into the kitchen. The hours dragged slowly by in a silence broken only by an occasional ring at the bell. About three she emerged from the house and climbed the area steps with her bag hooked over her arm. He watched the little black figure out of sight, watched a man in a white canvas hat ascend the steps to push a blue-printed circular through the letter-box. It had begun to rain a little. He returned to the breakfast-room and with the window wide open to the rustling coolness of the leaves, edged his way very slowly across from line to line of the obscure French print.

Sabathier none the less, and in spite of his unintelligible literariness, did begin to take shape and consistency. The man himself, breathing, and thinking, began to live for Lawford even in those few half-articulate pages, though not in quite so formidable a fashion as Mr Bethany had summed him up. But as the west began to lighten with the declining sun, the same old disquietude, the same old friendless and foreboding ennui stole over Lawford's solitude once more. He shut his books, placed a candlestick and two boxes of matches on the hall table, lit a bead of gas, and went out into the rainy-sweet streets again.

At a mean little barber's with a pole above his lettered door he went in to be shaved. And a few steps further on he sat down at the crumb-littered counter of a little baker's shop to have some tea. It pleased him almost to childishness to find how easily he could listen and even talk to the oiled and crimpy little barber, and to the pretty, consumptive-looking, print-dressed baker's wife. Whatever his face might now be conniving at, the Arthur Lawford of last week could never have hob-nobbed so affably with his social 'inferiors.'

For no reason in the world, unless to spend a moment or two longer in the friendly baker's shop, he bought six-penny-worth of cakes. He watched them as they were deposited one by one in the bag, and even asked for one sort to be exchanged for another, flushing a little at the pretty compliment he had ventured on.

He climbed out of the shop, and paused on the wooden doorstep. 'Do you happen to know Mr Herbert Herbert's?' he said.

The baker's wife glanced up at him with clear, reflective eyes. 'Mr Herbert's?—that must be some little way off, sir. I don't know any such name, and I know most, just round about like.'

'Well, yes, it is,' said Lawford, rather foolishly; 'I hardly know why I asked. It's past the churchyard at Widderstone.'

'Oh yes, sir,' she encouraged him.

'A big, wooden-looking house.'

'Really, sir. Wooden?'

Lawford looked into her face, but could find nothing more to say, so he smiled again rather absently, and ascended into the street.

He sat down outside the churchyard gate on the very bank where he had in the sourness of the nettles first opened Sabathier's Memoirs. The world lay still beneath the pale sky. Presently the little fat rector walked up the hill, his wrists still showing beneath his sleeves. Lawford meditatively watched him pass by. A small boy with a switch, a tiny nose, and a swinging gallipot, his cheeks lit with the sunset, followed soon after. Lawford beckoned him with his finger and held out the bag of tarts. He watched him, half incredulous of his prize, and with many a cautious look over his shoulder, pass out of sight. For a long while he sat alone, only the evening birds singing out of the greenness and silence of the churchyard. What a haunting inescapable riddle life was.

Colour suddenly faded out of the light streaming between the branches. And depression, always lying in ambush of the novelty of his freedom, began like mist to rise above his restless thoughts. It was all so devilish empty—this raft of the world floating under evening's shadow. How many sermons had he listened to, enriched with the simile of the ocean of life. Here they were, come home to roost. He had fallen asleep, ineffectual sailor that he was, and a thief out of the cloudy deep had stolen oar and sail and compass, leaving him adrift amid the riding of the waves.

'Are they worth, do you think, quite a penny?' suddenly inquired a quiet voice in the silence. He looked up into the almost colourless face, into the grey eyes beneath their clear narrow brows.

'I was thinking,' he said, 'what a curious thing life is, and wondering—'

'The first half is well worth the penny—its originality! I can't afford twopence. So you must *give* me what you were wondering.'

Lawford gazed rather blankly across the twilight fields. 'I was wondering,' he said with an oddly naive candour, 'how long it took one to sink.'

'They say, you know,' Grisel replied solemnly, 'drowned sailors float midway, suffering their sea change; purgatory. But what a splendid pennyworth. All pure philosophy!'

'"Philosophy!"' said Lawford; 'I am a perfect fool. Has your brother told you about me?'

She glanced at him quickly. 'We had a talk.'

'Then you do know—?' He stopped dead, and turned to her. 'You really realise it, looking at me now?'

'I realise,' she said gravely, 'that you look even a little more pale and haggard than when I saw you first the other night. We both, my brother and I, you know, thought for certain you'd come yesterday. In fact, I went into the Widderstone in the evening to look for you, knowing your nocturnal habits....' She glanced again at him with a kind of shy anxiety.

'Why—why is your brother so—why does he let me bore him so horribly?'

'Does he? He's tremendously interested; but then, he's pretty easily interested when he's interested at all. If he can possibly twist anything into the slightest show of a mystery, he will. But, of course, you won't, you can't, take all he says seriously. The tiniest pinch of salt, you know. He's an absolute fanatic at talking in the air. Besides, it doesn't really matter much.'

'In the air?'

'I mean if once a theory gets into his head—the more far-fetched, so long as it's original, the better—it flowers out into a positive miracle of incredibilities. And of course you can rout out evidence for anything under the sun from his dingy old folios. Why did he lend you that *particular* book?'

'Didn't he tell you that, then?'

'He said it was Sabathier.' She seemed to think intensely for the merest fraction of a moment, and turned. 'Honestly, though, I think he immensely exaggerated the likeness. As for...'

He touched her arm, and they stopped again, face to face. 'Tell me what difference exactly you see,' he said. 'I am quite myself again now, honestly; please tell me just the very worst you think.'

'I think, to begin with,' she began, with exaggerated candour, 'his is rather a detestable face.'

'And mine?' he said gravely.

'Why—very troubled; oh yes—but his was like some bird of prey. Yours—what mad stuff to talk like this!—not the least symptom, that I can see, of—why, the "prey," you know.'

They had come to the wicket in the dark thorny hedge. 'Would it be very dreadful to walk on a little—just to finish?'

'Very,' she said, turning as gravely at his side.

'What I wanted to say was—' began Lawford, and forgetting altogether the thread by which he hoped to lead up to what he really wanted to say, broke off lamely; 'I should have thought you would have absolutely despised a coward.'

'It would be rather absurd to despise what one so horribly well understands. Besides, we weren't cowards—we weren't cowards a bit. My childhood was one long, reiterated terror—nights and nights of it. But I never had the pluck to tell any one. No one so much as dreamt of the company I had. Ah, and you didn't see either that my heart was absolutely in my mouth, that I was shrivelled up with fear, even at sight of the fear on your face in the dark. There's absolutely nothing so catching. So, you see, I *do* know a little what nerves are; and dream too sometimes, though I don't choose charnelhouses if I can get a comfortable bed. A coward! May I really say that to ask my help was one of the bravest things in a man I ever heard of. Bullets—that kind of courage—no real woman cares twopence for bullets. An old aunt of mine stared a man right out of the house with the thing in her face. Anyhow, whether I may or not, I do say it. So now we are quits.'

'Will you—' began Lawford, and stopped. 'What I wanted to say was,' he jerked on, 'it is sheer horrible hypocrisy to be talking to you like this—though you will never have the faintest idea of what it has meant and done for me. I mean... And yet, and yet, I do feel when just for the least moment I forget what I am, and that isn't very often, when I forget what I have become and what I must go back to—I feel that I haven't any business to be talking with you at all. "Quits!" And here I am, an outcast from decent society. Ah, you don't know—'

She bent her head and laughed under her breath. 'You do really stumble on such delicious compliments. And yet, do you know, I think my brother would be immensely pleased to think you were an outcast from decent society if only he could be thought one too. He has been trying half his life to wither decent society with neglect and disdain—but it doesn't take the least notice. The deaf adder, you know. Besides, besides; what is all this meek talk? I detest meek talk—gods or men. Surely in the first and last resort all we are is ourselves. Something has happened; you are jangled, shaken. But to us, believe me, you are simply one of fewer friends—and I think, after struggling up Widderstone Lane hand in hand with you in the dark, I have a right to say "friends"—than I could count on one hand. What are we all if we only realized it? We talk of dignity and propriety, and we are like so many children playing with knucklebones in a giant's scullery. Come along, he will, some suppertime, for us, each in turn—and how many even will so much as look up from their play to wave us good-bye? that's what I mean—the plot of *silence* we are all in. If only I had my brother's lucidity, how much better I would have said all this. It is only, believe me, that I want ever so much to help you, if I may—even at risk, too,' she added, rather shakily, 'of having that help—well—I know it's little good.'

The lane had narrowed. They had climbed the arch of a narrow stone bridge that spanned the smooth dark Widder. A few late starlings were winging far above them. Darkness was coming on apace. They stood for awhile looking down into the black flowing water, with here and there the mild silver of a star dim leagues below. 'I am afraid,' said Grisel, looking quietly up, 'you have led me into talking most pitiless nonsense. How many hours, I wonder, did I lie awake in the dark last night, thinking of you? Honestly, I shall never, *never* forget that walk. It haunted me, on and on.'

'Thinking of me? Do you really mean that? Then it was not all imagination; it wasn't just the drowning man clutching at a straw?'

The grey eyes questioned him. 'You see,' he explained in a whisper, as if afraid of being overheard, 'it—it came back again, and—I don't mind a bit how much you laugh at me! I had been asleep, and had had a most awful dream, one of those dreams that seem to hint that some day *that* will be our real world, that some day we may awake where dreaming then will be of this; and I woke—came back—and there was a tremendous knocking going on downstairs. I knew there was no one else in the house—'

'No one else in the house? And you like this?'

'Yes,' said Lawford, stolidly, 'they were all out as it happened. And, of course,' he went on quickly, 'there was nothing for me to do but simply to go down and open the door. And yet, do you know, at first I simply couldn't move. I lit a candle, and then—then somehow I got to know that waiting for me was just—but there,' he broke off half-ashamed, 'I mustn't bother you with all this morbid stuff. Will your brother be in now, do you think?'

'My brother will be in, and, of course, expecting you. But as for "bother," believe me—well, did I quite deserve it?' She stooped towards him. 'You lit a candle—and then?'

They turned and retraced their way slowly up the hill.

'It came again.'

'It?'

'That—that presence, that shadow. I don't mean, of course, it's a real shadow. It comes, doesn't it, from—from within? As if from out of some unheard-of hiding place, where it has been lurking for ages and ages before one's childhood; at least, so it seems to me now. And yet although it does come from within, there it is, too, in front of you, before your eyes, feeding even on your fear, just watching, waiting for—What nonsense all this must seem to you!'

'Yes, yes; and then?'

'Then, and you must remember the poor old boy had been knocking all this time—my old friend—Mr Bethany, I mean—knocking and calling through the letter-box, thinking I was *in extremis*, or something; then—how shall I describe it?—well *you* came, your eyes, your face, as clear as when, you know, the night before last, we went up the hill together. And then...'

'And then?'

'And then, we—you and I, you know—simply drove him downstairs, and I could hear myself grunting as if it was really a physical effort; we drove him, step by step, downstairs. And—' He laughed outright, and boyishly continued his adventure. 'What do you think I did then, without the ghost of a smile, too, at the idiocy of the thing? I locked the poor beggar in the drawing-room. I saw him there, as plainly as I ever saw anything in my life, and the furniture glimmering, though it was pitch dark: I can't describe it. It all seemed so desperately real, absolutely vital then. It all seems so meaningless and impossible now. And yet, although I am utterly played out and done for, and however absurd it may *sound*, I wouldn't have lost it; I wouldn't go back for any bribe there is. I feel just as if a great bundle had been rolled off my back. Of course, the queerest, the most detestable part of the whole business is that *it*—the thing on the stairs—was this'—he lifted a grave and haggard face towards her again—'or rather *that*,' he pointed with his stick towards the starry churchyard. 'Sabathier,' he said.

Again they had paused together before the white gate, and this time Lawford pushed it open, and followed his companion up the narrow path.

She stayed a moment, her hand on the bell. 'Was it my brother who actually put that horrible idea into your mind?—about Sabathier?'

'Oh no, not really put it into my head,' said Lawford hollowly. 'He only found it there; lit it up.'

She laid her hand lightly on his arm. 'Whether he did or not,' she said with an earnestness that was almost an entreaty, 'of course, you *must* agree that we every one of us have some such experience—that kind of visitor, once at least, in a lifetime.' 'Ah, but,' began Lawford, turning forlornly away, 'you didn't see, you can't have realized—the change.'

She pulled the bell almost as if in some inward triumph. 'But don't you think,' she suggested, 'that that, like the other, might be, as it were, partly imagination too? If now you thought *back*....'

But a little old woman had opened the door, and the sentence, for the moment, was left unfinished.

CHAPTER SEVENTEEN

There was no one in the room, and no light, when they entered. For a moment Grisel stood by the open window, looking out. Then she turned impulsively. 'My brother, of course, will ask you too,' she said; 'we had made up our minds to do so if you came again; but I want you to promise me now that you won't dream of going back to-night. That surely would be tempting—well, not Providence. I couldn't rest if I thought you might be alone; like that again.' Her voice died away into the calling of the waters. A light moved across the dingy old rows of books and as his sister turned to go out Herbert appeared in the doorway, carrying a green-shaded lamp, with an old leather quarto under his arm.

'Ah, here you are,' he said. 'I guessed you had probably met.' He drew up, burdened, before his visitor. But his clear black glance, instead of wandering off at his first greeting, had intensified. And it was almost with an air of absorption that he turned away. He dumped his book on to a chair and it turned over with scattered leaves on to the floor. He put the lamp down and stooped after it, so that his next words came up muffled, and as if the remark had been forced out of him. 'You don't feel worse, I hope?' He got up and faced his visitor for the answer. And for the moment Lawford stood considering his symptoms.

'No,' he said almost gaily; 'I feel enormously better.' But Herbert's long, oval, questioning eyes beneath the sleek black hair were still fixed on his face. 'I am afraid, my dear fellow,' he said, with something more than his usual curiously indifferent courtesy, 'the struggle has frightfully pulled you to pieces.'

'The question is,' answered Lawford, with a kind of tired yet whimsical melancholy in his voice, 'though I am not sure that the answer very much matters—what's going to put me together again? It's the old story of Humpty Dumpty, Herbert. Besides, one thing you said has stuck out in a quite curious way in my memory. I wonder if you will remember?'

'What was that?' said Herbert with unfeigned curiosity.

'Why, you said even though Sabathier had failed, though I was still my own old stodgy self, that you thought the face—the face, you know, might work in. Somehow, sometimes I think it has. It does really rather haunt me. In that case—well, what then?' Lawford had himself listened to this involved explanation much as one watches the accomplishment of a difficult trick, marvelling more at its completion at all than at the difficulty involved in the doing of it.

'"Work in,"' repeated Herbert, like a rather blasé child confronted with a new mechanical toy; 'did I really say that? well, honestly, it wasn't bad; it's what one would expect on that hypothesis. You see, we are only different, as it were, in our differences. Once the foot's over the threshold, it's nine points of the law! But I don't remember saying it.' He shamefacedly and naively confessed it: 'I say such an awful lot of things. And I'm always changing my mind. It's a standing joke against me with my sister. She says the recording angel will have two sides to my account: Mondays, Wednesdays, and Fridays; and Tuesdays, Thursdays, and Saturdays—diametrically opposite convictions, and both kinds wrong. On Sundays I am all things to all men. As for Sabathier, by the way, I do want particularly to have another go at him. I've been thinking him over, and I'm afraid in some ways he won't quite wash. And that reminds me, did you read the poor chap?'

'I just grubbed through a page or two; but most of my French was left at school. What I did do, though, was to show the book to an old friend of ours—my wife's and mine—just to skim—a Mr Bethany. He's an old clergyman—our vicar, in fact.'

Herbert had sat down, and with eyes slightly narrowed was listening with peculiar attention. He smiled a little magnanimously. 'His verdict, I should think, must have been a perfect joy.'

'He said,' said Lawford, in his rather low, monotonous voice, 'he said it was precious poor stuff, that it reminded him of patchouli; and that Sabathier—the print I mean—looked like a foxy old roué. They were, I think, his exact words. We were alone together, last night.'

'You don't mean that he simply didn't see the faintest resemblance?'

Lawford nodded. 'But then,' he added simply, 'whenever he comes to see me now he leaves his spectacles at home.'

And at that, as if at some preconcerted signal, they both went off into a simple shout of laughter, unanimous and sustained.

But this first wild bout of laughter over, the first real bursting of the dam, perhaps, for years, Lawford found himself at a lower ebb than ever.

'You see,' he said presently, and while still his companion's face was smiling around the remembrance of his laughter like ripples after the splash of a stone, 'Bethany has been absolutely my sheet-anchor right through. And I was—it was—you can't possibly realise what a ghastly change it really was. I don't think any one ever will.'

Herbert opened his hand and looked reflectively into its palm before allowing himself to reply. 'I wonder, you know; I have been wondering a good deal; simply taking the other point of view for a moment; *was* it? I don't mean "ghastly" exactly (like, say, smallpox, G.P.I., elephantiasis), but was it quite so complete, so radical, as in the first sheer gust of astonishment you fancied?'

Lawford thought on a little further. 'You know how one sees oneself in a passion—why, how a child looks—the whole face darkened and drawn and possessed? That was the change. That's how it seems to come back to me. And something, somebody, dodging behind the eyes. Yes; more that than even any excessive change of feature, except, of course, that I also seemed—Shall I ever forget that first cold, stifling stare into the looking-glass! I certainly was much darker, even my hair. But I've told you all this before,' he added wearily, 'and the scores and scores of times I've thought it. I used to sit up there in the big spare bedroom my wife put me up in, simply gloating. My flesh seemed nothing more than an hallucination: there I was, haunting my body, an old grinning tenement, and all that I thought I wanted, and couldn't do without, all I valued and prided myself on—stacked up in the drizzling street below. Why, Herbert, our bodies *are* only glass or cloud. They melt, don't they, like wax in the sun once we're out. But those first few days don't make very pleasant thinking. Friday night was the first, when I sat there like a twitching waxwork, soberly debating between Bedlam here and Bedlam hereafter. I even sometimes wonder whether its very repetition has not dulled the memory or distorted it. My wife,' he added ingenuously, 'seems to think there are signs of a slight improvement—a going back, I mean. But I'm not sure whether she meant it.'

Herbert surveyed his visitor critically. 'You say "dark," he said; 'but surely, Lawford, your hair now is nearly grey; well-flecked at least.'

Although the remark carried nothing comparatively of a shock with it, yet it seemed to Lawford as if an electric current had passed over his scalp, coldly stirring every hair upon his head. But somehow or other it was easier to sit quietly on, to express no surprise, to let them do or say what they liked. 'Well' he retorted with an odd, crooked smile, 'you must remember I am a good deal older than I was last Saturday. I grew grey in the grave, Herbert.'

'But it's like this, you know,' said Herbert, rising excitedly, and at the next moment, on reflection, composedly reseating himself. 'How many of your people actually *saw* it? How many owned to its being as bad, as complete, as you made out? I don't want for a moment to cut right across what you said last night—our talk—but there are two million sides to every question, and as often as not the less conspicuous have sounder—well—roots. That's all.'

'I think really, do you know, I would rather not go over the detestable thing again. Not many; my wife, though, and a man I know called Danton, who—who's prejudiced. After all, I have myself to think about too. And right through, right through—there wasn't the least doubt of that—they all in their hearts knew it was me. They knew I was behind. I could feel that absolutely always; it's not just eyes and ears we use, there's us ourselves to consider, though God alone knows what that means. But the password was there, as you might say; and they all knew I knew it, all—except'—he looked up as if in bewilderment—'except just one, a poor old lady, a very old friend of my mother's, whom I—I Sabathiered!'

'Whom—you—Sabathiered!' repeated Herbert carefully, with infinite relish, looking sidelong at his visitor. 'And it is just precisely that....'

But at that moment his sister appeared in the doorway to say that supper was ready. And it was not until Herbert was actually engaged in carving a cold chicken that he followed up his advantage. 'Mr. Lawford, Grisel,' he said, 'has just enriched our jaded language with a new verb—to Sabathier. And if I may venture to define it in the presence of the distinguished neologist himself, it means, "To deal with histrionically"; or, rather, that's what it will mean a couple of hundred years hence. For the moment it means, "To act under the influence of subliminalization; To perplex, or bemuse, or estrange with *otherness*." Do tell us, Lawford, more about the little old lady.' He passed with her plate a little meaningful glance at his sister, and repeated, 'Do!'

'But I've been plaguing your sister enough already. You'll wish...' Lawford began, and turned his tired-out eyes towards those others awaiting them so frankly they seemed in their perfect friendliness a rest from all his troubles. 'You see,' he went on, 'what I kept on thinking and thinking of was to get a quite unbiased and unprejudiced view. She had known me for years, though we had not actually met more than once or twice since my mother's death. And there she was sitting with me at the other end of just such another little seat as'—he turned—to Herbert 'as ours, at Widderstone. It was on Bewley Common: I can see it all now; it was sunset. And I simply turned and asked her in a kind of a whining affected manner if she remembered me; and when after a long time she came round to owning that to all intents and purposes she did not—I professed to have made a mistake in recognising *her*. I think,' he added, glancing up from one to the other of his two strange friends, 'I think it was the meanest trick I can remember.'

'H'm,' said Herbert solemnly: 'I wish I had as sensitive a conscience. But as your old friend didn't recognise you, who's the worse? As for her not doing so, just think of the difference a few years makes to a man, and *any* severe shock. Life wears so infernally badly. Who, for that matter, does not change, even in character and yet who professes to see it? Mind, I don't say in essence! But then how many of the human ghosts one meets does one know in essence? One doesn't want to. It would be positively cataclysmic. And that's what brings me around to feel, Lawford, if I may venture to say so, that you may have brooded a little too keenly on—on your own case. Tell any one you feel ill; he will commiserate with you to positive nausea. Tell any priest your soul is in danger; will he wait for proof? It's misereres and penances world without end. Tell any woman you love her; will she, can she, should she, gainsay you? There you are. The cat's out of the bag, you see. My sister and I sat up half the night talking the thing over. I said I'd take the plunge. I said I'd risk appearing the crassest, contradictoriest wretch that ever drew breath. I don't deny that what I hinted at the other night must seem in part directly contrary to what I'm going to say now.'

He wheeled his black eyes as if for inspiration, and helped himself to salad. 'It's this,' he said. 'Isn't it possible, isn't it even probable that being ill, and overstrung, moping a little over things more or less out of the common ruck, and sitting there in a kind of trance—isn't it possible that you may have very largely *imagined* the change? Hypnotised yourself into believing it much worse—more profound, radical, acute—and simply absolutely hypnotizing others into thinking so, too. Christendom is just beginning to rediscover that there is such a thing as faith, that it is just possible that, say, megrims or melancholia may be removed at least as easily as mountains. The converse, of course, is obvious on the face of it. A man fails because he thinks himself a failure. It's the men that run away that lose the battle. Suppose then, Lawford'—he leaned forward, keen and suave—'suppose you have been and "Sabathiered" yourself!'

Lawford had grown accustomed during the last few days to finding himself gazing out like a child into reality, as if from the windows of a dream. He had in a sense followed this long, loosely stitched, preliminary argument; he had at least in part realised that he sat there between two clear friendly minds acting in the friendliest and most obvious collusion. But he was incapable of fixing his attention very closely on any single fragment of Herbert's apology, or of rousing himself into being much more than a dispassionate and not very interested spectator of the little melodrama that Fate, it appeared, had at the last moment decided rather capriciously to twist into a farce. He turned with a smile to the face so keenly fixed and enthusiastic with the question it had so laboriously led up to: 'But surely, I don't quite see...'

Herbert lifted his glass as if to his visitor's acumen and set it down again without tasting it. 'Why, my dear fellow,' he said triumphantly, 'even a dream must have a peg. Yours was this unforgettable old suicide. Candidly now, how much of Sabathier was actually yours? In spite of all that that fantastical fellow, Herbert, said last night, dead men *don't* tell tales. The last place in the world to look for a ghost is where his traitorous bones lie crumbling. Good heavens, think what irrefutable masses of evidence there would be at our finger-tips if every tombstone hid its ghost! No; the fellow just arrested you with his creepy epitaph: an epitaph, mind you, that is in a literary sense distinctly fertilizing. It catches one's fancy in its own crude way, as pages and pages of infinitely more complicated stuff take possession of, germinate, and sprout in one's imagination in another way. We are all psychical parasites. Why, given his epitaph, given the surroundings, I wager any sensitive consciousness could have guessed at his face; and guessing, as it were, would have feigned it. What do you think, Grisel?'

'I think, dear, you are talking absolute nonsense; what do they call it—"darkening counsel"? It's "the hair of the dog," Mr Lawford.'

'Well, then, you see,' said Herbert over a hasty mouthful, and turning again to his victim—'then you see, when you were just in the pink of condition to credit any idle tale you heard, then I came in. What, with the least impetus, can one *not* see by moonlight? The howl of a dog turns the midnight into a Brocken; the branch of a tree stoops out at you like a Beelzebub crusted with gadflies. I'd, mind you, sipped of the deadly old Huguenot too. I'd listened to your innocent prattle about the child kicking his toes out on death's cupboard door; what more likely thing in the world, then, than that with that moon, in that packed air, I should have swallowed the bait whole, and seen Sabathier in every crevice of your skin? I don't say there wasn't any resemblance; it was for the moment extraordinary; it was even when you were here the other night distinctly arresting. But now (poor old Grisel, I'm nearly done) all I want to say is this: that if we had the "foxy old roué" here now, and Grisel played Paris between the three of us, she'd hand over the apple not to you but to me.'

'I don't quite see where poor Paris comes in,' suggested Grisel meekly.

'No, nor do I,' said Herbert. 'All that I mean, sagacious child, is, that Mr Lawford no more resembles the poor wretch now than I resemble the Apollo Belvedere. If you had only heard my sister scolding me, railing at me for putting such ideas into your jangled head! They don't affect *me* one iota. I have, I suppose, what is usually called imagination; which merely means that I can sup with the devil, spoon for spoon, and could sleep in Bluebeard's linen-closet without turning a hair. You, if I am not very much mistaken, are not much troubled with that very unprofitable quality, and so, I suppose, when a crooked and bizarre fancy does edge into your mind it roots there.'

And that said, not without some little confusion, and covert glance of inquiry at his sister, Herbert made all the haste he could to catch up the course that his companions had already finished.

If only, Lawford thought, this insufferable weariness would lift awhile he could enjoy the quiet, absurd, heedless talk, and this very friendly topsy-turvy effort to ease his mind and soothe his nerves. He might even take an interest again in his 'case.'

'You see,' he said, turning to Grisel, 'I don't think it really very much matters how it all came about. I never could believe it would last. It may perhaps—some of it at least may be fancy. But then, what isn't? What *is* trustworthy? And now your brother tells me my hair's turning grey. I suppose I have been living too slowly, too sluggishly, and they thought it was high time to stir me up.'

He saw with extraordinary vividness the low panelled room; the still listening face; the white muslin shoulders and dark hair; and the eyes that seemed to recall some far-off desolate longing for home and childhood. It was all a dream. That was the end of the matter. Even now, perhaps, his tired old stupid body was lying hunched up, drenched with dew upon the little old seat under the mist-wreathed branches. Soon it would bestir itself and wake up and go off home—home to Sheila, to the old deadly round that once had seemed so natural and inevitable, to the old dull Lawford—eyes and brain and heart.

They returned up the dark shallow staircase to Herbert's book-room, and he talked on to very quiet and passive listeners in his own fantastic endless fashion. And ever and again Lawford would find himself intercepting fleeting and anxious glances at his face, glances almost of remorse and pity; and thought he detected beneath this irresponsible contradictory babble an unceasing effort to clear the sky, to lure away too pressing memories, to put his doubts and fears completely to rest.

Herbert even went so far as to plead guilty, when Grisel gave him the cue, of having a little heightened and overcoloured his story of the restless phantasmal old creature that haunted their queer wooden hauntable old house. And when they rose, laughing and yawning to take up their candles, it was, after all, after a rather animated discussion, with many a hair-raising ghost story brought in for proof between brother and sister, as to exactly how many times that snuff-coloured spectre had made his appearance; and, with less unanimity still, as to the precise manner in which he was in the habit of making his precipitant exit.

'You do at any rate acknowledge, Grisel, that the old creature does appear, and that you saw him yourself step out into space when you were sitting down there under the willow shelling peas. I've seen him twice for certain, once rather hazily; Sallie saw him so plainly she asked his business: that's five. I resign.'

'Acknowledge!' said Grisel; 'of course I do. I'd acknowledge anything in the world to save argument. Why, I don't know what I should do without him. If only, now Mr Lawford would give him a fair chance to show himself reading quietly here about ten minutes to one, or shelling peas even, if he prefers it. If only he'd stay long enough for *that*. Wouldn't it be the very thing for them both!'

'Of course,' said Herbert cordially, 'the very thing.'

Lawford looked up at neither of them. He shook his head.

But he needed little persuasion to stay at least one night. The prospect of that long solitary walk, of that tired stupid stooping figure dragging itself along the interminable country roads seemed a sheer impossibility. 'It is not—it isn't, I swear it—the other that keeps me back,' he had solemnly assured the friend that half smiled her relief at his acceptance, 'but—if you only knew how empty it's all got now; all reason gone even to go on at all.'

'But doesn't it follow? Of course it's empty. And now life is going to begin again. I assure you it is, I do indeed. Only, only have courage—just the will to win on.'

He said good-night; shut-to the latched door of his long low room, ceilinged with rafters close under the steep roof, its brown walls hung with quiet, dark, pondering and beautiful faces looking gravely across at him. And with his candle in his hand he sat down on the bedside. All speculation was gone. The noisy clock of his brain had run down again. He turned towards the old oval looking-glass on the dressing-table without the faintest stirring of interest, suspense, or anxiety. What did it matter what a man looked like—a now familiar but enfeebled and deprecating voice seemed to say. He knew that a change had come. Even Sheila had noticed it. And since then what had he not gone through? What now was here seemed of little moment, so far at least as this world was concerned.

At last with an effort he rose, crossed the uneven floor, and looked in unmovedly on what was his own poor face come back to him: changed indeed almost beyond belief from the sleek self-satisfied genial yet languid Arthur Lawford of the past years, and still haunted with some faint trace of the set and icy sharpness, and challenge, and affront of the dark Adventurer, but that—how immeasurably dimmed and blunted and faded. He had expected to find it so. Would it (the thought vanished across his mind) would it have been as unmistakably there had he come hot-foot, fearing, expecting to find the other? But—was he disappointed!

He hardly knew how long he stood there, leaning on his hands, surveying almost listlessly in the candle-light that lined, bedraggled, grey, hopeless countenance, those dark-socketed, smouldering eyes, whose pupils even now were so dilated that a casual glance would have failed to detect the least hint of any iris. 'It must have been something pretty bad you were, you know, or something pretty bad you did,' they seemed to be trying to say to him, 'to drag us down to this.'

He knelt down by force of habit to say his prayers; but no words came. Well, between earthly friends a betrayal such as this would have caused a livelong estrangement and hostility. The God the old Lawford used to pray to would forgive him, he thought wearily, if just for the present he was a little too sore at heart to play the hypocrite. But if, while kneeling, he said nothing, he saw a good many things in such tranquillity and clearness as the mere eyes of the body can share but rarely with their sisters of the imagination. And now it was Alice who looked mournfully out of the dark at him; and now the little old charwoman, Mrs Gull, with her bag hooked over her arm, climbed painfully up the area steps; and now it was the lean vexed face of a friend, nursing some restless and anxious grievance against him—Mr Bethany; and then and ever again it was the face of one who seemed pure dream and fantasy and yet... He listened intently and fancied even now he could hear the voices of brother and sister talking quietly and circumspectly together in the room beneath.

CHAPTER EIGHTEEN

A quiet knocking aroused him in the long, tranquil bedroom; and Herbert's head was poked into the room. 'There's a bath behind that door over there,' he whispered, 'or if you like I'm off for a bathe in the Widder. It's a luscious day. Shall I wait? All right,' and the head was withdrawn. 'Don't put much on,' came the voice at the panel; 'we'll be home again in twenty minutes.'

The green and brightness of the morning must have been prepared for overnight by spiders and the dew. Everywhere the gleaming nets were hung, and everywhere there rose a tiny splendour from the waterdrops, so clear and pure and changeable it seemed with their fire and colour they shook a tiny crystal music in the air. Herbert led the way along a clayey downward path beneath hazels tossing softly together their twigs of nuts, until they came out into a rounded hollow that, mounded with thyme, sloped gently down to the green banks of the Widder. The water poured like clearest glass beneath a rain of misty sunbeams.

'My sister always says that this is the very dell Boccaccio had in his mind's eye when he wrote the "Decameron." There really is something almost classic in those pines. And I'd sometimes swear with my eyes just out of the water I've seen Dryads half in hiding peeping between those beeches. Good Lord, Lawford, what a world we wretched moderns have made, and missed!'

The water was violently cold. It seemed to Lawford, as it swept up over his body, and as he plunged his night-distorted eyes beneath its blazing surface, that it was charged with some strange, powerful enchantment to wash away in its icy clearness even the memory of the dull and tarnished days behind him. If one could but tie up anyhow that stained bundle of inconsequent memories called life, and fling it into a cupboard remoter even than Bluebeard's, and lock the door, and drop the quickly-rusting key into these living waters!

He dressed himself with window thrown open to the blackbirds and thrushes, and the occasional shrill solitary whistling of a robin. But, like the sour-sweet fragrance of the brier, its wandering desolate burst of music had power to wake memory, and carried him instantly back to that first aimless descent into the evening gloom of Widderstone from which it was in vain to hope ever to climb again. Surely never a more ghoulish face looked out on its man before than that which confronted him as with borrowed razor he stood shaving those sunken chaps, that angular chin.

And even now, beneath the lantern of broad daylight, just as within that other face had lurked the undeniable ghost and presence of himself, so beneath the sunken features seemed to float, tenuous as smoke, scarcely less elusive than a dream, between eye and object, the sinister darkness of the face that in those two bouts with fear he had by some strange miracle managed to repel.

'Work in,' the chance phrase came back. It had worked in in sober earnest; and so far as the living of the next few weeks went, surely it might prove an ally without which he simply could not conceive himself as struggling on at all.

But as dexterous minds as even restless Sabathier's had him just now in safe and kindly keeping. All the quiet October morning Herbert kept him talking and stooping over his extraordinary collection of books.

'The point is,' he explained to Lawford, standing amid a positive archipelago of precious 'finds,' with his foot hoisted onto a chair and a patched-up, sea-stained folio on his knee, 'I honestly detest the mere give and take of what we are fools enough to call life. I don't deny Life's there,' he swept his hand towards the open window—'in that frantic Tophet we call London; but there's no focus, no point of vantage. Even a scribbler only gets it piecemeal and through a dulled medium. We learn to read before we know how to see; we swallow our tastes, convictions, and emotions whole; so that nine-tenths of the world's nectar is merely honeydew.' He smiled pleasantly into the fixed vacancy of his visitor's face. 'That's why I've just gone on,' he continued amiably, 'collecting this particular kind of stuff—what you might call riff-raff. There's not a book here, Lawford, that hasn't at least a glimmer of the real thing in it—just Life, seen through a living eye, and felt. As for literature, and style, and all that gallimaufry, don't fear for them if your author has the ghost of a hint of genius in his making.'

'But surely,' said Lawford, trying for the twentieth time to pretend to himself that these endless books carried the faintest savour of the delight to him which they must, he rather forlornly supposed, shower upon Herbert, 'surely genius is a very rare thing!'

'Rare! the world simply swarms with it. But before you can bottle it up in a book it's got to be articulate. Just for a single instant imagine yourself Falstaff, and if there weren't hundreds of Falstaffs in every generation, to be examples of his ungodly life, he'd be as dead as a doornail to-morrow—imagine yourself Falstaff, and being so, sitting down to write "Henry IV," or "The Merry Wives." It's simply preposterous. You wouldn't be such a fool as to waste the time. A mere Elizabethan scribbler comes along with a gift of expression and an observant eye, lifts the bloated old tippler clean out of life, and swims down the ages as the greatest genius the world has ever seen. Whereas, surely, though you mustn't let me bore you with all this piffle, it's Falstaff is the genius, and W. S. merely a talented reporter.

'Lear, Macbeth, Mercutio—they live on their own, as it were. The newspapers are full of them, if we were only the Shakespeares to see it. Have you ever been in a Police Court? Have you ever *watched* tradesmen behind their counters? My soul, the secrets walking in the streets! You jostle them at every corner. There's a Polonius in every first-class railway carriage, and as many Juliets as there are boarding-schools. What the devil are *you*, my dear chap, but genius itself, with all the world brand new upon your shoulders? And who'd have thought it of you ten days ago?

'It's simply and solely because we're all, poor wretches, dumb—dumb as butts of Malmsez; dumb as drummerless drums. Here am I, ass that I am, trickling out this—this whey that no more expresses me than Tupper does Sappho. But that's what I want to mean. How inexhaustibly rich everything is, if you only stick to life. Here it is packed away behind these rotting covers, just the real thing, no respectable stodge; no mere parasitic stuff; not more than a dozen poets; scores of outcasts and vagabonds—and the real thing in vagabonds is pretty rare in print, I can tell you. We're all, every one of us, sodden with facts, drugged with the second-hand, and barnacled with respectability until—until the touch comes. Goodness knows where from; but there's no mistaking it; oh no!'

'But what,' said Lawford uneasily, 'what on earth do you mean by the touch?'

'I mean when you cease to be a puppet only and sit up in the gallery too. When you squeeze through to the other side. When you suffer a kind of conversion of the mind; become aware of your senses. When you get a living inkling. When you become articulate to yourself. When you *see*.'

'I am awfully stupid,' Lawford murmured, 'but even now I don't really follow you a bit. But when, as you say, you do become articulate to yourself, what happens then?'

'Why, then,' said Herbert with a shrug almost of despair, 'then begins the weary tramp back. One by one drop off the truisms, and the Grundyisms, and the pedantries, and all the stillborn claptrap of the marketplace sloughs off. Then one can seriously begin to think about saving one's soul.'

'Saving one's soul,' groaned Lawford; 'why, I am not even sure of my own body yet.' He walked slowly over to the window and with every thought in his head as quiet as doves on a sunny wall, stared out into the garden of green things growing, leaves fading and falling water. 'I tell you what,' he said, turning irresolutely, 'I wonder if you could possibly find time to write me out a translation of Sabathier. My French is much too hazy to let me really get at the chap. He's gone now; but I really should like to know what kind of stuff exactly he has left behind.'

'Oh, Sabathier!' said Herbert, laughing. 'What do you think of that, Grisel?' he asked, turning to his sister, who at that moment had looked in at the door. 'Here's Mr Lawford asking me to make a translation of Sabathier. Lunch, Lawford.'

Lawford sighed. And not until he had slowly descended half the narrow uneven stairs that led down to the dining-room did he fully realise the guile of a sister that could induce a hopeless bookworm to waste a whole morning over the stupidest of companions, simply to keep his tired-out mind from rankling, and give his Sabathier a chance to go to roost.

'I think, do you know,' he managed to blurt out at last 'I think I ought to be getting home again. The house is empty—and '

'You shall go this evening,' said Herbert, 'if you really must insist on it. But honestly, Lawford, we both think that after what the last few days must have been, it is merely common sense to take a rest. How can you possibly rest with a dozen empty rooms echoing every thought you think? There's nothing more to worry about; you agree to that. Send your people a note saying that you are here, safe and sound. Give them a chance of lighting a fire, and driving in the fatted calf. Stay on with us just the week out.'

Lawford turned from one to the other of the two friendly faces. But what was dimly in his mind refused to express itself. 'I think, you know, I—' he began falteringly.

'But it's just this thinking that's the deuce—this preposterous habit of having continually to make up one's mind. Off with his head, Grisel! My sister's going to take you for a picnic; we go every other fine afternoon; and you can argue it out with her.'

Once alone again with Grisel, however, Lawford found talking unnecessary. Silences seemed to fall between them as quietly and restfully as evening flows into night. They walked on slowly through the fading woods, and when they had reached the top of the hill that sloped down to the dark and foamless Widder they sat down in the honey-scented sunshine on a knoll of heather and bracken, and Grisel lighted the little spirit-kettle she had brought with her, and busied herself very methodically over making tea.

That done, she clasped her hands round her knees, and sat now gossiping, now silent, in the pale autumnal beauty. There was a bird wistfully twittering in the branches overhead, and ever and again a withered leaf would slip circling down from the motionless beech boughs arched in their stillness above their heads beneath the thin blue sky.

'Men, you know,' she began again suddenly, starting out of reverie, 'really are absurdly blind; and just a little bit absurdly kindly stupid. How many times have I been at the point of laughing out at my brother's delicious naive subtleties. But you do, you will, understand, Mr Lawford, that he was, that we are both "doing our best"—to make amends?'

'I understand—I do indeed—a tenth part of all your kindness.'

'Yes, but that's just it—that horrible word "kindness"! If ever there were two utterly self-absorbed people, without a trace, with an absolute horror of kindness, it is just my brother and I. It's most of it false and most of it useless. We all surely must take what comes in this topsy-turvy world. I believe in saying out:—that the more one thinks about life the worse it becomes. There are only two kinds of happiness in this world—a wooden post's and Prometheus's. And who ever heard of any one having the impudence to be kind to Prometheus? As for a miserable "medium" like me, not quite a post and leagues and leagues from even envying a Prometheus, she's better for the powder without the jam. But that's all nothing. What I can't help thinking—and it's not a bit giving my brother away, because we both think it—that it was partly our thoughtlessness that added at least something to—to the rest. It was perfectly absurd. He saw you were ill; he saw—he must have seen even in that first Sunday talk—that your nerves were all askew. And who doesn't know what "nerves" means nowadays? And yet he deliberately chattered. He loves it—just at large, you know, like me. I told him before I came out that I intended, if I could, to say all this. And now it's said you'll please forgive me for going back to it.'

'Please don't talk about forgiveness. But when you say he chattered, you mean about Sabathier, of course. And that, you know, I don't care a fig for now. We can settle all that between ourselves—him and me, I mean. And now tell me candidly again—Is there any "prey" in my face now?'

She looked up fleetingly into his eyes, leant back her head and laughed. '"Prey," there never was a glimpse.'

'And "change"?' Their eyes met again in an infinitely brief, infinitely bewildering argument.

'Really, really, scarcely perceptible,' she assured him, 'except, of course, how horribly, horribly ill you look. And that only seems to prove to me you must be hiding something else. No illusion on earth could—could have done that to your face.'

'You think, I know,' he persisted, 'that I must be persuaded and cosseted and humoured. Yes, you do; it's my poor old sanity that's really in both your minds. Perhaps I am—not absolutely sound. Anyhow. I've been watching it in your looks at each other all the time. And I can never, never say, never tell you what you have done for me. But you see, after all, we did win through; I keep on telling myself that. So that now it's purely from the most selfish and practical motives that I want you to be perfectly frank with me. I have to go back, you know; and some of them, one or two of my friends I mean, are not all on my side. Think of me as I was when you came into the room, three centuries ago, and you turned and looked, frowning at me in the candle-light; remember that and look at me now. What is the difference? Does it shock you? Does it make the whole world seem a trick, a sham? Does it simply sour your life to think such a thing possible? Oh, the hours I've spent gloating on Widderstone's miserable mask of skin and bone, as I was saying to your brother only last night, and never knew until they shuffled me that the old self too was nothing better than a stifling suffocating mask.'

'But don't you see,' she argued softly, turning her face away a little, 'you were a stranger then (though I certainly didn't *mean* to frown). And then a little while after we were, well, just human beings, shoulder to shoulder, and if friendship does not mean that, I don't know what it does mean. And now, you are—well, just you: the you, you know, of three centuries ago! And if you mean to ask me whether at any precise moment I have been conscious that this you I am now speaking to was not the you of last night, or of that dark climb up the hill, why, it is simply frantic to think it could ever be necessary to say over and over again, No. But if you mean, Have you changed else? All I could answer is, Don't we all change as we grow to know one another? What were just features, what just dingily represented one, as it were, is forgotten, or rather gets remembered. Of course, the first glimpse is the landscape under lightning as it were. But afterwards isn't it surely like the alphabet to a child; what was first a queer angular scrawl becomes A, and is always ever after A, undistinguished, half-forgotten, yet standing at last for goodness knows what real wonderful things—or for just the dry bones of soulless words? Is that it?' She stole a sidelong glance into his brooding face, leaning her head on her hand.

'Yes, yes,' came the rather dissatisfied reply. 'I do agree; perfectly. But then, you see—I told you I was going to talk of nothing but myself—what did at first happen to me was something much worse, and, I suppose, something quite different from that.'

'And yet, didn't you tell us, that of all your friends not one really denied in their hearts your—what they would call, I suppose—your *identity*; except that poor little offended old lady. And even she, if my intuition is worth a penny piece, even she when you go soon and talk to her will own that she did know you, and that it was not because you were a stranger that she was offended, but because you so ungenerously pretended to be one. That was a little mad, now, if you like!'

'Oh yes,' said Lawford, 'I am going to ask her forgiveness. I don't know what I didn't vow to take her for a peace-offering if the chance should ever come—and the courage—to make my peace with her. But now that the chance has come, and I think the courage, it is the desire that's gone. I don't seem to care either way. I feel as if I had got past making my peace with any one.'

But this time no answer helped him out.

'After all,' he went plodding on, 'there is more than just the mere day to day to consider. And one doesn't realise that one's face actually *is* one's fortune without a shock. And that *that* gone, one is, as your brother said, just like a bee come back to the wrong hive. It undermines,' he smiled rather bitterly, 'one's views rather. And it certainly shifts one's friends. If it hadn't been just for my old'—he stopped dead, and again pushed slowly on—'if it hadn't been for our old friend, Mr Bethany, I doubt if we should now have had a soul on our side. I once read somewhere that wolves always chase the old and weak and maimed out of the pack. And after all, what do *we* do? Where do we keep the homeless and the insane? And yet, you know,' he added ruminatingly, 'it is not as if mine was ever a particularly lovely or lovable face! While as for the poor wretch behind it, well, I really cannot see what meaning, or life even, he had before—'

'Before?'

Lawford met bravely the clear whimsical eyes. 'Before, I was Sabathiered.'

Grisel laughed outright.

'You think,' he retorted almost bitterly, 'you think I am talking like a child.'

'Yes,' she sighed cheerfully, 'I was quite envying you.'

'Well, there I am,' said Lawford inconsequently. 'And now; well, now, I suppose, the whole thing's to begin again. I can't help beginning to wonder what the meaning of it all is; why one's duty should always seem so very stupid a thing. And then, too, what *can* there be on earth that even a buried Sabathier could desire?' He glanced up in a really animated perplexity at the still, dark face turned in the evening light towards the darkening valley. And perplexity deepened into a disquieted frown—like that of a child who is roused suddenly from a daydream by the half-forgotten question of a stranger. He turned his eyes almost furtively away as if afraid of disturbing her; and for awhile they sat in silence... At last he turned again almost shyly. 'I hope some day you will let me bring my daughter to see you.'

'Yes, yes,' said Grisel eagerly; 'we should both *love* it, of course. Isn't it curious?—I simply *knew* you had a daughter. Sheer intuition!'

'I say "some day,"' said Lawford; 'I know, though, that that some day will never come.'

'Wait; just wait,' replied the quiet confident voice, 'that will come too. One thing at a time, Mr Lawford. You've won your old self back again; you'll win your old love of life back again in a little while; never fear. Oh, don't I know that awful Land's End after illness; and that longing, too, that gnawing longing, too, for Ultima Thule. So, it's a bargain between us that you bring your daughter soon.' She busied herself over the tea things. 'And, of course,' she added, as if it were an afterthought, looking across at him in the pale green sunlight as she knelt, 'you simply won't think of going back to-night.... Solitude, I really do think, solitude just now would be absolute madness. You'll write to-day and go, perhaps, to-morrow!'

Lawford looked across in his mind at his square ungainly house, full-fronting the afternoon sun. He tried to repress a shudder. 'I think, do you know, I ought to go to-day.'

'Well, why not? Why not? Just to reassure yourself that all's well. And come back here to sleep. If you'd really promise that I'd drive you in. I'd love it. There's the jolliest little governess-cart we sometimes hire for our picnics. May I? You've no idea how much easier in our minds my brother and I would be if you would. And then to-morrow, or at any rate the next day, you shall be surrendered, whole and in your right mind. There, that's a bargain too. Now we must hurry.'

CHAPTER NINETEEN

Herbert himself went down to order the governess cart, and packed them in with a rug. And in the dusk Grisel set Lawford down at the corner of his road and drove on to an old bookseller's with a commission from her brother, promising to return for him in an hour. Dust and a few straws lay at rest as if in some abstruse arrangement on the stones of the porch just as the last faint whirling gust of sunset had left them. Shut lids of sightless indifference seemed to greet the wanderer from the curtained windows.

He opened the door and went in. For a moment he stood in the vacant hall; then he peeped first into the blind-drawn dining-room, faintly, dingily sweet, like an empty wine-bottle. He went softly on a few paces and just opening the door looked in on the faintly glittering twilight of the drawing-room. But the congealed stump of candle that he had set in the corner as a final rancorous challenge to the beaten Shade was gone. He slowly and deliberately ascended the stairs, conscious of a peculiar sense of ownership of what in even so brief an absence had taken on so queer a look of strangeness. It was almost as if he might be some lone heir come in the rather mournful dusk to view what melancholy fate had unexpectedly bestowed on him.

'Work in'—what on earth else could this chill sense of strangeness mean? Would he ever free his memory from that one haphazard, haunting hint? And as he stood in the doorway of the big, calm room, which seemed even now to be stirring with the restless shadow of these last few far-away days; now pacing sullenly to and fro; now sitting hunched-up to think; and now lying impotent in a vain, hopeless endeavour only for the breath of a moment to forget—he awoke out of reverie to find himself smiling at the thought that a changed face was practically at the mercy of an incredulous world, whereas a changed heart was no one's deadly dull affair but its owner's. The merest breath of pity even stole over him for the Sabathier who after all had dared and had needed, perhaps, nothing like so arrogant and merciless a *coup de grâce* to realise that he had so ignominiously failed.

'But there, that's done!' he exclaimed out loud, not without a tinge of regret that theories, however brilliant and bizarre, could never now be anything else—that now indeed that the symptoms had gone, the 'malady,' for all who had not been actually admitted into the shocked circle, was become nothing more than an inanely 'tall' story; stuffing not even savoury enough for a goose. How wide exactly, he wondered, would Sheila's discreet, shocked circle prove? He stood once more before the looking-glass, hearing again Grisel's words in the still green shadow of the beech-tree, 'Except of course, horribly, horribly ill.' 'What a fool, what a coward she thinks I am!'

There was still nearly an hour to be spent in this great barn of faded interests. He lit a candle and descended into the kitchen. A mouse went scampering to its hole as he pushed open the door. The memory of that ravenous morning meal nauseated him. It was sour and very still here; he stood erect; the air smelt faint of earth. In the breakfast-room the bookcase still swung open. Late evening mantled the garden; and in sheer ennui again he sat down to the table, and turned for a last not unfriendly hob-a-nob with his poor old friend Sabathier. He would take the thing back. Herbert, of course, was going to translate it for him. Now if the patient old Frenchman had stormed Herbert instead—that surely would have been something like a coup! Those frenzied books. The absurd talk of the man. Herbert was perfectly right—he could have entertained fifty old Huguenots without turning a hair. 'I'm such an awful stodge.'

He turned the woolly leaves over very slowly. He frowned impatiently, and from the end backwards turned them over again. Then he laid the book softly down on the table and sat back. He stared with narrowed lids into the flame of his quiet friendly candle. Every trace, every shred of portrait and memoir were gone. Once more, deliberately, punctiliously, he examined page by page the blurred and unfamiliar French—the sooty heads, the long, lean noses, the baggy eyes passing like figures in a peepshow one by one under his hand—to the last fragmentary and dexterously mended leaf. Yes, Sabathier was gone. Quite the old slow Lawford smile crept over his face at the discovery. It was a smile a little sheepish too, as he thought of Sheila's quiet vigilance.

And the next instant he had looked up sharply, with a sudden peculiar shrug, and a kind of cry, like the first thin cry of an awakened child, in his mind. Without a moment's hesitation he climbed swiftly upstairs again to the big sepulchral bedroom. He pressed with his fingernail the tiny spring in the looking-glass. The empty drawer flew open. There were finger-marks still in the dust.

Yet, strangely enough, beneath all the clashing thoughts that came flocking into his mind as he stood with the empty drawer in his hand, was a wounding yet still a little amused pity for his old friend Mr Bethany. So far as he himself was concerned the discovery—well, he would have plenty of time to consider everything that could possibly now concern himself. Anyhow, it could only simplify matters.

He remembered waking to that old wave of sickening horror on the first unhappy morning; he remembered the keen yet owlish old face blinking its deathless friendliness at him, and the steady pressure of the cold, skinny hand. As for Sheila, she had never done anything by halves; certainly not when it came to throwing over a friend no longer necessary to one's social satisfaction. But she would edge out cleverly, magnanimously, triumphantly enough, no doubt, when the day of reckoning should come, the day when, her nets wide spread, her bait prepared, he must stand up before her outraged circle and positively prove himself her lawful husband, perhaps even to the very imprint of his thumb.

'Poor old thing!' he said again; and this time his pity was shared almost equally between both witnesses to Mr Bethany's ingenuous little document, the loss of which had fallen so softly and pathetically that he felt only ashamed of having discovered it so soon.

He shut back the tell-tale drawer, and after trying to collect his thoughts in case anything should have been forgotten, he turned with a deep trembling sigh to descend the stairs. But on the landing he drew back at the sound of voices, and then a footstep. Soon came the sound of a key in the lock. He blew out his candle and leant listening over the balusters.

'Who's there?' he called quietly.

'Me, sir,' came the feeble reply out of the darkness.

'What is it, Ada? What have you come for?'

'Only, sir, to see that all was safe, and you were in, sir.'

'Yes,' he said. 'All's safe; and I am in. What if I had been out?' It was like dropping tiny pebbles into a deep well—so long after came the answering feeble splash.

'Then I was to go back, sir.' And a moment after the discreet voice floated up with the faintest tinge of effrontery out of the hush. 'Is that Dr Ferguson, too sir?'

'No, Ada; and please tell your mistress from me that Dr Ferguson is unlikely to call again.' A keen but rather forlorn smile passed over his face. 'He's dining with friends no doubt at Holloway. But of course if she should want to see him he will see her to-morrow at any hour at Mrs Lovat's. And—Ada!'

'Yes, sir?'

'Say that I'm a little better; your mistress will be relieved to hear that I'm a little better; still not *quite* myself say, but, I think, a little better.'

'Yes, sir; and I'm sure I'm very glad to hear it,' came fainter still.

'What voice was that I heard just now?'

'Miss Alice's, sir; but she came quite against my wishes, and I hope you won't repeat it, sir. She promised if she came that mistress shouldn't know. I was only afraid she might disturb you, or—or Dr Ferguson. And did you say, sir, that I was to tell mistress that he *might* be coming back?'

'Ah, that I don't know; so perhaps it would be as well not to mention him at all. Is Miss Alice there?'

'I said I would tell her if you were alone. But I hope you'll understand that it was only because she begged so. Mistress has gone to St Peter's bazaar; and that's how it was.'

'I quite understand. Beckon to her.'

There came a hasty step in the hall and a hurried murmur of explanation. Lawford heard her call as she ran up the stairs; and the next moment he had Alice's hand in his and they were groping together through the gloaming back into the solitude of the empty room again.

'Don't be alarmed, dear,' he heard himself imploring. 'Just hold tight to that clear common sense, and above all you won't tell? It must be our secret; a dead, dead secret from every one, even your mother, for just a little while; just a mere two days or so—in case. I'm—I'm better, dear.'

He fumbled with the little box of matches, dropped one, broke another; but at last the candle-flame dipped, brightened, and with the door shut and the last pale blueness of dusk at the window Lawford turned and looked at his daughter. She stood with eyes wide open, like the eyes of a child walking in its sleep; then twisted her fingers more tightly within his. 'Oh, dearest, how ill, how ill you look,' she whispered. 'But there, never mind—never mind. It was all a miserable dream, then; it won't, it can't come back? I don't think I could bear its coming back. And mother told me such curious things; as if I were a child and understood nothing. And even after I knew that you were you—I mean before I sat up here in the dark to see you—she said that you were gone and would never come back; that a terrible thing had happened—a disgrace which we must never speak of; and that all the other was only a pretence to keep people from talking. But I did not believe then, and how could I believe afterwards?'

'There, never mind now, dear, what she said. It was all meant for the best, perhaps. But here I am; and not nearly so ill as I look, Alice; and there's nothing more to trouble ourselves about; not even if it should be necessary for me to go away for a time. And this is our secret, mind; ours only; just a dead secret between you and me.'

They sat for awhile without speaking or stirring. And faintly along the hushed road Lawford heard in the silence a leisurely indolent beat of little hoofs approaching, and the sound of wheels. A sudden wave of feeling swept over him. He took Alice's quiet loving face in his hands and kissed her passionately. 'Do not so much as think of me yet, or doubt, or question: only love me, dearest. And soon—and soon—'

'We'll just begin again, just begin again, won't we? all three of us together, just as we used to be. I didn't mean to have said all those horrid things about mother. She was only dreadfully anxious and meant everything for the best. You'll let me tell her soon?'

The haggard face turned slowly, listening. 'I hear, I understand, but I can't think very clearly now, Alice; I can't, dear; my miserable old tangled nerves. I just stumble along as best I can. You'll understand better when you get to be a poor old thing like me. We must do the best we can. And of course you'll see, Dillie, how awfully important it is not to raise false hopes. You understand? I mustn't risk the least thing in the world, must I? And now goodbye; only for a few hours now. And not a word, not a word to a single living soul.'

He extinguished the candle again, and led the way to the top of the stairs. 'Are you there, Ada?'

'Yes, sir,' answered the quiet imperturbable voice from under the black straw brim. Alice went slowly down, but at the foot of the stairs, looking out into the cold, blue, lamplit street she paused as if at a sudden recollection, and ran hastily up again.

'There was nothing more, dear?' She said, leaning back to peer up.

'"Nothing more?" What?'

She stood panting a little in the darkness, listening to some cautious yet uneasy thought that seemed to haunt her mind. 'I thought—it seemed there was something we had not said, something I could not understand. But there, it is nothing! You know what a fanciful old silly I am. You do love me? Quite as much as ever?'

'More, sweetheart, more!'

'Good-night again, then; and God bless you, dear.'

The outer door closed softly, the footsteps died away. Lawford still hesitated. He took hold of the stairs above his head as he stood on the landing and leaned his head upon his hands, striving calmly to disentangle the perplexity of his thoughts. His pulses were beating in his ear with a low muffled roar. He looked down between the blinds to where against the blue of the road beneath the straggling yellow beams of the lamp stood the little cart and drooping, shaggy pony, and Grisel sitting quietly there awaiting him. He shut his eyes as if in hope by some convulsive effort of mind to break through this subtle glasslike atmosphere of dream that had stolen over consciousness, and blotted out the significance, almost the meaning of the past. He turned abruptly. Empty as the empty rooms around him, unanswering were mind and heart. Life was a tale told by an idiot—signifying nothing.

He paused at the head of the staircase. And even then the doubt confronted him: Would he ever come back? Who knows? he thought; and again stood pondering, arguing, denying. At last he seemed to have come to a decision. He made his way downstairs, opened and left ajar a long narrow window in a passage to the garden beyond the kitchen. He turned on his heel as he reached the gate and waved his hand as if in a kind of forlorn mockery towards the darkly glittering windows. The drowsy pony awoke at touch of the whip.

Grisel lifted the rug and squeezed a little closer into the corner. She had drawn a veil over her face, so that to Lawford her eyes seemed to be dreaming in a little darkness of their own as he laid his hand on the side of the cart. 'It's a most curious thing,' he said, 'but peeping down at you just now when the sound of the wheels came, a memory came clearly back to me of years and years ago—of my mother. She used to come to fetch me at school in a little cart like this, and a little pony just like this, with a thick dusty coat. And once I remember I was simply sick of everything, a failure, and fagged out, and all that, and was looking out in the twilight; I fancy even it was autumn too. It was a little side staircase window; I was horribly homesick. And she came quite unexpectedly. I shall never forget it—the misery, and then, her coming.' He lifted his eyes, cowed with the incessant struggle, and watched her face for some time in silence. 'Ought I to stay?'

'I see no "ought,"' she said. 'No one is there?'

'Only a miserable broken voice out of a broken cage—called Conscience.'

'Don't you think, perhaps, that even *that* has a good many disguises—convention, cowardice, weakness, ennui; they all take their turn at hooting in its feathers? You must, you really must have rest. You don't know; you don't see; I do. Just a little snap, some one last exquisite thread gives way, and then it is all over. You see I have even to try to frighten you, for I can't tell you how you distress me.'

'Why do I distress you?—my face, my story you mean?'

'No; I mean you: your trouble, that horrible empty house, and—oh, dear me, yes, your courage too.'

'Listen,' said Lawford, stooping forward. He could scarcely see the pale, veiled face through this mist that had risen up over his eyes. 'I have no courage apart from you; no courage and no hope. Ask me to come!—a stranger with no history, no mockery, no miserable rant of a grave and darkness and fear behind me. Are we not all haunted—every one? That forgotten, and the fool I was, and the vacillating, and the pretence—oh, how it all sweeps clear before me; without a will, without a hope or glimpse or whisper of courage. Be just the memory of my mother, the face, the friend I've never seen; the voice that every dream leaves echoing. Ask me to come.'

She sat unstirring; and then as if by some uncontrollable impulse stooped a little closer to him and laid her gloved hand on his.

'I hear, you know; I hear too,' she whispered. 'But we mustn't listen. Come now. It's growing late.'

The little village echoed back from its stone walls the clatter of the pony's hoofs. Night had darkened to its deepest when their lamp shone white on the wicket in the hedge. They had scarcely spoken. Lawford had simply watched pass by, almost without a thought, the arching trees, the darkening fields; had watched rise up in a mist of primrose light the harvest moon to shine in saffron on the faces and shoulders of the few wayfarers they met, or who passed them by. The still grave face beneath the shadow of its veil had never turned, though the moon poured all her flood of brilliance upon the dark profile. And once when as if in sudden alarm he had lifted his head and looked at her, a sudden doubt had assailed him so instantly that he had half put out his hand to touch her, and had as quickly withdrawn it, lest her beauty and stillness should be, even as the moment's fancy had suggested, only a far-gone memory returned in dream.

Herbert hailed them from the darkness of an open window. He came down, and they talked a little in the cold air of the garden. He lit a cigarette, and climbed languidly into the cart, and drove the drowsy little pony off into the moonlight.

CHAPTER TWENTY

It was a quiet supper the three friends sat down to. Herbert sat narrowing his eyes over his thoughts, which, when the fancy took him, he scattered out upon the others' silence. Lawford apparently had not yet shaken himself free from the sorcery of the moonlight. His eyes shone dark and full like those of a child who has trespassed beyond its hour for bed, and sits marvelling at reality in a waking dream.

Long after they had bidden each other good-night, long after Herbert had trodden on tiptoe with his candle past his closed door, Lawford sat leaning on his arms at the open window, staring out across the motionless moonlit trees that seemed to stand like draped and dreaming pilgrims, come to the peace of their Nirvana at last beside the crashing music of the waters. And he himself, the self that never sleeps beneath the tides and waves of consciousness, was listening, too, almost as unmovedly and unheedingly to the thoughts that clashed in conflict through his brain.

Why, in a strange transitory life was one the slave of these small cares? What if even in that dark pit beneath, which seemed to whisper Lethe to the tumultuous, swirling waters—what if there, too, were merely a beginning again, and to seek a slumbering refuge there merely a blind and reiterated plunge into the heat and tumult of another day? Who was that poor, dark, homeless ghoul, Sabathier? Who was this Helen of an impossible dream? Her face with its strange smile, her eyes with their still pity and rapt courage had taken hope away. 'Here's not your rest,' cried one insistent voice; 'she is the mystery that haunts day and night, past all the changing of the restless hours. Chance has given you back eyes to see, a heart that can be broken. Chance and the stirrings of a long-gone life have torn down the veil age spins so thick and fast. Pride and ambition; what dull fools men are! Effort and duty, what dull fools men are!' He listened on and on to these phantom pleadings and to the rather coarse old Lawford conscience grunting them mercilessly down, too weary even to try to rest.

Rooks at dawn came sweeping beneath the turquoise of the sky. He saw their sharp-beaked heads turn this way, that way, as they floated on outspread wings across the misty world. Except for the hoarse roar of the water under the huge thin-leafed trees, not a sound was stirring. 'One thing,' he seemed to hear himself mutter as he turned with a shiver from the morning air, 'it won't be for long. You can, at least, poor devil, wait the last act out.' If in this foolish hustling mob of the world, hired anywhere and anywhen for the one poor dubious wage of a penny—if it was only his own small dull part to carry a mock spear, and shout huzza with the rest—there was nothing for it, he grunted obstinately to himself, shout he would with the loudest.

He threw himself on to the bed with eyes so wearied with want of sleep it seemed they had lost their livelong skill in finding it. Not the echo of triumph nor even a sigh of relief stirred the torpor of his mind. He knew vaguely that what had been the misery and madness of the last few days was gone. But the thought had no power to move him now. Sheila's good sense, and Mr Bethany's stubborn loyalty were alike old stories that had lost their savour and meaning. Gone, too, was the need for that portentous family gathering that had sat so often in his fancy during these last few days around his dining-room table, discussing with futile decorum the problem of how to hush him up, to muffle him down. Half dreaming, half awake, he saw the familiar door slowly open and, like the timely hero in a melodrama, his own figure appear before the stricken and astonished company. His eyes opened half-fearfully, and glanced up in the morning twilight. Their perplexity gave place to a quiet, almost vacant smile; the lids slowly closed again, and at last the lean hands twitched awhile in sleep.

Next morning he spent rummaging among the old books, dipping listlessly here and there as the tasteless fancy took him, while Herbert sat writing with serene face and lifted eyebrows at his open window. But the unfamiliar long S's, the close type, and the spelling of the musty old books wearied eye and mind. What he read, too, however far-fetched, or lively, or sententious, or gross, seemed either to be of the same texture as what had become his everyday experience, and so baffled him with its nearness, or else was only the meaningless ramblings of an idle pen. And this, he thought to himself, looking covertly up at the spruce clear-cut profile at the window, this is what Herbert had called Life.

'Am I interrupting you, Herbert; are you very busy?' he asked at last, taking refuge on a chair in a far corner of the room.

'Bless me, no; not a bit—not a bit,' said Herbert amiably, laying down his pen. 'I'm afraid the old leatherjackets have been boring you. It's a habit this beastly reading; this gorge and glint and fever all at second-hand—purely a bad habit, like morphia, like laudanum. But once in, you know there's no recovery. Anyhow, I'm neck-deep, and to struggle would be simply to drown.'

'I was only going to say how sorry I am for having left Sabathier at home.'

'My dear fellow—' began Herbert reassuringly.

'It was only because I wanted so very much to have your translation. I get muddled up with other things groping through the dictionary.'

Herbert surveyed him critically. 'What exactly is your interest now, Lawford? You don't mean that my old "theory" has left any sting now?'

'No sting; oh no. I was only curious. But you yourself still think it really, don't you?'

Herbert turned for a moment to the open window.

'I was simply trying then to find something to fit the facts as you experienced them. But now that the facts have gone—and they have, haven't they?—exit, of course, my theory!'

'I see,' was the cryptic answer. 'And yet, Herbert,' Lawford solemnly began again, 'it has changed me; even in my way of thinking. When I shut my eyes now—I only discovered it by chance—I see immediately faces quite strange to me; or places, sometimes thronged with people; and once an old well with some one sitting in the shadow. I can't tell you how clearly, and yet it is all altogether different from a dream. Even when I sit with my eyes open, I am conscious, as it were, of a kind of faint, colourless mirage. In the old days—I mean before Widderstone, what I saw was only what I'd seen already. Nothing came uncalled for, unexplained. This makes the old life seem so blank; I did not know what extraordinarily *real* things I was doing without. And whether for that reason or another, I can't quite make out what in fact I did want then, and was always fretting and striving for. I can see no wisdom or purpose in anything now but to get to one's journey's end as quickly and bravely as one can. And even then, even if we do call life a journey, and death the inn we shall reach at last in the evening when it's over; that, too, I feel will be only as brief a stopping-place as any other inn would be. Our experience here is so scanty and shallow—nothing more than the moment of the continual present. Surely that must go on, even if one does call it eternity. And so we shall all have to begin again. Probably Sabathier himself.... But there, what on earth *are* we, Herbert, when all is said? Who is it has—has done all this for us—what kind of self? And to what possible end? Is it that the clockwork has been wound up and must still jolt on a while with jarring wheels? Will it never run down, do you think?'

Herbert smiled faintly, but made no answer.

'You see,' continued Lawford, in the same quiet, dispassionate undertone, 'I wouldn't mind if it was only myself. But there are so many of us, so many selves, I mean; and they all seem to have a voice in the matter. What is the reality to this infernal dream?'

'The reality is, Lawford, that you are fretting your life out over this rotten illusion. Be guided by me just this once. We'll go, all three of us, a good ten-mile walk to-day, and thoroughly tire you out. And to-night you shall sleep here—a really sound, refreshing sleep. Then to-morrow, whole and hale, back you shall go; honestly. It's only professional strong men should ask questions. Babes like you and me must keep to slops.'

So, though Lawford made no answer, it was agreed. Before noon the three of them had set out on their walk across the fields. And after rambling on just as caprice took them, past reddening blackberry bushes and copses of hazel, and flaming beech, they sat down to spread out their meal on the slope of a hill, overlooking quiet ploughed fields and grazing cattle. Herbert stretched himself with his back to the earth, and his placid face to the pale vacant sky, while Lawford, even more dispirited after his walk, wandered up to the crest of the hill.

At the foot of the hill, upon the other side, lay a farm and its out-buildings, and a pool of water beneath a group of elms. It was vacant in the sunlight, and the water vividly green with a scum of weed. And about half a mile beyond stood a cluster of cottages and an old towered church. He gazed idly down, listening vaguely to the wailing of a curlew flitting anxiously to and fro above the broken solitude of its green hill. And it seemed as if a thin and dark cloud began to be quietly withdrawn from over his eyes. Hill and wailing cry and barn and water faded out. And he was staring as if in an endless stillness at an open window against which the sun was beating in a bristling torrent of gold, while out of the garden beyond came the voice of some evening bird singing with such an unspeakable ecstasy of grief it seemed it must be perched upon the confines of another world. The light gathered to a radiance almost intolerable, driving back with its raining beams some memory, forlorn, remorseless, remote. His body stood dark and senseless, rocking in the air on the hillside as if bereft of its spirit. Then his hands were drawn over his eyes. He turned unsteadily and made his way, as if through a thick, drizzling haze, slowly back.

'What is that—there?' he said almost menacingly, standing with bloodshot eyes looking down upon Herbert.

'"That!"—what?' said Herbert, glancing up startled from his book. 'Why, what's wrong, Lawford?'

'That,' said Lawford sullenly, yet with a faintly mournful cadence in his voice; 'those fields and that old empty farm—that village over there? Why did you bring me here?'

Grisel had not stirred. 'The village...'

'Ssh!' she said, catching her brother's sleeve; 'that's Detcham, yes, Detcham.'

Lawford turned wide vacant eyes on her. He shook his head and shuddered. 'No, no; not Detcham. I know it; I know it; but it has gone out of my mind. Not Detcham; I've been there before; don't look at me. Horrible, horrible. It takes me back—I can't think. I stood there, trying, trying; it's all in a blur. Don't ask me—a dream.'

Grisel leaned forward and touched his hand. 'Don't think; don't even try. Why should you? We can't; we *mustn't* go back.'

Lawford, still gazing fixedly, turned again a darkened face towards the steep of the hill. 'I think, you know,' he said, stooping and whispering, '*he* would know—the window and the sun and the singing. And oh, of course it was too late. You understand—too late. And once... you can't go back; oh no. You won't leave me? You see, if you go, it would only be all. I could not be quite so alone. But Detcham—Detcham? perhaps you will not trust me—tell me? That was not the name.' He shuddered violently and turned dog-like beseeching eyes. 'To-morrow—yes, to-morrow,' he said, 'I will promise anything if you will not leave me now. Once—' But again the thread running so faintly through that inextricable maze of memory eluded him. 'So long as you won't leave me now!' he implored her.

She was vainly trying to win back her composure, and could not answer him at once....

In the evening after supper Grisel sat her guest down in front of a big wood fire in the old book-room, where, staring into the playing flames, he could fall at peace into the almost motionless reverie which he seemed merely to harass and weary himself by trying to disperse. She opened the little piano at the far end of the room and played on and on as fancy led—Chopin and Beethoven, a fugue from Bach, and lovely forlorn old English airs, till the music seemed not only a voice persuading, pondering, and lamenting, but gathered about itself the hollow surge of the water and the darkness; wistful and clear, as the thoughts of a solitary child. Ever and again a log burnt through its strength, and falling amid sparks, stirred, like a restless animal, the stillness; or Herbert in his corner lifted his head to glance towards his visitor, and to turn another page. At last the music, too, fell silent, and Lawford stood up with his candle in his hand and eyed with a strange fixity brother and sister. His glance wandered slowly round the quiet flame-lit room.

'You won't,' he said, stooping towards them as if in extreme confidence, 'you won't much notice? They come and go. I try not to—to speak. It's the only way through. It is not that I don't know they're only dreams. But if once the—the others thought there had been any tampering'—he tapped his forehead meaningly—'here: if once they thought *that*, it would, you know, be quite over then. How could I prove...?' He turned cautiously towards the door, and with laborious significance nodded his head at them.

Herbert bent down and held out his long hands to the fire. 'Tampering, my dear chap: That's what the lump said to the leaven.'

'Yes, yes,' said Lawford, putting out his hand, 'but you know what I mean, Herbert. Anything I tried to do then would be quite, quite hopeless. That would be poisoning the wells.'

They watched him out of the room, and listened till quite distinctly in the still night-shaded house they heard his door gently close. Then, as if by consent, they turned and looked long and questioningly into each other's faces.

'Then you are not afraid?' Herbert said quietly.

Grisel gazed steadily on, and almost imperceptibly shook her head.

'You mean?' he questioned her; but still he had again to read her answer in her eyes.

'Oh, very well, Grisel,' he said quietly, 'you know best,' and returned once more to his writing.

For an hour or two Lawford slept heavily, so heavily that when a little after midnight he awoke, with his face towards the uncurtained window, though for many minutes he lay brightly confronting all Orion, that from blazing helm to flaming dog at heel filled high the glimmering square, he could not lift or stir his cold and leaden limbs. He rose at last and threw off the burden of his bedclothes, and rested awhile, as if freed from the heaviness of an unrememberable nightmare. But so clear was his mind and so extraordinarily refreshed he seemed in body that sleep for many hours would not return again. And he spent almost all the remainder of the lagging darkness pacing softly to and fro; one face only before his eyes, the one sure thing, the one thing unattainable in a world of phantoms.

Herbert waited on in vain for his guest next morning, and after wandering up and down the mossy lawn at the back of the house, went off cheerfully at last alone for his dip. When he returned Lawford was in his place at the breakfast-table. He sat on, moody and constrained, until even Herbert's haphazard talk trickled low.

'I fancy my sister is nursing a headache,' he said at last, 'but she'll be down soon. And I'm afraid from the looks of you, Lawford, your night was not particularly restful.' He felt his way very heedfully. 'Perhaps we walked you a little too far yesterday. We are so used to tramping that—' Lawford kept thoughtful eyes fixed on the deprecating face.

'I see what it is, Herbert—you are humouring me again. I have been wracking my brains in vain to remember what exactly *did* happen yesterday. I feel as if it was all sunk oceans deep in sleep. I get so far—and then I'm done. It won't give up a hint. But you really mustn't think I'm an invalid, or—or in my second childhood. The truth is,' he added, 'it's only my *first*, come back again. But now that I've got so far, now that I'm really better, I—' He broke off rather vacantly, as if afraid of his own confidence. 'I must be getting on,' he summed up with an effort, 'and that's the solemn fact. I keep on forgetting I'm—I'm a ratepayer!'

Herbert sat round in his chair. 'You see, Lawford, the very term is little else than Double-Dutch to me. As a matter of fact Grisel sends all my hush-money to the horrible people that do the cleaning up, as it were. I can't catch their drift. Government to me is merely the spectacle of the clever, or the specious, managing the dull. It deals merely with the physical, and just the fringe of consciousness. I am not joking. I think I follow you. All I mean is that the obligations—mainly tepid, I take it—that are luring you back to the fold would be the very ones that would scare me quickest off. The imagination, the appeal faded: we're dead.'

Lawford opened his mouth; '*Temporarily* tepid,' he at last all but coughed out.

'Oh yes, of course,' said Herbert intelligently. 'Only temporarily. It's this beastly gregariousness that's the devil. The very thought of it undoes me—with an absolute shock of sheepishness. I suddenly realise my human nakedness: that here we are, little better than naked animals, bleating behind our illusory wattles on the slopes of—of infinity. And nakedness, after all, is a wholesome thing to realize only when one thinks too much of one's clothes. I peer sometimes, feebly enough, out of my wool, and it seems to me that all these busybodies, all these fact-devourers, all this news-reading rabble, are nothing brighter than very dull-witted children trying to play an imaginative game, much too deep for their poor reasons. I don't mean that *your* wanting to go home is anything gregarious, but I do think *their* insisting on your coming back at once might be. And I know you won't visit this stuff on me as anything more than just my "scum," as Grisel calls the fine flower of my maiden meditations. All that I really *want* to say is that we should both be more than delighted if you'd stay just as long as it will not be a bore for you to stay. Stay till you're heartily tired of us. Go back now, if you *must*; tell them how much better you are. Bolt off to a nerve specialist. He'll say complete rest—change of scene, and all that. They all do. Instinct via intellect. And why not take your rest here? We are such miserably dull company to one another it would be a greater pleasure to have you with us than I can say. I mean it from the very bottom of my heart. Do!'

Lawford listened. 'I wish—,' he began, and stopped dead again. 'Anyhow, I'll go back. I am afraid, Herbert, I've been playing truant. It was all very well while—To tell you the truth I can't think *quite* straight yet. But it won't last for ever. Besides—well, anyhow, I'll go back.'

'Right you are,' said Herbert, pretending to be cheerful. 'You can't expect, you really can't, everything to come right straight away. Just have patience. And now, let's go out and sit in the sun. They've mixed September up with May.'

And about half an hour afterwards he glanced up from his book to find his visitor fast asleep in his garden chair.

Grisel had taken her brother's place, with a little pile of needlework beside her on the grass, when Lawford again opened his eyes under the rosy shade of a parasol. He watched her for a while, without speaking.

'How long have I been asleep?' he said at last.

She started and looked up from her needle.

'That depends on how long you have been awake,' she said, smiling. 'My brother tells me,' she went on, beginning to stitch, 'that you have made up your mind to leave us to-day. Perhaps we are only flattering ourselves it has been a rest. But if it has—is that, do you think, quite wise?'

He leant forward and hid his face in his hands. 'It's because—it's because it's the only "must" I can see.'

'But even "musts"—well, we have to be sure even of "musts," haven't we? Are *you*?' She glanced up and for an instant their eyes met, and the falling water seemed to be sounding out of a distance so remote it might be but the echo of a dream. She stooped once more over her work.

'Supposing,' he said very slowly, and almost as if speaking to himself, 'supposing Sabathier—and you know he's merely like a friend now one mustn't be seen talking to—supposing he came back; what then?'

'Oh, but Sabathier's gone: he never really came. It was only a fancy—a mood. It was only you—another you.'

'Who was that yesterday, then?'

She glanced at him swiftly and knew the question was but a venture.

'Yesterday?'

'Oh, very well,' he said fretfully, 'you too! But if he did, if he did, come really back: "prey" and all?'

'What is the riddle?' she said, taking a deep breath and facing him brightly.

'Would *my* "must" still be *his*?' The face he raised to her, as he leaned forward under the direct light of the sun, was so colourless, cadaverous and haggard, the thought crossed her mind that it did indeed seem little more than a shadowy mask that but one hour of darkness might dispel.

'You said, you know, we did win through. Why then should we be even thinking of defeat now?'

'"We"!'

'Oh no, you!' she cried triumphantly.

'You do not answer my question.'

'Nor you mine! It *was* a glorious victory. Is there the ghost of a reason why you should cast your mind back? Is there, now?'

'Only,' said Lawford, looking patiently up into her face, 'only because I love you': and listened in the silence to the words as one may watch a bird that has escaped for ever and irrevocably out of its cage, steadily flying on and on till lost to sight.

For an instant the grey eyes faltered. 'But that, surely,' she began in a low voice, still steadily sewing, 'that was our compact last night—that you should let me help, that you should trust me just as you trusted the mother years ago who came in the little cart with the shaggy dusty pony to the homesick boy watching at the window. Perhaps,' she added, her fingers trembling, 'in this odd shuffle of souls and faces, I *am* that mother, and most frightfully anxious you should not give in. Why, even because of the tiredness, even because the cause seems vain, you must still fight on—wouldn't she have said it? Surely there are prizes, a daughter, a career, no end! And even they gone—still the self undimmed, undaunted, that took its drubbing like a man.'

'I know you know I'm all but crazed; you see this wretched mind all littered and broken down; look at me like that, then. Forget even you have befriended me and pretended—Why must I blunder on and on like this? Oh, Grisel, my friend, my friend, if only you loved me!'

Tears clouded her eyes. She turned vaguely as if for a hiding-place. 'We can't talk here. How mad the day is. Listen, listen! I do—I do love you—mother and woman and friend—from the very moment you came. It's all so clear, so clear: *that*, and your miserable "must," my friend. Come, we will go away by ourselves a little, and talk. That way. I'll meet you by the gate.'

CHAPTER TWENTY-ONE

She came out into the sunlight, and they went through the little gate together. She walked quickly, without speaking, over the bridge, past a little cottage whose hollyhocks leaned fading above its low flint wall. Skirting a field of stubble, she struck into a wood by a path that ran steeply up the hillside. And by and by they came to a glen where the woodmen of a score of years ago had felled the trees, leaving a green hollow of saplings in the midst of their towering neighbours.

'There,' she said, holding out her hand to him, 'now we are alone. Just six hours or so—and then the sun will be there,' she pointed to the tree-tops to the west, 'and then you will have to go; for good, for good—you your way, and I mine. What a tangle—a tangle is this life of ours. Could I have dreamt we should ever be talking like this, you and I? Friends of an hour. What will you think of me? Does it matter? Don't speak. Say nothing—poor face, poor hands. If only there were something to look to—to pray to!' She bent over his hand and pressed it to her breast. 'What worlds we've seen together, you and I. And then—another parting.'

They wandered on a little way, and came back and listened to the first few birds that flew up into the higher branches, noonday being past, to sing.

They talked, and were silent, and talked again with out question, or sadness, or regret, or reproach; she mocking even at themselves, mocking at this 'change'—'Why, and yet without it, would you ever even have dreamed once a poor fool of a Frenchman went to his restless grave for me—for me? Need we understand? Were we told to pry? Who made us human must be human too. Why must we take such care, and make such a fret—this soul? I know it, I know it; it is all we have—"to save," they say, poor creatures. No, never to *spend*, and so they daren't for a solitary instant lift it on the finger from its cage. Well, we have; and now, soon, back it must go, back it must go, and try its best to whistle the day out. And yet, do you know, perhaps the very freedom does a little shake its—its monotony. It's true, you see, they have lived a long time; these Worldly Wisefolk they were wise before they were swaddled....

'There, and you are hungry?' she asked him, laughing in his eyes. 'Of course, of course you are—scarcely a mouthful since that first still wonderful supper. And you haven't slept a wink, except like a tired-out child after its first party, on that old garden chair. I sat and watched, and yes, almost hoped you'd never wake in case—in case. Come along, see, down there. I can't go home just yet. There's a little old inn—we'll go and sit down there—as if we were really trying to be romantic! I know the woman quite well; we can talk there—just the day out.'

They sat at a little table in the garden of 'The Cherry Trees,' its thick green apple branches burdened with ripened fruit. And Grisel tried to persuade him to eat and drink, 'for to-morrow we die,' she said, her hands trembling, her face as it were veiled with a faint mysterious light.

'There are dozens and dozens of old stories, you know,' she said, leaning on her elbows, 'dozens and dozens, meaning only us. You must, you must eat; look, just an apple. We've got to say goodbye. And faintness will double the difficulty.' She lightly touched his hand as if to compel him to smile with her. 'There, I'll peel it; and this is Eden; and soon it will be the cool of the evening. And then, oh yes, the voice will come. What nonsense I am talking. Never mind.'

They sat on in the quiet sunshine, and a spider slid softly through the air and with busy claws set to its nets; and those small ghosts the robins went whistling restlessly among the heavy boughs.

A child presently came out of the porch of the inn into the garden, and stood with its battered doll in its arms, softly watching them awhile. But when Grisel smiled and tried to coax her over, she burst out laughing and ran in again.

Lawford stooped forward on his chair with a groan. 'You see,' he said, 'the whole world mocks me. You say "this evening"; need it be, must it be this evening? If you only knew how far they have driven me. If you only knew what we should only detest each other for saying and for listening to. The whole thing's dulled and staled. Who wants a changeling? Who wants a painted bird? Who does not loathe the converted?—and I'm converted to Sabathier's God. Should we be sitting here talking like this if it were not so? I can't, I can't go back.'

She rose and stood with her hand pressed over her mouth, watching him.

'Won't you understand?' he continued. 'I am an outcast—a felon caught red-handed, come in the flesh to a hideous and righteous judgment. I hear myself saying all these things; and yet, Grisel, I do, I do love you with all the dull best I ever had. Not now, then; I don't ask new even. I can, I would begin again. God knows my face has changed enough even as it is. Think of me as that poor wandering ghost of yours;

how easily I could hide away—in your memory; and just wait, wait for you. In time even this wild futile madness too would fade away. Then I could come back. May I try?'

'I can't answer you. I can't reason. Only, still, I do know, talk, put off, forget as I may, must is must. Right and wrong, who knows what *they* mean, except that one's to be done and one's to be forsworn; or—forgive, my friend, the truest thing I ever said—or else we lose the savour of both. Oh, then, and I know, too, you'd weary of me. I know you, Monsieur Nicholas, better than you can ever know yourself, though you have risen from your grave. You follow a dream, no voice or face or flesh and blood; and not to do what the one old raven within you cries you *must,* would be in time to hate the very sound of my footsteps. You shall go back, poor turncoat, and face the clearness, the utterly more difficult, bald, and heartless clearness, as together we faced the dark. Life is a little while. And though I have no words to tell what always are and must be foolish reasons because they are not reasons at all but ghosts of memory, I know in my heart that to face the worst is your only hope of peace. Should I have staked so much on your finding that, and now throw up the game? Don't let us talk any more. I'll walk half the way, perhaps. Perhaps I will walk *all* the way. I think my brother guesses—at least *my* madness. I've talked and talked him nearly past his patience. And then, when you are quite safely, oh yes, quite safely and soundly gone, then I shall go away for a little, so that we can't even hear each other speak, except in dreams. Life!—well, I always thought it was much too plain a tale to have as dull an ending. And with us the powers beyond have played a newer trick, that's all. Another hour, and we will go. Till then there's just the solitary walk home and only the dull old haunted house that hoards as many ghosts as we ourselves to watch our coming.'

Evening began to shine between the trees; they seemed to stand aflame, with a melancholy rapture in their uplifted boughs above their fading coats. The fields of the garnered harvest shone with a golden stillness, awhir with shimmering flocks of starlings. And the old birds that had sung in the spring sang now amid the same leaves, grown older too to give them harbourage.

Herbert was sitting in his room when they returned, nursing his teacup on his knee while he pretended to be reading, with elbow propped on the table.

'Here's Nicholas Sabathier, my dear, come to say goodbye awhile,' said Grisel. She stood for a moment in her white gown, her face turned towards the clear green twilight of the open window. 'I have promised to walk part of the way with him. But I think first we must have some tea. No; he flatly refuses to be driven. We are going to walk.'

The two friends were left alone, face to face with a rather difficult silence, only the least degree of nervousness apparent, so far as Herbert was concerned, in that odd aloof sustained air of impersonality that had so baffled his companion in their first queer talk together.

'Your sister said just now, Herbert,' blurted Lawford at last. '"Here's Nicholas Sabathier come to say goodbye" well, I—what I want you to understand is that it *is* Sabathier, the worst he ever was; but also that it *is* "goodbye."'

Herbert slowly turned. 'I don't quite see why "goodbye," Lawford. And—frankly, there is nothing to explain. We have chosen to live such a very out-of-the-way life,' he went on, as if following up a train of thought.... 'The truth is if one wants to live at all—one's own life, I mean—there's no time for many friends. And just steadfastly regarding your neighbour's tail as you follow it down into the Nowhere—it's that that seems to me the deadliest form of hypnotism. One must simply go one's own way, doing one's best to free one's mind of cant—and I dare say clearing some excellent stuff out with the rubbish. One consequence is that I don't think, however foolhardy it may be to say so, I don't think I care a groat for any opinion as human as my own, good or bad. My sister's a million times a better woman than I am a man. What possibly could there be, then, for me to say?' He turned with a nervous smile. 'Why should it be goodbye?'

Lawford glanced involuntarily towards the door that stood in shadow duskily ajar. 'Well,' he said, 'we have talked, and we think it must be that, until, at least,' he smiled faintly, 'I can come as quietly as your old ghost you told me of; and in that case it may not be so very long to wait.'

Their eyes met fleetingly across the still, listening room. 'The more I think of it,' Lawford pushed slowly on, 'the less I understand the frantic purposelessness of all that has happened to me. Until I went down, as you said, "a godsend of a little Miss Muffet," and the inconceivable farce came off, I was fairly happy, fairly contented to dance my little wooden dance and wait till the showman should put me down into his box again. And now—well, here I am. The whole thing has gone by and scarcely left a trace of its visit. Here I am for all my friends to swear to; and yet, Herbert, if you'll forgive me troubling you with this stuff about myself, not a single belief, or thought, or desire remains unchanged. You will remember all that, I hope. It's not, of course, the ghost of an apology, only the mere facts.'

Herbert rose and paced slowly across to the window. 'The longer I live, Lawford, the more I curse this futile gift of speech. Here am I, wanting to tell you, to say out frankly what, if mind could appeal direct to mind, would be merely as the wind passing through the leaves of a tree with just one—one multitudinous rustle, but which, if I tried to put into words—well, daybreak would find us still groping on....' He turned; a peculiar wry smile on his face. 'It's a dumb world: but there we are. And some day you'll come again.'

'Well,' said Lawford, as if with an almost hopeless effort to turn thought into such primitive speech, 'that's where we stand, then.' He got up suddenly like a man awakened in the midst of unforeseen danger, 'Where is your sister?' he cried, looking into the shadow. And as if in actual answer to his entreaty, they heard the clinking of the cups on the little, old, green lacquer tray she was at that moment carrying into the room. She sat down on the window seat and put the tray down beside her. 'It will be before dark even now,' she said, glancing out at the faintly burning skies.

They had trudged on together with almost as deep a sense of physical exhaustion as peasants have who have been labouring in the fields since daybreak. And a little beyond the village, before the last, long road began that led in presently to the housed and scrupulous suburb, she stopped with a sob beside an old scarred milestone by the wayside. 'This—is as far as I can go,' she said. She stooped, and laid her hand on the cold moss-grown surface of the stone. 'Even now it's wet with dew.' She rose again and looked strangely into his face. 'Yes, yes, here it is,' she said, 'oh, and worse, worse than any fear. But nothing now can trouble you again of that. We're both at least past that.'

'Grisel,' he said, 'forgive me, but I can't—I can't go on.'

'Don't think, don't think,' she said, taking his hands, and lifting them to her bosom. 'It's only how the day goes; and it has all, my one dear, happened scores and scores of times before—mother and child and friend—and lovers that are all these too, like us. We mustn't cry out. Perhaps it was all before even we could speak—this sorrow came. Take all the hope and all the future: and then may come our chance.'

'What's life to me now. You said the desire would come back; that I should shake myself free. I could if you would help me. I don't know what you are or what your meaning is, only that I love you; care for nothing, wish for nothing but to see you and think of you. A flat, dull voice keeps saying that I have no right to be telling you all this. You will know best. I know I am nothing. I ask nothing. If we love one another, what is there else to say?'

'Nothing, nothing to say, except only goodbye. What could you tell me that I have not told myself over and over again? Reason's gone. Thinking's gone. Now I am only sure.' She smiled shadowily. 'What peace did *he* find who couldn't, perhaps, like you, face the last goodbye?'

They stood in utter solitude awhile in the evening gloom. The air was as still and cold as some grey unfathomable untraversed sea. Above them uncountable clouds drifted slowly across space.

'Why do they all keep whispering together?' he said in a low voice, with cowering face. 'Oh if you knew, Grisel, how they have hemmed me in; how they have come pressing in through the narrow gate I left ajar. Only to mock and mislead. It's all dark and unintelligible.'

He touched her hand, peering out of the shadows that seemed to him to be gathering between their faces. He drew her closer and touched her lips with his fingers. Her beauty seemed to his distorted senses to fill earth and sky. This, then, was the presence, the grave and lovely overshadowing dream whose surrender made life a torment, and death the near fold of an immortal, starry veil. She broke from him with a faint cry. And he found himself running and running, just as he had run that other night, with death instead of life for inspiration, towards his earthly home.

CHAPTER TWENTY-TWO

He was utterly wearied, but he walked on for a long while with a dogged unglancing pertinacity and without looking behind him. Then he rested under the dew-sodden hedgeside and buried his face in his hands. Once, indeed, he did turn and grind his way back with hard uplifted face for many minutes, but at the meeting with an old woman who in the late dusk passed him unheeded on the road, he stopped again, and after standing awhile looking down upon the dust, trying to gather up the tangled threads of his thoughts, he once more set off homewards.

It was clear, starry, and quite dark when he reached the house. The lamp at the roadside obscurely lit its breadth and height. Lamplight within, too, was showing yellow between the Venetian blinds; a cold gas-jet gleamed out of the basement window. He seemed bereft now of all desire or emotion, simply the passive witness of things external in a calm which, though he scarcely realised its cause, was an exquisite solace and relief. His senses were intensely sharpened with sleeplessness. The faintest sound belled clear and keen on his ear. The thinnest beam of light besprinkled his eyes with curious brilliance.

As quietly as some nocturnal creature he ascended the steps to the porch, and leaning between stone pilaster and wall, listened intently for any rumour of those within.

He heard a clear, rather languid and delicate voice quietly speak on until it broke into a little peal of laughter, followed, when it fell silent by Sheila's—rapid, rich, and low. The first speaker seemed to be standing. Probably, then, his evening visitors had only just come in, or were preparing to depart. He inserted his latchkey and gently pushed at the cumbersome door. It was locked against him. With not the faintest thought of resentment or surprise, he turned back, stooped over the balustrade and looked down into the kitchen. Nothing there was visible but a narrow strip of the white table, on which lay a black cotton glove, and beyond, the glint of a copper pan. What made all these mute and inanimate things so coldly hostile?

An extreme, almost nauseous distaste filled him at the thought of knocking for admission, of confronting Ada, possibly even Sheila, in the cold echoing gloom of the detestable porch; of meeting the first wild, almost metallic, flash of recognition. He swept softly down again, and paused at the open gate. Once before the voices of the night had called him: they would not summon him forever in vain. He raised his eyes again towards the window. Who were these visitors met together to drum the alien out? He narrowed his lids and smiled up at the vacuous unfriendly house. Then wheeling, on a sudden impulse he groped his way down the gravel path that led into the garden. As he had left it, the long white window was ajar.

With extreme caution he pushed it noiselessly up, and climbed in, and stood listening again in the black passage on the other side. When he had fully recovered his breath, and the knocking of his heart was stilled, he trod on softly, till turning the corner he came in sight of the kitchen door. It was now narrowly open, just enough, perhaps, to admit a cat; and as he softly approached, looking steadily in, he could see Ada sitting at the empty table, beneath the single whistling chandelier, in her black dress and black straw hat. She was reading apparently; but her back was turned to him and he could not distinguish her arm beyond the elbow. Then almost in an instant he discovered, as, drawn up and unstirring he gazed on, that she was not reading, but had covertly and instantaneously raised her eyes from the print on the table beneath, and was transfixedly listening too. He turned his eyes away and waited. When again he peered in she had apparently bent once more over her magazine, and he stole on.

One by one, with a thin remote exultation in his progress, he mounted the kitchen stairs, and with each deliberate and groping step the voices above him became more clearly audible. At last, in the darkness of the hall, but faintly stirred by the gleam of lamplight from the chink of the dining-room door, he stood on the threshold of the drawing-room door and could hear with varying distinctness what those friendly voices were so absorbedly discussing. His ear seemed as exquisite as some contrivance of science, registering passively the least sound, the faintest syllable, and like it, in no sense meddling with the thought that speech conveyed. He simply stood listening, fixed and motionless, like some uncouth statue in the leafy hollow of a garden, stony, unspeculating.

'Oh, but you either refuse to believe, Bettie, or you won't understand that it's far worse than that.' Sheila seemed to be upbraiding, or at least reasoning with, the last speaker. 'Ask Mr Danton—he actually *saw* him.'

'"Saw him,"' repeated a thick, still voice. 'He stood there, in that very doorway, Mrs Lovat, and positively railed at me. He stood there and streamed out all the names he could lay his tongue to. I wasn't—unfriendly to the poor beggar. When Bethany let me into it I thought it was simply—I did indeed, Mrs Lawford—a monstrous exaggeration. Flatly, I didn't believe it; shall I say that? But when I stood face to face with him, I could have taken my oath that that was no more poor old Arthur Lawford than—well, I won't repeat what particular word occurred to me. But there,' the corpulent shrug was almost audible, 'we all know what old Bethany is. A sterling old chap, mind you, so far as mere character is concerned; the right man in the right place; but as gullible and as soft-hearted as a tom-tit. I've said all this before, I know, Mrs Lawford, and been properly snubbed for my pains. But if I had been Bethany I'd have sifted the whole story at the beginning, the moment he put his foot into the house. Look at that Tichborne fellow—went for months and months, just picking up one day what he floored old Hawkins—wasn't it?—with the next. But of course,' he added gloomily, 'now that's all too late. He's moaned himself into a tolerably tight corner. I'd just like to see, though, a British jury comparing this claimant with his photograph, 'pon my word I would. Where would he be then, do you think?'

'But my dear Mr Danton,' went on the clear, languid voice Lawford had heard break so light-heartedly into laughter, 'you don't mean to tell me that a woman doesn't know her own husband when she sees him—or, for the matter of that, when she doesn't see him? If Tom came home from a ramble as handsome as Apollo to-morrow, I'd recognise him at the very first blush—literally! He'd go nuzzling off to get his slippers, or complain that the lamps had been smoking, or hunt the house down for last week's paper. Oh, besides, Tom's Tom—and there's an end of it.'

'That's precisely what I think, Mrs Lovat; one is saturated with one's personality, as it were.'

'You see, that's just it! That's just exactly every woman's husband all over; he is saturated with his personality. Bravo, Mr Craik!'

'Good Lord,' said Danton softly. 'I don't deny it!'

'But that,' broke in Sheila crisply—'that's just precisely what I asked you all to come in for. It's because I know now, apart altogether from the mere evidence, that—that he is Arthur. Mind, I don't say I ever really doubted. I was only so utterly shocked, I suppose. I positively put posers to him; but his memory was perfect in spite of the shock which would have killed a—a more sensitive nature.' She had risen, it seemed, and was moving with all her splendid impressiveness of silk and presence across the general line of vision. But the hall was dark and still; her eyes were dimmed with light. Lawford could survey her there unmoved.

'Are you there, Ada?' she called discreetly.

'Yes, ma'am,' answered the faint voice from below.

'You have not heard anything—no knock?'

'No, ma'am, no knock.'

'The door is open if you should call.'

'Yes, ma'am.'

'The girl's scared out of her wits,' said Sheila returning to her audience. 'I've told you all that miserable Ferguson story—a piece of calm, callous presence of mind I should never have dreamed my husband capable of. And the curious thing is—at least, it is no longer curious in the light of the ghastly facts I am only waiting for Mr Bethany to tell you—from the very first she instinctively detested the very mention of his name.'

'I believe, you know,' said Mr Craik with some decision, 'that servants must have the same wonderful instinct as dogs and children; they are natural, *intuitive* judges of character.'

'Yes,' said Sheila gravely, 'and it's only through that that I got to hear of the—the mysterious friend in the little pony-carriage. Ada's magnificently loyal—I will say that.'

'I don't want to suggest anything, Mrs Lawford,' began Mr Craik rather hurriedly, 'but wouldn't it perhaps be wiser not to wait for Mr Bethany? It is not at all unusual for him to be kept a considerable time in the vestry after service, and to-day is the Feast of St Michael's and all Angels, you know. Mightn't your husband be—er—coming back, don't you think?'

'Craik's right, Mrs Lawford; it's not a bit of good waiting. Bethany would stick there till midnight if any old woman's spiritual state could keep her going so long. Here we all are, and at any moment we may be interrupted. Mind you, I promise nothing—only that there shall be no scene. But here I am, and if he does come knocking and ringing and lunging out in the disgusting manner he—well, all I ask is permission to speak for *you*. 'Pon my soul, to think what you must have gone through! It isn't the place for ladies just now—honestly it ain't.'

'Besides, supposing the romantic lady of the pony-carriage has friends? Are *you* a pugilist, Mr Craik?'

'I hope I could give some little account of myself, Mrs Lovat; but you need have no anxiety about that.'

'There, Mr Danton. So as there is not the least cause for anxiety even if poor Arthur *should* return to his earthly home, may we share your dreadful story at once, Sheila; and then, perhaps, hear Mr Bethany's exposition of it when he *does* arrive? We are amply guarded.'

'Honestly, you know, you are a bit of a sceptic, Mrs Lovat,' pleaded Danton playfully. 'I've *seen* him.'

'And seeing is disbelieving, I suppose. Now then, Sheila.'

'I don't think there's the least chance of Arthur returning to-night,' said Sheila solemnly. 'I am perfectly well aware it's best to be as cheerful as one can—and as resolved; but I think, Bettie, when even you know the whole horrible secret, you won't think Mr Danton was—was horrified for nothing. The ghastly, the awful truth is that my husband—there is no other word for it—is—possessed!'

'"Possessed," Sheila! What in the name of all the creeps is that?'

'Well, I dare say Mr Craik will explain it much better than I can. By a devil, dear.' The voice was perfectly poised and restrained, and Mr Craik did not see fit for the moment to embellish the definition.

Lawford, with an almost wooden immobility, listened on.

'But *the* devil, or *a* devil? Isn't there a distinction?' inquired Mrs Lovat.

'It's in the Bible, Bettie, over and over again. It was quite a common thing in the Middle Ages; I think I'm right in saying that, am I not, Mr Craik?' Mr Craik must have solemnly nodded or abundantly looked his unwilling affirmation. 'And what *has* been,' continued Sheila temperately, 'I suppose may be again.'

'When the fellow began raving at me the other night,' began Danton huskily, as if out of an unfathomable pit of reflection, 'among other things he said that I haven't any wish to remember was that I was a sceptic. And Bethany said *ditto* to it. I don't mind being called a sceptic: why, I said myself Mrs Lovat was a sceptic just now! But when it comes to "devils," Mrs Lawford—I may be convinced about the other, but "devils"! Well, I've been in the City nearly twenty-five years, and it's my impression human nature can raise all the devils *we* shall ever need. And another thing,' he added, as if inspired, and with an immensely intelligent blink, 'is it just precisely that word in the Revised Version—eh, Craik?'

'I'll certainly look it up, Danton. But I take it that Mrs Lawford is not so much insisting on the word, as on the—the manifestation. And I'm bound to confess that the Society for Psychical Research, which has among its members quite eminent and entirely trustworthy men of *science*—I am bound to admit they have some very curious stories to tell. The old idea was, you know, that there are seventy-two princely devils, and as many as seven million—er—commoners. It may very well sound quaint to *our* ears, Mrs Lovat; but there it is. But whether that has any bearing on—on what you were saying, Danton, I can't say. Perhaps Mrs Lawford will throw a little more light on the subject when she tells us on what precise facts her—her distressing theory is based.'

Lawford had soundlessly stolen a pace or two nearer, and by stooping forward a little he could, each in turn, scrutinise the little intent company sitting over his story around the lamp at the further end of the table; squatting like little children with their twigs and pins, fishing for wonders on the brink of the unknown.

'Yes,' Mrs Lovat was saying, 'I quite agree, Mr Craik. Seventy-two princes, and no princesses. Oh, these masculine prejudices! But do throw a little more *modern* light on the subject, Sheila.'

'I mean this,' said Sheila firmly. 'When I went in for the last time to say good-bye—and of course it was at his own wish that I did leave him; and precisely *why* he wished it is now unhappily only too apparent—I had brought him some money from the bank—fifty pounds, I think; yes, fifty pounds. And quite by the merest chance I glanced down, in passing, at a book he had apparently been reading, a book which he seemed very anxious to conceal with his hand. Arthur is not a great reader, though I believe he studied a little before we were married, and—well, I detest anything like subterfuge, and I said it out without thinking, "Why, you're reading French, Arthur!" He turned deathly white but made no answer.'

'And can't you even confide to us the title, Sheila?' sighed Mrs Lovat reproachfully.

'Wait a minute,' said Sheila; 'you shall make as much fun of the thing as you like, Bettie, when I've finished. I don't know why, but that peculiar, stealthy look haunted me. "Why French?" I kept asking myself. "Why French?" Arthur hasn't opened a French book for years. He doesn't even approve of the *entente*. His argument was that we ought to be friends with the Germans because they are more hostile. Never mind. When Ada came back the next evening and said he was out, I came the following morning—by myself—and knocked. No one answered, and I let myself in. His bed had not been slept in. There were candles and matches all over the house—one even burnt nearly to the stick on the floor in the corner of the drawing-room. I suppose it was foolish, but I was alone, and just that, somehow, horrified me. It seemed to point to such a peculiar state of mind. I hesitated; what was the use of looking further? Yet something seemed to say to me—and it was surely providential—"Go downstairs!" And there in the breakfast-room the first thing I saw on the table was this book—a dingy, ragged, bleared, patched-up, oh, a horrible, a loathsome little book (and I have read bits too here and there); and beside it was my own little school dictionary, my own child's——' She looked up sharply. 'What was that? Did anybody call?'

'Nobody *I* heard,' said Danton, staring stonily round.

'It may have been the passing of the wind,' suggested Mr Craik, after a pause.

'Peep between the blinds, Mr Craik; it may be poor Mr Bethany confronting Pneumonia in the porch.'

'There's no one there, Mrs Lovat,' said the curate, returning softly from his errand. 'Please continue your—your narrative, Mrs Lawford.'

'We are panting for the "devil," my dear.'

'Well, I sat down and, very much against my inclination, turned over the pages. It was full of the most revolting confessions and trials, so far as I could see. In fact, I think the book was merely an amateur collection of—of horrors. And the faces, the portraits! Well, then, can you imagine my feelings when towards the end of the book about thirty pages from the end, I came upon this—gloating up at me from the table in my house before my very eyes?'

She cast a rapid glance over her shoulder, and gathering up her silk skirt, drew out, from the pocket beneath, the few crumpled pages, and passed them without a word to Danton. Lawford kept him plainly in view, as, lowering his great face, he slowly stooped, and holding the loose leaves with both fat hands between his knees, stared into the portrait. Then he truculently lifted his cropped head.

'What did I say?' he said. 'What did I *say?* What did I tell old Bethany in this very room? What d'ye think of that, Mrs Lovat, for a portrait of Arthur Lawford? What d'ye make of that, Craik—eh? Devil—eh?'

Mrs Lovat glanced with arched eyebrows, and with her finger-tips handed the sheets on to her neighbour, who gazed with a settled and mournful frown and returned them to Sheila.

She took the pages, folded them and replaced them carefully in her pocket. She swept her hands over her skirts, and turned to Danton.

'You agree,' she inquired softly, 'it's like?'

'Like! It's the livin' livid image. The livin' image,' he repeated, stretching out his arm, 'as he stood there that very night.'

'What will you say, then,' said Sheila, quietly, 'What will you say if I tell you that that man, Nicholas de Sabathier, has been in his grave for over a hundred years?'

Danton's little eyes seemed, if anything, to draw back even further into his head. 'I'd say, Mrs Lawford, if you'll excuse the word, that it might be a damn horrible coincidence—I'd go farther, an almost incredible coincidence. But if you want the sober truth, I'd say it was nothing more than a crafty, clever, abominable piece of trickery. That's what I'd say. Oh, you don't know, Mrs Lovat. When a scamp's a scamp, he'll stop at nothing. *I* could tell you some tales.'

'Ah, but that's not all,' said Sheila, eyeing them steadfastly one by one. 'We all of us know that my husband's story was that he had gone down to Widderstone—into the churchyard, for his convalescent ramble; that story's true. We all know that he said he had had a fit, a heart attack, and that a kind of—of stupor had come over him. I believe on my honour that's true too. But no one knows but he himself and Mr Bethany and I, that it was a wretched broken grave, quite at the bottom of the hill, that he chose for his resting place, nor—and I can't get the scene out of my head—nor that the name on that one solitary tombstone down there was—was...this!'

Danton rolled his eyes. 'I don't begin to follow,' he said stubbornly.

'You don't mean,' said Mr Craik, who had not removed his gaze from Sheila's face, 'I am not to take it that you mean, Mrs Lawford, the—the other?'

'Yes,' said Sheila, '*his*'—she patted her skirts—'Sabathier's.'

'You mean,' said Mrs Lovat crisply, 'that the man in the grave is the man in the book, and that the man in the book is—is poor Arthur's changed face?'

Sheila nodded.

Danton rose cumbrously from his chair, looking beadily down on his three friends.

'Oh, but you know, it isn't—it isn't right,' he began. 'Lord! I can see him now. Glassy—yes, that's the very word I said—glassy. It won't do, Mrs Lawford; on my solemn honour, it won't do. I don't deny it, call it what you like; yes, devils, if you like. But what I say as a practical man is that it's just rank—that's what it is! Bethany's had too much rope. The time's gone by for sentiment and all that foolery. Mercy's all very well, but after all it's justice that clinches the bargain. There's only one way:

we must catch him; we must lay the poor wretch by the heels before it's too late. No publicity, God bless me, no. We'd have all the rags in London on us. They'd pillory us nine days on end. We'd never live it down. No, we must just hush it up—a home or something; an asylum. For my part,' he turned like a huge toad, his chin low in his collar—'and I'd say the same if it was my own brother, and, after all, he is your husband, Mrs Lawford—I'd sooner he was in his grave. It takes two to play at that game, that's what I say. To lay himself open! I can't stand it—honestly, I can't stand it. And yet,' he jerked his chin over the peak of his collar towards the ladies, 'and yet you say he's being fetched; comes creeping home, and is fetched at dark by a—a lady in a pony-carriage. God bless me! It's rank. What,' he broke out violently again, 'what was he doing there in a cemetery after dark? Do you think that beastly Frenchman would have played such a trick on Craik here? Would he have tried his little game on me? Deviltry be it, if you prefer the word, and all deference to you, Mrs Lawford. But I know this—a couple of hundred years ago they would have burnt a man at the stake for less than a tenth of this. Ask Craik here. I don't know how, and I don't know when: his mother, I've always heard say, was a little eccentric; but the truth is he's managed by some unholy legerdemain to get the thing at his finger's ends; that's what it is. Think of that unspeakable book. Left open on the table! Look at his Ferguson game. It's our solemn duty to keep him for good and all out of mischief. It reflects all round. There's no getting out of it; we're all in it. And tar sticks. And then there's poor little Alice to consider, and—and you yourself, Mrs. Lawford: I wouldn't give the fellow—friend though he was, in a way—it isn't safe to give him five minutes' freedom. We've simply got to save you from yourself, Mrs Lawford; that's what it is—and from old-fashioned sentiment. And I only wish Bethany was here now to dispute it!'

He stirred himself down, as it were, into his clothes, and stood in the middle of the hearthrug, gently oscillating, with his hands behind his back. But at some faint rumour out of the silent house his posture suddenly stiffened, and he lifted a little, with heavy, steady lids, his head.

'What is the matter, Danton?' said Mr Craik in a small voice; 'why are you listening?'

'I wasn't listening,' said Danton stoutly, 'I was thinking.'

At the same moment, at the creak of a footstep on the kitchen stairs, Lawford also had drawn soundlessly back into the darkness of the empty drawing-room.

'While Mr Danton is "thinking," Sheila,' Mrs Lovat was softly interposing, 'do please listen a moment to *me*. Do you mean really that that Frenchman—the one you've pocketed—is the poor creature in the grave?'

'Yes, Mrs Lawford,' said Mr Craik, putting out his face a little, 'are we to take it that you mean that?'

'It's the same date, dear, the same name even to the spelling; what possibly else can I think?'

'And that the poor creature in the grave actually climbed up out of the darkness and—well, what?'

'I know no more than you do *now*, Bettie. But the two faces—you must remember you haven't seen my husband *since*.' You must remember you haven't heard the peculiar—the most peculiar things he—Arthur himself—has said to me. Things such as a wife... And not in jest, Bettie; I assure you....'

'And Mr Bethany?' interpolated Mr Craik modestly, feeling his way.

'Pah, Bethany, Craik! He'd back Old Nick himself if he came with a good tale. We've got to act; we've got to settle his hash before he does any mischief.'

'Well,' began Mrs Lovat, smiling a little remorsefully beneath the arch of her raised eyebrows, 'I sincerely hope you'll all forgive me; but I really am, heart and soul, with Old Nick, as Mr Danton seems on intimate terms enough to call him. Dead, he is really immensely alluring; and alive, I think, awfully—just awfully pitiful and—and pathetic. But if I know anything of Arthur he won't be beaten by a Frenchman. As for just the portrait, I think, do you know, I almost prefer dark men'—she glanced up at the face immediately in front of the clock—'at least,' she added softly, 'when they are not looking very vindictive. I suppose people are fairly often possessed, Mr Craik? *How* many "deadly sins" are there?'

'As a matter of fact, Mrs Lovat, there are seven. But I think in this case Mrs Lawford intends to suggest not so much that—that her husband is in that condition; habitual sin, you know—grave enough, of course, I own—but that he is actually being compelled, even to the extent of a more or less complete change of physiognomy, to follow the biddings of some atrocious spiritual influence. It is no breach of confidence to say that I have myself been present at a death-bed where the struggle against what I may call the end was perfectly awful to witness. I don't profess to follow all the ramifications of the affair, but though possibly Mr Danton may seem a little harsh, such harshness, if I may venture to intercede, is not necessarily "vindictive." And—and personal security is a consideration.'

'If you only knew the awful fear, the awful uncertainty I have been in, Bettie! Oh, it is worse, infinitely worse, than you can possibly imagine. I have myself heard the Voice speak out of him—a high, hard, nasal voice. I've seen what Mr Danton calls the "glassiness" come into his face, and an expression so wild and so appallingly depraved, as it were, that I have had to hurry downstairs to hide myself from the thought. I'm willing to sacrifice everything for my own husband and for Alice; but can it be expected of me to go on harbouring....' Lawford listened on in vain for a moment; poor Sheila, it seemed, had all but broken down.

'Look here, Mrs Lawford,' began Danton huskily, 'you really mustn't give way; you really mustn't. It's awful, unspeakably awful, I admit. But here we are; friends, in the midst of friends. And there's absolutely nothing—What's that? Eh? Who is it?... Oh, the maid!'

Ada stood in the doorway looking in. 'All I've come to ask, ma'am,' she said in a low voice, 'is, am I to stay downstairs any longer? And are you aware there's somebody in the house?'

'What's that? What's that you're saying?' broke out the husky voice again. 'Control yourself! Speak gently! What's that?'

'Begging your pardon, sir, I'm perfectly under control. And all I say is that I can't stay any longer alone downstairs there. There's somebody in the house.'

A concentrated hush seemed to have fallen on the little assembly.

'"Somebody"—but who?' said Sheila out of the silence. 'You come up here, Ada, with these idle fancies. Who's in the house? There has been no knock—no footstep.'

'No knock, no footstep, ma'am, that I've heard. It's Dr Ferguson, ma'am. He was here that first night; and he's been here ever since. He was here when I came on Tuesday; and he was here last night. And he's here now. I can't be deceived by my own feelings. It's not right, it's not out-spoken to keep me in the dark like this. And if you have no objection, I would like to go home.'

Lawford in his utter weariness had nearly closed the door and now sat bent up on a chair, wondering vaguely when this poor play was coming to an end, longing with an intensity almost beyond endurance for the keen night air, the open sky. But still his ears drank in every tiniest sound or stir. He heard Danton's lowered voice muttering his arguments. He heard Ada quietly sniffing in the darkness of the hall.

And this was his world! This was his life's panorama, creaking on at every jolt. This was the 'must' Grisel had sent him back to—these poor fools packed together in a panic at an old stale tale! Well, they would all come out presently, and cluster; and the crested, cackling fellow would lead them safely away out of the haunted farmyard.

He started out of his reverie at Danton's voice close at hand.

'Look here, my good girl, we haven't the least intention of keeping you in the dark. If you want to leave your mistress like this in the midst of her anxieties she says you can go and welcome. But it's not a bit of good in the world coming up with these cock-and-bull stories. The truth is your master's mad, that's the sober truth of it—hopelessly insane, you understand; and we've got to find him. But nothing's to be said, d'ye see? It's got to be done without fuss or scandal. But if there's any witness wanted, or anything of that kind, why, here you are; and,' he dropped his voice to an almost inaudible hoot, 'and well worth your while! You did see him, eh? Step into the trap, and all that?'

Ada stood silent a moment. 'I don't know, sir,' she began quietly, 'by what right you speak to me about what you call my cock-and-bull stories. If the master is mad, all I can say to *anybody* is I'm very sorry to hear it. I came to my mistress, sir, if you please; and I prefer to take my orders from one who has a right to give them. Did I understand you to say, ma'am, that you wouldn't want me any more this evening?'

Sheila had swept solemnly to the door. 'Mr Danton meant all that he said quite kindly, Ada. I can perfectly understand your feelings—perfectly. And I'm very much obliged to you for all your kindness to me in very trying circumstances. We are all agreed—we are forced to the terrible conclusion which—which Mr Danton has just—expressed. And I know I can rely on your discretion. Don't stay on a moment if you really are afraid. But when you say "some one" Ada, do you mean—some one like you or me; or do you mean—the other?'

'I've been sitting in the kitchen, ma'am, unable to move. I'm watched everywhere. The other evening I went into the drawing-room—I was alone in the house—and... I can't describe it. It wasn't dark; and yet it was all still and black, like the ruins after a fire. I don't mean I saw it, only that it was like a scene. And then the watching—I am quite aware to some it may sound all fancy. But I'm not superstitious, never was. I only mean—that I can't sit alone here. I daren't. Else, I'm quite myself. So if so be you don't want me any more; if I can't be of any further use to you or to—to Mr. Lawford, I'd prefer to go home.'

'Very well, Ada; thank you. You can go out this way.'

The door was unchained and unbolted, and 'Good-night' said. And Sheila swept back in sombre pomp to her absorbed friends.

'She's quite a good creature at heart,' she explained frankly, as if to disclaim any finesse, 'and almost quixotically loyal. But what really did she mean, do you think? She is so obstinate. That maddening "some one"! How they do repeat themselves. It can't be my husband; not Dr Ferguson, I mean. You don't suppose—oh surely, not "some one" else!' Again the dark silence of the house seemed to drift in on the little company.

Mr Craik cleared his throat. 'I failed to catch quite all that the maid said,' he murmured apologetically; 'but I certainly did gather it was to some kind of—of emanation she was referring. And the "ruin," you know. I'm not a mystic; and yet do you know, that somehow seemed to me almost offensively suggestive of—of demonic influence. You don't suppose, Mrs Lawford—and of course I wouldn't for a moment venture on such a conjecture unsupported—but even if this restless spirit (let us call it) did succeed in making a footing, it might possibly be rather in the nature of a lodging than a permanent residence. Moreover we are, I think, bound to remember that probably in all spheres of existence like attracts like; even the Gadarene episode seems to suggest a possible *multiplication!*' he peered largely. 'You don't suppose, Mrs Lawford...?'

'I think Mr Craik doesn't quite relish having to break the news, Sheila dear,' explained Mrs Lovat soothingly, 'that perhaps Sabathier's *out*. Which really is quite a heavenly suggestion, for in that case your husband would be in, wouldn't he? Just our old stolid Arthur again, you know. And next Mr Craik is suggesting, and it certainly does seem rather fascinating, that poor Ada's got mixed up with the Frenchman's friends, or perhaps, even, with one of the seventy-two Princes Royal. I know women can't, or mustn't reason, Mr Danton, but you do, I hope, just catch the drift?'

Danton started. 'I wasn't really listening to the girl,' he explained nonchalantly, shrugging his black shoulders and pursing up his eyes. 'Personally, Mrs Lovat, I'd pack the baggage off to-night, box and all. But it's not my business.'

'You mustn't be depressed—must he, Mr Craik? After all, my dear man, the business, as you call it, is not exactly entailed. But really, Sheila, I think it must be getting very late. Mr Bethany won't come now. And the dear old thing ought certainly to have his say before we go any further; *oughtn't* he, Mr Danton? So what's the use of worriting poor Ada's ghost any longer. And as for poor Arthur—I haven't the faintest desire in the world to hear the little cart drive up, simply in case it should be to leave your unfortunate husband behind it, Sheila. What it must be to be alone all night in this house with a dead and buried Frenchman's face—well, I shudder, dear!'

'And yet, Mrs Lovat,' said Mr Craik, with some little show of returning bravado, 'as we make our bed, you know.'

'But in this case, you see,' she replied reflectively, 'if all accounts are true, Mr Craik, it's manifestly the wicked Frenchman who has made the bed, and Sheila who refu—— But look; Mr Danton is fretting to get home.'

'If you'll all go to the door,' said Danton, seizing a fleeting opportunity to raise his eyebrows more expressively even than if he had again shrugged his shoulders at Sheila, 'I'll put out the light.'

The night air flowed into the dark house as Danton hastily groped his way out of the dining-room.

'There's only one thing,' said Sheila slowly. 'When I last saw my husband, you know, he was, I think, the least bit better. He was always stubbornly convinced it would all come right in time. That's why, I think, he's been spending his—his evenings away from home. But supposing it did?'

'For my part,' said Mrs Lovat, breathing the faint wind that was rising out of the west, 'I'd sigh; I'd rub my eyes; I'd thank God for such an exciting dream; and I'd turn comfortably over and go to sleep again. I'm all for Arthur—absolutely—back against the wall.'

'For my part,' said Danton, looming in the dusk, 'friend or no friend, I'd cut the—I'd cut him dead. But don't fret, Mrs Lawford, devil or no devil, he's gone for good.'

'And for my part—' began Mr Craik; but the door at that moment slammed.

Voices, however, broke out almost immediately in the porch. And after a hurried consultation, Lawford in his stagnant retreat heard the door softly reopen, and the striking of a match. And Mr Craik, followed closely by Danton's great body, stole circumspectly across his dim chink, and the first adventurer went stumbling down the kitchen staircase.

'I suppose,' muttered Lawford, turning his head in the darkness, 'they have come back to put out the kitchen gas.'

Danton began a busy tuneless whistle between his teeth.

'Coming, Craik?' he called thickly, after a long pause.

Apparently no answer had been returned to his inquiry: he waited a little longer, with legs apart, and eyeballs enveloped in brooding darkness. 'I'll just go and tell the ladies you're coming,' he suddenly bawled down the hollow. 'Do you hear, Craik? They're alone, you know.' And with that he resolutely wheeled and rapidly made his way down the steps into the garden. Some few moments afterwards Mr Craik shook himself free of the basement, hastened at a spirited trot to rejoin his companions, and in his absence of mind omitted to shut the front door.

CHAPTER TWENTY-THREE

Lawford sat on in the darkness, and now one sentence and now another of their talk would repeat itself in his memory, in much the same way as one listlessly turns over an antiquated diary, to read here and there a flattened and almost meaningless sentiment. Sometimes a footstep passed echoing along the path under the trees, then his thoughts would leave him, and he would listen and listen till it had died quite out. It was all so very far away. And they too—these talkers—so very far away; as remote and yet as clear as the characters in a play when they have made their final bow, and have left the curtained stage, and one is standing uncompanioned and nearly the last of the spectators, and the lights that have summoned back reality again are being extinguished. It was only by painful effort of mind that he kept recalling himself to himself—why he was here; what it all meant; that this was indeed actuality.

Yet, after all, this by now was his customary loneliness: there was little else he desired for the present than the hospitality of the dark. He glanced around him in the clear, black, stirless air. Here and there, it seemed, a humped or spindled form held against all comers its passive place. Here and there a tiny faintness of light played. Night after night these chairs and tables kept their blank vigil. Why, he thought, pleased as an overtired child with the fancy, in a sense they were always alone, shut up in a kind of senselessness—just like us all. But what—what, he had suddenly risen from his chair to ask himself—what on earth are they alone with? No precise answer had been forthcoming to that question. But as in turning in the doorway, he looked out into the night, flashing here and there in dark spaces of the sky above the withering apple leaves—the long dark wall and quiet untrodden road—with the tumultuous beating of the stars—one thing at least he was conscious of having learned in these last few days: he knew what kind of a place he was alone *in*.

It seemed to weave a spell over him, to call up a nostalgia he had lost all remembrance of since childhood. And that queer homesickness, at any rate, was all Sabathier's doing, he thought, smiling in his rather careworn fashion. Sabathier! It was this mystery, bereft now of all fear, and this beauty together, that made life the endless, changing and yet changeless, thing it was. And yet mystery and loveliness alike were only really appreciable with one's legs, as it were, dangling down over into the grave.

Just with one's lantern lit, on the edge of the whispering unknown, and a reiterated going back out of the solitude into the light and warmth, to the voices and glancing of eyes, to say good-bye:—that after all was this life on earth for those who watched as well as acted. What if one's earthly home were empty?—still the restless fretted traveller must tarry; 'for the horrible worst of it is, my friend,' he said, as if to some silent companion listening behind him, 'the worst of it is, *your* way was just simply, solely suicide.' What was it Herbert had called it? Yes, a cul-de-sac—black, lofty, immensely still and old and picturesque, but none the less merely a contemptible cul-de-sac; no abiding place, scarcely even sufficing with its flagstones for a groan from the fugitive and deluded refugee. There was no peace for the wicked. The question of course then came in—Was there any peace anywhere, for anybody?

He smiled at a sudden odd remembrance of a quiet, sardonic old aunt whom he used to stay with as a child. 'Children should be seen and not heard,' she would say, peering at him over his favourite pudding.

His eyes rested vacantly on the darkling street. He fell again into reverie, gigantically brooded over by shapes only imagination dimly conceived of: the remote alleys of his mind astir with a shadowy and ceaseless traffic which it wasn't at least *this* life's business to hearken after, or regard. And as he stood there in a mysteriously thronging peaceful solitude such as he had never known before, faintly out of the silence broke the sound of approaching hoofs. His heart seemed to gather itself close; a momentary blindness veiled his eyes, so wildly had his blood surged up into cheek and brain. He remained, caught up, with head slightly inclined, listening, as, with an interminable tardiness, measureless anguished hope died down into nothing in his mind.

Cold and heavy, his heart began to beat again, as if to catch up those laggard moments. He turned with an infinite revulsion of feeling to look out on the lamps of the old fly that had drawn up at his gate.

He watched incuriously a little old lady rather arduously alight, pause, and look up at his darkened windows, and after a momentary hesitation, and a word over her shoulder to the cabman, stoop and fumble at the iron latch. He watched her with a kind of wondering aversion, still scarcely tinged with curiosity. She had succeeded in lifting the latch and in pushing her way through, and was even now steadily advancing towards him along the tiled path. And a minute after he recognised with the strangest reactions the quiet old figure that had shared a sunset with him ages and ages ago—his mother's old schoolfellow, Miss Sinnet.

He was already ransacking the still faintly-perfumed dining-room for matches, and had just succeeded in relighting the still-warm lamp, when he heard her quiet step in the porch, even felt her peering in, in the gloom, with all her years' trickling customariness behind her, a little dubious of knocking on a wide-open door.

But the lamp lit Lawford went out again and welcomed his visitor. 'I am alone,' he was explaining gravely, 'my wife's away and the whole house topsy-turvy. How very, very kind of you!'

The old lady was breathing a little heavily after her ascent of the steep steps, and seemed not to have noticed his outstretched hand. None the less she followed him in, and when she was well advanced into the lighted room, she sighed deeply, raised her veil over the front of her bonnet, and leisurely took out her spectacles.

'I suppose,' she was explaining in a little quiet voice, 'you *are* Mr Arthur Lawford, but as I did not catch sight of a light in any of the windows I began to fear that the cabman might have set me down at the wrong house.'

She raised her head, and first through, and then over her spectacles she deliberately and steadfastly regarded him.

'Yes,' she said to herself, and turned, not as it seemed entirely with satisfaction, to look for a chair. He wheeled the most comfortable up to the table.

'I have been visiting my old friend Miss Tucker—Rev W. Tucker's daughter—she, I knew, could give me your address; and sure enough she did. Your road, d'ye see, was on my way home. And I determined, in spite of the hour, just to inquire. You must understand, Mr Lawford, there was something that I rather particularly wanted to say to you. But there!—you're looking sadly, sadly ill; and,' she glanced round a little inquisitively, 'I think my story had better wait for a more convenient occasion.'

'Not at all, Miss Sinnet; please not,' Lawford assured her, 'really. I have been ill, but I'm now practically quite myself again. My wife and daughter have gone away for a few days; and I follow to-morrow, so if you'll forgive such a very poor welcome, it may be my—my only chance. Do please let me hear.'

The old lady leant back in her chair, placed her hands on its arms and softly panted, while out of the rather broad serenity of her face she sat blinking up at her companion as if after a long talk, instead of at the beginning of one. 'No,' she repeated reflectively, 'I don't like your looks at all; yet here we are, enjoying beautiful autumn weather, Mr Lawford, why not make use of it?'

'Oh yes,' said Lawford, 'I do. I have been making tremendous use of it.'

Her eyelid flickered at his candid glance. 'And does your business permit of much walking?'

'Well, I've been malingering these last few days idling at home; but I am usually more or less my own man, Miss Sinnet. I walk a little.'

'H'm, but not much in my direction, Mr Lawford?' she quizzed him.

'All horrible indolence, Miss Sinnet. But I often—often think of you; and especially just lately.'

'Well, now,' she wriggled round her head to get a better view of him rather stiffly seated on his chair, 'that's very peculiar; because I too have been thinking lately a great deal of you. And yet—I fancy I shall succeed in mystifying you presently—not precisely of you, but of somebody else!'

'You do mystify me—"somebody else"!' he replied gallantly. 'And that is the story, I suppose?'

'That's the story,' repeated Miss Sinnet with some little triumph. 'Now, let me see; it was on Saturday last—yes, Saturday evening; a wonderful sunset; Bewley Heath.'

'Oh yes; my daughter's favourite walk.'

'And your daughter's age now?'

'She's nearly sixteen; Alice, you know.'

'Ah, yes, Alice; to be sure. It *is* a beautiful walk, and if fine, I generally take mine there too. It's near; there's shade; it's very little frequented; and I can wander and muse undisturbed. And that I think is pretty well all that an old woman like me is fit for, Mr Lawford. "Nearly sixteen!" Is it possible? Dear, dear me? But let me get on. On my way home from the Heath, you may be aware, before one reaches the road again, there's a somewhat steep ascent. I haven't the strength I had, and whether I'm fatigued or not, I have always made it a rule to rest awhile on a most convenient little seat at the summit, admire the view—what I can see of it—and then make my way quietly, quietly home. On Saturday, however, and it most rarely occurs—once, I remember, when a very civil nursemaid was sitting with two charmingly behaved little children in the sunshine, and I heard they were my old friend Major Loder's *son's* children—on Saturday, as I was saying, my own particular little haunt was already occupied.' She glanced back at him from out of her thoughts, as it were. 'By a gentleman. I say, gentleman; though I must confess that his conduct—perhaps, too, a little something even in his appearance, somewhat belied the term. Anyhow, gentleman let us call him.'

Lawford, all attention, nodded, and encouragingly smiled.

'I'm not one of those tiresome, suspicious people, Mr Lawford, who distrust strangers. I have never been molested, and I have enjoyed many and many a most interesting, and sometimes instructive, talk with an individual whom I've never seen in my life before, and this side of the grave perhaps, am never likely to see again.' She lifted her head with pursed lips, and gravely yet still flickeringly regarded him once more. 'Well, I made some trifling remark—the weather, the view, what-not,' she explained with a little jerk of her shoulder—'and to my extreme astonishment he turned and addressed me by name—Miss Sinnet. Unmistakably—Sinnet. Now, perhaps, and very rightly, you won't considered *that* a very peculiar thing to do? But you will recollect, Mr Lawford, that I had been sitting there a considerable time. Surely, now, if you had recognised my face you would have addressed me at once?'

'Was he, do you think, Miss Sinnet, a little uncertain, perhaps?'

'Never mind, never mind; let me get on with my story first. The next thing my gentleman does is more mysterious still. His whole manner was a little peculiar, perhaps—a certain restlessness, what, in fact, one might be almost tempted to call a certain furtiveness of behaviour. Never mind. What he does next is to ask me a riddle! Perhaps you won't think *that* was peculiar either?'

'What was the riddle?' smiled Lawford.

'Why, to be sure, to guess his name! Simply guided, so I surmised, by some very faint resemblance in his face to his *mother*, who was, he assured me, an old schoolfellow of mine at *Brighton*. I thought and thought. I confess the adventure was beginning to be a little perplexing. But of course, very, very few of my old schoolfellows remain distinctly in my memory now; and I fear *that* grows more treacherous the longer I live. Their faces as girls are clear enough. But later in life most of them drifted out of sight—many, alas, are dead; and, well, at last I narrowed my man down to one. And who now, do you suppose *that* was?'

Lawford sustained an expression of abysmal mystification. 'Do tell me—who?'

'Your own poor dear mother, Mr Lawford.'

'*He* said so?'

'No, no,' said the old lady, with some vexation, closing her eyes. '*I* said so. He asked me to guess. And I guessed Mary Lawford; now do you see?'

'Yes, yes. But *was* he like her, Miss Sinnet? That was really very, very extraordinary. Did you see *any* likeness in his face?'

Miss Sinnet very deliberately took her spectacles out of their case again. 'Now, see here, sir; this is being practical, isn't it? I'm just going to take a leisurely glance at yours. But you mustn't let me forget the time. You must look after the time for me.'

'It's about a quarter to ten,' said Lawford, having glanced first at the stopped clock on the chimney-piece and then at his watch. He then sat quite still and endeavoured to sit at ease, while the old lady lifted her bonneted head and ever so gravely and benignly surveyed him.

'H'm,' she said at last. 'There's no mistaking *you*. It's Mary's chin, and Mary's brow—with just a little something, perhaps, of her dreamy eye. But you haven't all her looks, Mr Lawford, by any manner of means. She was a very beautiful girl, and so vivacious, so fanciful—it was, I suppose the foreign strain showing itself. Even marriage did not quite succeed in spoiling her.'

'The foreign strain?' Lawford glanced with a kind of fleeting fixity at the quiet old figure. 'The foreign strain?'

Your mother's maiden name, my dear Mr Lawford, surely memory does not deceive me in that, was van der Gucht. *That*, I believe, is a foreign name.'

'Ah, yes,' said Lawford, his rising thoughts sinking quietly to rest again. 'Van der Gucht, of course. I—how stupid of me!'

'As a matter of fact, your mother was very proud of her Dutch blood. But there,' she flung out little fin-like sleeves, 'if you don't let me keep to my story I shall go back as uneasy as I came. And you didn't,' she added even more fretfully, 'you didn't tell me the time.'

Lawford stared at his watch again for some few moments without replying. 'It's a few minutes to ten,' he said at last.

'Dear me! And I'm keeping the cabman! I must hurry on. Well, now, I put it to you; you shall be my father confessor—though I detest the idea in real life—was I wrong? Was I justified in professing to the poor fellow that I detected a likeness when there was extremely little likeness there?'

'What! None at all!' cried Lawford; 'not the faintest trace?'

'My dear good Mr Lawford,' she expostulated, patting her lap, 'there's very little more than a trace of my dear beautiful Mary in *you*, her own son. How could there be—how could you expect it in him, a complete stranger? No, it was nothing but my own foolish kindliness. It might have been Mary's son for all that I could recollect. I haven't for years, please remember, had the pleasure of receiving a visit from *you*. I am firmly of opinion that I was justified. My motive was entirely benevolent. And then—to my positive amazement—well, I won't say hard things of the absent; but he suddenly turns round on me with a "Thank you, Miss Bennett." Bennett, hark ye! Perhaps you won't agree that I had any justification in being vexed and—and affronted at *that*.'

'I think, Miss Sinnet,' said Lawford solemnly, 'that you were perfectly justified. Oh, perfectly. I wonder even you had the patience to give the real Arthur Lawford a chance to ask your forgiveness for—for the stranger.'

'Well, candidly,' said Miss Sinnett severely. 'I was very much scandalised; and I shouldn't be here now telling you my story if it hadn't been for your mother.'

'My mother!'

The old lady rather grimly enjoyed his confusion. 'Yes, Mr Lawford, your mother. I don't know why—something in his manner, something in his face—so dejected, so unhappy, so—if it is not uncharitablnesse to say it—so wild: it has haunted me: I haven't been able to put the matter out of my mind. I have lain awake in my bed thinking of him. Why did he speak to me, I keep asking myself. Why did he play me so very aimless a trick? How had he learned my name? Why was he sitting there so solitary and so dejected? And worse even than that, what has become of him? A little more patience, a little more charity, perhaps—what might I not have done for him? The whole thing has harassed and distressed me more than I can say. Would you believe it, I have actually twice, and on one occasion, three times in a day made my way to the seat—hoping to see him there. And I am not so young as I was. And then, as I say, to crown all, I had a most remarkable dream about your mother. But that's my own affair. Elderly people like me are used—well, perhaps I won't say used—we're not surprised or disturbed by visits from those who have gone before. We live, in a sense, among the tombs; though I would not have you fancy it's in any way a morbid or unhappy life to lead. We don't talk about it—certainly not to young people. Let them enjoy their Eden while they can; though there's plenty of apples, I fear, on the Tree yet, Mr Lawford.'

She leant forward and whispered it with a big, simple smile:—'We don't even discuss it much among ourselves. But as one gets nearer and nearer to the wicket-gate there's other company around one than you'll find in—in the directory. And that is why I have just come on here tonight. Very probably my errand may seem to have no meaning for you. You look ill, but you don't appear to be in any great trouble or adversity, as I feared in my—well, there—as I feared you might be. I must say, though, it seems a terribly empty house. And no lights, too!'

She slowly, with a little trembling nodding of her bonnet, turned her head and glanced quietly, fixedly, and unflinchingly, out of the half-open door. 'But that's not my affair.' And again she looked at him for a little while.

Then she stooped forward and touched him kindly and trustingly on the knee. 'Trouble or no trouble,' she said, 'it's never too late to remind a man of his mother. And I'm sure, Mr Lawford, I'm very glad to hear you are struggling up out of your illness again. We must keep a brave heart, forty or seventy, whichever we may be: "While the evil days come not nor the years draw nigh when thou shalt say, I have no pleasure in them," though they have not come to me even yet; and I trust from the bottom of my heart, not to *you*.'

She looked at him without a trace of emotion or constraint in her large, quiet face, and their eyes met for a moment in that brief, fixed, baffling fashion that seems to prove that mankind is after all but a dumb masked creature saddled with the vain illusion of speech.

'And now that I've eased my conscience,' said the old lady, pulling down her veil, 'I must beg pardon for intruding at such an hour of the evening. And may I have your arm down those dreadful steps? Really, Mr Lawford, judging from the houses they erect for us, the builders must have a very peculiar notion of mankind. Is the fly still there? I expressly told the man to wait, and what I am going to do if—!'

'He's there,' Lawford reassured her, craning his neck in their slow progress to catch a peep into the quiet road. And like a flock of birds scared by a chance comer at their feeding in some deserted field, a whirring cloud of memories swept softly up in his mind—memories whose import he made no effort to discover. None the less, the leisurely descent became in their company something of a real experience even in such a brimming week.

'I hope, some day, you will really tell me your dream?' he said, pushing the old lady's silk skirts in after her as she slowly climbed into the carriage.

'Ah, my dear Lawford, when you are my age,' she called back to him, groping her way into the rather musty gloom, 'you'll dream such dreams for yourself. Life's not what's just the fashion. And there are queerer things to be seen and heard just quietly in one's solitude than this busy life gives us time to discover. But as for my mystifying Bewley acquaintance—I confess I cannot make head or tail of him.'

'Was he,' said Lawford rather vaguely, looking up into the dim white face that with its plumes filled nearly the whole carriage window, 'was his face very unpleasing?'

She raised a gloved hand. 'It has haunted me, haunted me, Mr Lawford; its—its conflict! Poor fellow; I hope, I do hope, he faced his trouble out. But I shall never see him again.'

He squeezed the trembling, kindly old hand. 'I bet, Miss Sinnet,' he said earnestly, 'even your having *thought* kindly of the poor beggar eased his mind—whoever he may have been. I assure you, assure you of that.'

'Ay, but I did more than *think*,' replied the old lady with a chuckle that might have seemed even a little derisive if it had not been so profoundly magnanimous.

He watched the old black fly roll slowly off, and still smiling at Miss Sinnet's inscrutable finesse went back into the house. 'And now, my friend,' he said, addressing peacefully the thronging darkness, 'the time's nearly up for me to go too.'

He had made up his mind. Or, rather, it seemed as if in the unregarded silences of this last long talk his mind had made up itself. Only among impossibilities had he the shadow of a choice. In this old haunted house, amid this shallow turmoil no practicable clue could show itself of a way out. He would go away for a while.

He left the door ajar behind him for the moments still left, and stood for a while thinking. Then, lamp in hand, he descended into the breakfast-room for pen, ink, and paper. He sat for some time in that underground calm, nibbling his pen like a harassed and self-conscious schoolboy. At last he began:

'MY DEAR SHEILA,—I must tell you, to begin with, that the *change* has now all passed away. I am—as near as man can be—completely myself again. And next: that I overheard all that was said tonight in the dining-room.

'I'm sorry for listening; but it's no good going over all that now. Here I am, and, as you said, for Alice's sake we must make the best of it. I am going away for a while, to get, if I can, a chance to quiet down. I suppose every one comes sooner or later to a time in life when there is nothing else to be done but just shut one's eyes and blunder on. And that's all I can do now—blunder on....'

He paused, and suddenly, at the echo of the words in his mind, a revulsion of feeling—shame and hatred of himself surged up, and he tore his letter into tiny pieces. Once more he began, 'my dear Sheila,' dropped his pen, sat on for a long time, cold and inert, harbouring almost unendurably a pitiful, hopeless longing.... He would write to Grisel another day.

He leant back in his chair, his fingers pressed against his eyelids. And clearer than those which myriad-hued reality can ever present, pictures of the imagination swam up before his eyes. It seemed, indeed, that even now some ghost, some revenant of himself was sitting there, in the old green churchyard, roofed only with a thousand thousand stars. The breath of darkness stirred softly on his cheek. Some little scampering shape slipped by. A bird on high cried weirdly, solemnly, over the globe. He shuddered faintly, and looked out again into the small lamplit room.

Here, too, was quite as inexplicable a coming and going. A fly was walking on the table beneath his eyes, with the uneasy gait of one that has outlived his hour and most of his companions. Mice were scampering and shrieking in the empty kitchen. And all about him, in the viewless air, the phantoms of another life passed by, unmindful of his motionless body. He fell into a lethargy of the senses, and only gradually became aware after a while of the strange long-drawn sigh of rain at the window. He rose and opened it. The night air flowed in, chilled with its waters and faintly fragrant of the dust. It soothed away all thought for a while. He turned back to his chair. He would wait until the rain had lulled before starting....

A little before midnight the door was softly, and with extreme care, pushed open, and Mr Bethany's old face, with an intense and sharpened scrutiny, looked in on the lamplit room. And as if still intent on the least sound within the empty walls around him, he came near, and stooping across the table, stared through his spectacles at the sidelong face of his friend, so still, with hands so lightly laid on the arms of his chair that the old man had need to watch closely to detect in his heavy slumber the slow measured rise and fall of his breast.

He turned wearily away muttering a little, between an immeasurable relief and a now almost intolerable medley of vexations. What *was* this monstrous web of Craik's? What *had* the creature been nodding and ducketing about?—those whisperings, that tattling? And what in the end, when you were old and sour and out-strategied, what was the end to be of this urgent dream called Life? He sat quietly down and drew his hands over his face, pushed his lean knotted fingers up under his spectacles, then sat blinking—and softly slowly deciphered the solitary 'My dear Sheila' on Lawford's note-paper. 'H'm,' he muttered, and looked up again at the dark still eyelids that in the strange torpor of sleep might yet be dimly conveying to the dreaming brain behind them some hint of his presence. 'I wish to goodness, you wonderful old creature,' he muttered, wagging his head, 'I wish to goodness you'd wake up.'

For some time he sat on, listening to the still soft downpour on the fading leaves. 'They don't come to *me,*' he said softly again; with a tiny smile on his old face. 'It's that old medieval Craik: with a face like a last year's rookery!' And again he sat, with head a little sidelong, listening now to the infinitesimal sounds of life without, now to the thoughts within, and ever and again he gazed steadfastly on Lawford.

At last it seemed in the haunted quietness other thoughts came to him. A cloud, as it were of youth, drew over the wrinkled skin, composed the birdlike keenness; his head nodded. Once, like Lawford in the darkness at Widderstone, he glanced up sharply across the lamplight at his phantasmagorical shadowy companion, heard the steady surge of multitudinous rain-drops, like the roar of Time's winged chariot hurrying near; then he too, with spectacles awry, bobbed on in his chair, a weary old sentinel on the outskirts of his friend's denuded battlefield.

Printed in Great Britain
by Amazon

30848377R00111